THE JUDGE WHO THOUGHT HE WAS GOD

by

C. E. CANFIELD

Bloomington, IN Milton Keynes, UK

authorHOUSE

AuthorHouse™
1663 Liberty Drive, Suite 200
Bloomington, IN 47403
www.authorhouse.com
Phone: 1-800-839-8640

AuthorHouse™ UK Ltd.
500 Avebury Boulevard
Central Milton Keynes, MK9 2BE
www.authorhouse.co.uk
Phone: 08001974150

First published by AuthorHouse 6/15/2006

ISBN: 1-4259-2048-9 (sc)

Printed in the United States of America
Bloomington, Indiana

This book is printed on acid-free paper.

Date: July 23rd, 1962. Time: 0600 hours. The place: Easton Pennsylvania, a young girl came in the front door of the hospital, took about three steps inside the entrance and collapsed on the floor. The receptionist looked up just as she fell. She saw the pool of water on the floor and knew right away what was happening. She called the birthing center for a doctor and a gurney. She was wheeled into a labor- room. No sooner had they closed the door when she gave birth to a girl. The doctor asked, "What was her name? Where did she live? Did she have any insurance? Did she want someone called? Did she have a husband, maybe a boyfriend, someone?"

The girl would not talk. They thought at first she must be deaf, as all during the birth not once did she cry. It seemed she had no feelings for pain. They gave her some medication to make her sleep. The doctor figured she would talk when she woke up. She woke at four in the afternoon. She looked around and saw the nurse dozing in a chair next to the bed. She asked the nurse for a drink of ice water, as her mouth was very dry. Those were the first words she had spoken since entering the hospital. The nurse came back with a paper cup filled with cold water. The girl took a sip. It felt good going down, the nurse asked if she was hungry, she said, "Yes." The nurse sent down for a tray of food. When it came, she had it down it two mouthfuls, she was starved. The nurse went out to tell the charge nurse that the girl was awake. By the time the charge nurse had gotten around to her room the girl was sound asleep again. The next morning when breakfast came, the girl ate all of it with no trouble. She was told that the doctor was coming up to see her. The nurse left the room, and the girl slipped out of bed and found her clothes. They had been washed, folded, and put in the closet. She dressed, turned the water on in the bathroom a little, just enough to make someone think she was taking a shower, and closed the door. She went over to the door in her room, opened it, and looked up and down the hallway. Everyone was busy and paying no attention, coming or going. She walked down the hall, took the stairs down to the first floor and walked out the front door, no trouble at all. She looked around; everything looked strange to her. Looking up she saw the sign, Easton General Hospital. She remembered the hospital now, but for some reason she had to run. She did not know which way to go, didn't have any money. There was a bunch of something in her pocket. Reaching for it, she found a paper bag, inside was a bunch of money. Where did it come from? Was it stolen? Were the cops after her? There were many questions that needed a lot of answers.

Inside the hospital, the doctor knocked on her door and walked in. She was not in bed. Maybe she's in the bathroom he thought. He could hear the water running. The nurse came in and also found the bed empty. Water was running in the bathroom, she must be taking a shower. It was shift-changing time and reports had to be made out, I'll have the next shift nurse go in and see her. She can tell her she has a beautiful, blue-eyed, blonde, little girl." A half hour later the doctor came back. The room was the same as when he was there before. He called the desk; was the girl having tests or something? The nurse said, "No, she should be in her room." After checking the bathroom and finding it empty, and the water still running he sounded the alarm. The hospital staff was put on alert. All the doors and exits were watched. The police were called, along with the DCF and the FBI. The newborn baby was still in the hospital but the girl was nowhere to be found. The police sent out an all points bulletin to all the police cars: *WANTED, Be on the lookout for a blonde girl, five feet four inches tall, medium build. This girl has left the Easton General Hospital and needs medical treatment at once.*

She started walking, not sure of which direction to go in. An elderly couple was walking toward her. She asked, "Which way is the bus terminal?" They told her they were unsure. She walked a little further down the street. A man was standing on the corner waiting for the light to change. She asked him about the bus terminal, and he said, "He would be going right past it." They walked together to the end of the block. There was the bus terminal. She thanked the man and went inside. She had to use the ladies' room; looking around she found the door and started to go inside, just as a woman was coming out. No one else was inside. She went inside one of the stalls. She felt wet in the groin area. Looking down she saw bloodstains on her underwear. She let out a little gasp, "Oh my god... I left my baby back at the hospital." She cleaned herself the best she could. She folded some toilet paper and put it in her underwear just in case she began bleeding again. Outside she washed her face and hands, and dried them with paper towels. She went back inside one of the stalls, took out the paper bag and started counting. There were five, ten, fifty, and hundred dollar bills. She put them in order and started counting again, starting with the hundreds and working her way down to the fives... eight hundred and ninety-five dollars. Where would she have gotten all that money? Did she rob a bank, or steal it from someone? She could not remember... she folded it very carefully and tucked most of it in her bra, saving a little and putting it back in her bag. If someone robbed her, they wouldn't get much.

Her mind was still a blank. Where am I? What city is this? What state am I in? How did I get here? Was I supposed to meet someone here, or was I running away from someone? What about the baby? Who was the father, was I married, and did I have any more children? If I went back to the hospital, would I be arrested? She didn't remember her name. How was she going to tell the police what they wanted to know if she herself didn't know? Would they believe her? She was tired and sore. Looking around at the posters on the wall, she figured she was in Pennsylvania, maybe in Homer. She saw that name somewhere. What made her come here? A man's voice broke into her thoughts. She looked around and saw a man in a blue uniform standing there. "Pardon me, but you look confused," he said in a friendly voice. He asked if he could be of help. The man was in his mid to late twenties. She shook her head and said she was waiting for her sister-in-law who was one hour late. Thoughts were running through her mind, "I hope he doesn't ask what bus or where she's coming from..." He again broke into her thoughts. "How about a cup of coffee or something?" It's my coffee break and I hate to eat alone." At first she was going to say no and walk away, but the way he said it was like they'd been old friends all their lives. She was hungry, and needed someone to talk to, answer some questions...and tell her problems to.

They went over to the cafeteria. He ordered two coffees and two buttered hard rolls. He brought them back to the table and sat down. They talked about the weather and this and that for about fifteen minutes. Never once did he ask her name of where she was from, and he never told her his name either. They were laughing about something when his two-way radio beeped. He answered the call, shook his head and said he would go right away. He looked at the girl said, "I have to go to work... there's a fight downstairs. I hope you'll be here when I get back," and he left. He was such a nice man, and she knew no one, so she decided to wait. Ten minutes later he came back holding his arm. She rushed over to help him back to his seat. He said that he'd be OK. But he had to go back to the station and change clothes. "Your sister-in-law hasn't arrived," he asked? She shook her head, saying in a low voice, "I guess she's not coming." He asked where she was staying in town because he would like to see her again. She told him she had just come in herself and hadn't gotten a place yet. The beeper went off again. He answered it. Looking at the girl, he said he would keep his eyes open and signed off. He said with a smile on his face, "If you can't find a place to sleep tonight, I'll give you my address. You can sleep there tonight. I have two bedrooms, so there will be enough room for you and the doors have inside locks." He gave her his card and took off for the station house.

All of a sudden she remembered she still had her maternity dress on. It was wrapped around her almost twice. I've got to buy a new dress, underwear, comb and toothbrush... it was getting late, and the stores would be closing in an hour. She got up from the table and went over to the phone booth, looking in the yellow pages for consignment shops. She found a few but didn't know where they were. Looking in the front of the book, she found a map of the city. It said the city was Easton and the state was Pennsylvania. What was she doing in Easton PA? Looking at the streets, she found a store only two blocks from where she was. Finding the shop, she looked in the window before going in just to make sure the place was OK. Once inside she went right to the dress department.

A young girl came over and asked if she could help. Going through the racks, she had found a few, but it dawned on her that she wasn't sure of her size. She told the girl she just had a baby and wasn't sure of her sizes. The girl said, "No problem, I'll get a measuring tape." She came back with the tape and started measuring. They came up with several, and she picked the first one...blue with white trim, and a belt. She thought at least I don't have to buy one. The dress was made to order. Looking around the shop, she found some underwear and a small pocketbook. She went back to the dressing room to change. She took some money out of her bra; a twenty-dollar bill and a five-dollar, as well the money she had in her back pocket, and put it all in her new pocketbook. She paid the girl $21.90 and left, feeling now almost like a new person. All she needed now was a shower and a place to stay tonight.

Next-door was a small hotel. She went in and asked the price of a room for the night. The price was $75.00. She said thank you and left. On the corner was a phone booth. Looking in the yellow pages, she found another one only a few blocks away. The phone on the front desk rang. "Windsor Hotel," the clerk answered. She asked, "How much is your cheapest room for the night?" Without looking at the price book, he said "Eighty-five dollars with a private toilet." She said thank you and hung up. Changing things in her pocket to her bag, she came across the card that the man at the bus terminal had given her. She found out his name was Chris Young. Looking in the phone book again, she found the street that he lived on, it was four blocks away. She was too tired to walk. Just then a cab pulled up to let some people out. She asked the cabby to take her to the address and building number. He said "Lady, that's what I'm here for," and away they went. The cabby left her off right at the door. The fare was $1.75. She gave him two dollars and said thank you. Walking up two flights of stairs was not easy for her. She found the door, waited until she breathe normally again and knocked on the door. The door opened a little way and the young girl said, "Can I help you?" She wasn't expecting to see anyone. She told the girl that Chris had told her she could stay the night but if it was an inconvenience, she would move on.

The girl said, "You must be the woman my father told me was coming. Please come in. My name is Christine, like my father's, except mine is a girl's name. People call me Chrissie." Just then the phone rang. Chrissie answered it. She said she was OK, and that she had company, talking for a few minutes and then hanging up. "Would you like to take a shower?" The girl said yes, if it was OK with her. Still no name was given. She has been trying to think of a name, an easy one... "June". It was summertime and June would fit right in. After her shower the two of them sat and talked. Chrissie told her all about herself and the school she went to. How much she liked the teachers. Then out of the blue she said, "What shall I call you? My father said not to pry, but I have to call you something..."My name is June." Chrissie said, "That's better. Now we can be friends."

Looking at the time, Chrissie said that her father should be home any minute. June was upset to think that her father would leave her alone at this hour of the night. She figured Chrissie to be ten and a half or eleven years old. Not old enough to be by herself. Just then a knock came at the door. Without hesitating Chrissie ran and opened the door. There stood the same good-looking man in a blue uniform. He picked her up, gave her a kiss and a big hug, and put her back down. He then turned and saw the girl.

Chrissie said, "Daddy, June has a name and we are good friends now." "That's good," said her father, "Did you have supper?" Chrissie said she had it before June came. "I believe it's bedtime for my little princess. Take a shower and put on clean PJs, brush your teeth, give me a big hug and kiss, say good night to June and hop into bed."

After all that was done, and Chrissie was sleeping, Chris said, "I think we should have a good talk." Let me go first." Back at the terminal when I came back you had left. I picked up your coffee cup and took it with me back to the station. I was afraid you might be running from the law, so I had a fingerprint check done. Everything came back OK. At least you don't have a police record. However, I did find out where you are from. What happened to you, and why you were at the bus terminal? First I want you to know I didn't mean to pry into your private life but I could see you were confused about a lot of things. That second call I got on my radio was a lookout for a girl fitting your description, dress and all. You are wanted back at the hospital. I wasn't sure why, so I called the hospital and found out you just had a baby girl. But you were dazed and confused. You walked out not knowing where to go, that's when I met you. Your name is Alma Canfield. You are 26 years old and lived in Freeport Maine. You lived with your boyfriend for about four years. He was very abusive when he had been drinking, which seemed like most of the time. You left him one morning after he had gone to work. You went to your mother's, and told her you needed help, and couldn't stand the abuse any longer. You also told her you were five months pregnant. You had left your job at the courthouse where you were a court secretary. But being pregnant you had missed a lot of time. Your boyfriend was not happy that you left your job and that you were pregnant and slapped you around. Your mother had been saving money so she could go see her sister in Pennsylvania. I have not yet found out what happened between you being five months pregnant and the time you had the baby... I called the hospital and the baby, when it is big enough, will go to a foster home for the time being. A report has been filled out with your name as the mother. Because you came to the hospital and not knowing who you were, there will be no charges against you. However, in order to get your baby back you must prove you are able, health-wise and financially, to care for your baby. Plus, you have to pay all charges for the present care of your little girl. That's all for tonight, but please don't run off again. You would only make matters worse for yourself. Only because you have a good record as a court employee are you able to stay out of jail. Tomorrow when I come home we will hear your side of the story. I sure hope your memory comes back.

"Chrissie will be going to school tomorrow. I get her ready in the morning and my neighbor takes her to school with her two children, and she brings her home at night. She should be home by 4:30. I get home about the same time as she does. Tonight I had a lot of work to do, so I was a little late. Chrissie told me you were here. That's your bedroom over there. We will try to be quiet in the morning, but we are not used to having guests." She had no nightclothes. Then she thought, I might as well wear my underclothes. They'll both be gone in the morning. She went into the bedroom and turned on the light. There on the bed was a pair of ladies pajamas. She wondered where they came from. No words were ever spoken about his wife that is, if he ever had one but the girl? When we were talking she never mentioned anything about her mother. It was late and she was real tired. Tomorrow is another day, and she would try to figure things out then. She pulled the covers back, and there on the pillow was a note: "Please have a good night's sleep Chrissie."

When she woke up the clock said 10:15. She wondered where she was. Then it dawned on her: that nice policeman and the nice little girl. It was coming back to her now. She had slept for almost ten hours. She was still pretty sore in the groin. At least there was no blood to be seen-- only some clots on the toilet paper. The first thing to do was to wash her underclothes. That way they should be dry before they get home. Next she went into the kitchen. On the table was a box of cornflakes, a bowl with a spoon in it, sugar, and a cup with a tea bag and a note. "Hope you had a good night's sleep, the milk is in the fridge sorry we are out of juice." While she was eating she started remembering things. Like when she was a little girl her father would say "Come here bitch and clean this mess up on the floor." He had spilled something or, "Hey bitch take the garbage out" If I said anything to him he would say, "Go to your room, bitch." If I didn't do what he wanted me to do, he would pull down my panties and slap me so hard I could hardly walk. He forced his self on my mother one night and she screamed, swore, and hit him, and all he did was laugh. Nine months later they had a little baby girl. He wouldn't let my mother go to the hospital that would take all his drinking money and more. So she had the baby at home. My father was a lumberjack, cutting trees and bring them out to a road on sleds. That's all he knew, sometimes he would be gone for a week or more. My mother would be happy then. When he was home he was drunk most of the time. If my mother needed money for food or cloth to make us dresses he would yell, "Go out and earn it, bitch." She would go around the neighborhood looking for work. I remember my sister being very sick one year. My mother wanted to take her to the doctor's. My father said "There's nothing wrong with her, leave her alone. The little bitch just has a cold. I'm not spending good beer money on medicine." Two weeks later she died, she had pneumonia. He made a big thing out of the funeral, crying, telling everyone he loved her and all that. "Her mother should have taken her to the doctor's..." He passed the hat around for funeral expenses. Later that day he went down to the beer garden and got drunk.

That day changed everything, my mother was heartbroken. She was about to leave him, she started saving pennies. When one day he came home coughing up blood, he wanted to go to the doctor's, and my mother said, "I don't have any money for doctors, take care of yourself'." He stayed home for two weeks in bed. My mother would only give him hot tea. She had no money to throw away on medicine. He begged her, she would only say, "Bastard go buy your own medicine and food." He said, "He was sorry he treated her and the kids the way he did," she wouldn't listen. He was losing weight and still coughing up blood. About a month later he died. My mother found $250.00 in his pocket. The bartender said, "He owed him $200.00 for drinks he had never paid for. He told my mother if she wanted, she could work there, and he would take it out of her wages. She said, "OK." She was a nice looking lady, big busted, but not fat.

My mother was in her early forties when my father died. I was going to night school to be a secretary. My mother was taking in boarders and needed the room. I moved in with my boyfriend, one night I went over to see my mother. I went in the back door I heard her laughing, and moaning. Saying, "I love it... I love it... deeper... deeper oh god I never had it so good, don't stop now... play with my tits... OH... OH... oh... oh god." I looked in the bedroom and there they were both naked with him on top of her. I left without them knowing I was there. I was pretty upset with my mother for what she was doing, but... I guess she was lonely. My father never gave her any attention; we were all bitches to him. I stayed with my boyfriend for four years. I finished school and got a job at the courthouse in town. I was promoted to court secretary. I remember doing that for two years. I loved the job...everyone was so nice to me. After I became pregnant I lost a lot of time because of morning sickness. They covered for me, but the workload got to be too much. They had to get another secretary. I was put on short time. I couldn't take the abuse at home and at the courthouse too, so I quit. That's when my boyfriend slapped me around. He was drinking a lot and was very nasty when he was drunk. He was like my father and I wasn't going to stand for it. I went to my mother and told her I was leaving. She cried and didn't want me to go. I told her I had to, she went into the bedroom and came out with a paper bag. She told me where in Pennsylvania to go. She said, "A salesman at the bar was going there, maybe I could ride down with him? She called and he said, "He would like the company. We where going down I-95 in Connecticut when a trailer truck crossed the center divider and smashed head on into us. That's all

I remember till now. When Chrissie came home from school, she found me on the couch. When I woke up I told her I had a very bad headache. She went and made me a hot cup of tea. When Chris came home I told him everything I could remember. He told me he had checked all the police departments from the Maine state line down to the New York state line. He had a report on the accident. The driver of the car died. The truck driver was not hurt, but a girl was in the hospital for months. Then they lost track of her. They said, "You and the baby got banged up pretty bad. You needed a lot of rehabilitation treatment after that and you were moved to a rehabilitation hospital. They didn't know your name, but you fit the description I gave them. That's why they lost track of you.

She asked for an aspirin, this headache would not go away and she was having cramps also. She asked, "Was there a good doctor around here,?" Chris told her there was one about three blocks away, it was a clinic. She got up early the next morning so she would be the first one in line. They asked her a million questions-- full name, address, phone number, age, weight, height, ever pregnant, number of children. Do you use drugs... alcohol... smoke... and more? She told them she just had a baby, had cramps and a very bad headache, and couldn't remember much. They put her in a room and told her to take off all her clothes. A woman Doctor came in, she seemed nice at first. She put on a pair of rubber gloves and said, "Bend over. Now sit down with your legs spread." After the examination was over, she told me to go home, there's nothing wrong with me. My head was ready to explode. I asked her if she was going to take my blood -pressure? She said, "She didn't have time for that because there was a room full of patients outside." I also asked, "If she was going to draw blood for testing? She said, "Come back next week-- if I have time I will do it then." I asked the girl at the desk how much I owed. She said $10.00. I gave her the money and ran out of there fast.

It was getting close to noon now and I was getting hungry, but I was afraid to eat because I felt dizzy. I still had two and a half blocks to go. I felt like vomiting. My head was pounding. I leaned against a building for support. Some guy came along and asked if I needed a fix. I didn't know what the matter was. The Doctor said I was OK. A police car came by...it slowed down but didn't stop. If this head would only stop hurting, it was getting worse. I was crying, I wanted to get to Chris's apartment. The police car came by again only this time it stopped. They got out of the car and came over to me. At first they thought I needed a fix. I told them I don't do drugs. They both laughed, and said, "We don't either. Get up and go to some other place." I asked if they would take me to my friend's apartment. They asked me what the number was, I told them and said, "I was a friend of Chris Young and please contact him for me." When they heard Chris' name, things changed. They helped me into the police car and took me to the apartment. They helped me inside and said they would call Chris right now.

When Chris got home, I was on the floor banging my head against the wall. He picked me up and carried me to the car. The nearest hospital was five blocks away. It wasn't Griffin, but a closer one. I passed out in the car. When I came to, it was two days later in the afternoon. Chrissie was there holding my hand and talking to me. When she saw my eyes were open she let out a cry. A nurse came running in the room. "Thank god you're here, we almost lost you. I'll get the Doctor at once." And she left. Chrissie picked up the phone and called her father. He was so happy to hear the good news. He would stop in after work. He was there in fifteen minutes instead. The doctor was just coming in the door when Chris arrived. "She has a blood clot on the brain. If that woman's doctor had taken her blood pressure like she should have, she would have noticed something was wrong. A blood test and a CAT scan showed the problem. You brought her in the hospital just in time. Another few hours and it would have been too late. She will need surgery at once; all we will need is some information. As yet we don't know too much about her. We should talk with her own doctor first." Chris tried to explain that she was from out of state and had just moved here. The doctor said, "they would need some release forms filled out before surgery...permission for blood transfusions, insurance, and so on. With all that taken care of, we should be operating the first thing in the morning." Chris walked out with the doctor, when they got down the hall, Chris asked, "What her chances were? I know the operation is a bad one." The doctor said," She may not make it, but we will do everything in our power to pull her through. Now you had better get down to the admitting office and fill out a bunch of paperwork."

This was going to be something he knew very little about. He had no idea if she had any insurance, and if she didn't, how was she going to pay this bill. This was going to be a big problem. He went down stairs and asked for the supervisor. The lady came out and asked, "If she could help? They sat down and he explained the situation to her. She was very sympathetic-- "However, the hospital does not run on sympathy." Doctors have to be paid; nurses, equipment, lights, heat, maintenance, and much more. I'm sorry about your friend but we will need the money for the operation. Otherwise, I'm sorry." She started to get up. He asked if there was some plan that the hospital had that she could work out with the money. The women said, "What if she does not make it, the hospital would still lose... I'm sorry." He thought for a moment. "How would it be if I signed for her? I'm a police officer here in the city and have a little money saved up. Would that help?" She said, "Do you have insurance?" He said, "yes, but she does not... right?" "This operation will cost approximately Forty thousand dollars. How can you justify the cost when you make $60.00 a week? Pay rent. You have a little girl to take care of, food to buy and other essentials, how could you possible pay for it?" "Please, this women will die tomorrow without this operation." The woman got up and left. His heart was broken, putting money before human life. He went back to the station house, thanked the officer of the day for giving him the time off. The sergeant came over and asked how she was doing? Chris told him about the problem he had at the hospital. "I don't know what I'm going to do. I can't let her die; at least with the operation she will have a fighting chance." The sergeant told him to go home maybe something can be worked out.

He went back to the hospital, explained the situation to the doctor, went in, and saw Alma, kissed her for the first time and wished her luck. Picked up Chrissie and went to church and prayed for a miracle... then went home. He made a sandwich for both of them and got ready for bed. Later Chrissie came into the bedroom; she asked if he was sleeping? He told her he couldn't. She asked if she could sleep with him tonight. She hadn't done that in a long ...long time. She and her father talked just about all night. It was after three am when they dozed off.

The phone rang and woke Chris up; it was the Doctor at the hospital. The operation was a success, they removed the clot and she should be fine. . He looked at the clock; it was a little after ten am. He asked the Doctor to please repeat what he just said. The Doctor laughed, she's going to be ok... He asked, " How can that be, he hadn't been able to get that much money together?" He was confused; first he never slept that late before. He wanted to get up early so he could tell her the bad news himself. He didn't know how he was going to pay back the money to whom ever paid for the operation. He was going around in circles. He got dressed, woke up Chrissie who was still sleeping and told her the good news. It was too late for her to go to school now, and she wanted to go to the hospital and see Alma. Chris called the school and explained to the teacher what happened. The teacher was very understanding. Chrissie was so excited and happy she didn't feel like eating breakfast. Chris made a light snack and off they went. When they got to the hospital they went directly to Alma's room. Her head was all bandaged up and she was sleeping.

He went down to the office and asked for the supervisor. He was told she was not working today but the assistant was in, he said he would like to talk to her. He was surprised when a man came out. Chris explained everything to him, he said he found no reason why she could not have had the operation, and the bill was paid in full. That can't be Chris said, she knows no one here and I don't have that kind of money. The man smiled and said, "The sergeant at the police station sent a driver over last night with a letter and a check from the police charity fund. That you have been paying into each week for just such a thing as this. Fortunately there was enough money in the bank to cover it." Chris sat down and cried. His brother officers did this for me and Alma. She regained consciousness two days later; outside of a little headache she was fine.

She was in the hospital a few days over a week. The doctor wanted her to go for rehab. But she said she was doing fine and didn't need it, she would rest at the apartment for a few days then look for work. The doctor suggested she take a month off but she had too many bills to pay. After two weeks she was back to her old self again. No headaches and her memory were coming back.

She now remembers what happened after the accident. She was in a hospital for two months. They were worried she was going to lose the baby. She didn't write down the address of her aunt figuring she would remember. She left the house in such a hurry that she forgot her wallet with all her ID cards in it. After they released her from the general hospital she was sent to a rehabilitation hospital. It was called Gaylord. Her back and left leg were badly damaged in the crash. She also had a bad gash in her head. The trucking company had insurance and covered all the bills. She never asked for a settlement, she just signed a release like they told her to. Little did she know what lay ahead?

Chris was very good to her; he waited on her hand and foot till she was able to take care of herself. She hadn't gone to see her baby yet. She has talked with the people that are taking care of her a number of times. The D.C.F. people are out there all the time, checking to make sure everything is OK. They have been checking Alma also. Making sure everything is going well with her. She has been thinking and thinking for a proper name. She wasn't in to much of hurry. The people call her baby blue eyes. She sleeps all night and smiles all the time. Alma can't wait to see her. The only problem was they lived about a two hour drive from here. Chris told her he would drive her out anytime she wants.

Her aunt's address is starting to come to her. She looked up their last name in the phone book. There were only eight names listed. All she had to do was remember her street name...Chris never tried to kiss her only that one time in the hospital. She was glad in a way, she liked Chris and she loved Chrissie but she wasn't in the mood for romance. Close friends, yes, but heavy romance, no. She had to find an apartment and live on her own. She started looking in the papers; they all were in the six hundred dollar range and up. But she still kept looking. A few weeks later, she was talking with Chrissie's neighbor telling her how she would like to find a small place and go back to work. Chris has done more for me then I could ever have hoped for. The lady said she would keep her eyes and ears open. If something came up she would call her. Two week later, the neighbor called and said she heard there was a tenant moving out and she should see the superintendent right away, which she did. He said, "Yes there was a tenant moving out, but the place needed painting and cleaned up first. It would take a couple of weeks before it would be ready. The rent was six hundred a month." She said, "That was more then she could afford at the present time, because she had no job. But just as soon as she was working she could pay the rent." The super said, "She could have it for 6 months at $500.00 a month, then he would have to get the full price." Going back to the apartment she was singing and dancing all the way. The super said she could use the furniture but they needed some repairs and a coat of paint. That would be another less expense she would have. A small can of paint, paintbrush, and some sand paper. However she hadn't seen the furniture as yet. She was hoping that's all they needed. Back at the apartment she was singing, when Chrissie came home. She told Chrissie the good news. Chrissie became very quiet. She didn't want Alma to leave. She told Chrissie she was still going to be in the same building, only one flight up and she can come and see her and stay as long as she wants. When Chris came home she couldn't wait to tell him the good news. She had just two weeks to find a job and start working; she had a lot of bills to pay. She wanted her daughter; pay the hospital and give Chrissie money for new clothes come spring.

Chris was not a happy man; he thought a lot of Alma and had hoped she would be there, a very long time. But there were no commitments between them. No words were ever spoken. She wanted independence not that she wasn't grateful for all that he had done for her these past few months. Alma would always help Chrissie with her schoolwork every day, now things would be different. Chris and Chrissie were not very happy. The good thing about it was, she was only up stairs.

The next day Chris asked around to see if any jobs were available. At the present time nothing was open.

A few days later one of the secretaries told Chris that she heard one of the court secretaries was leaving. She was going to have a baby and that was going to leave them short. That was Alma's specialty. He was sad to see her go but he understood, and was willing to help in any way. At least she was in the same building and would see each other often he hoped. The next day she went and applied for the job. She was well versed on court procedure after working in Maine. Things were very different here in Pennsylvania. But because of Chris and her experience, she was given the job. She worked hard and caught on fast and was well liked. Chrissie would come up every night with her homework so things weren't that bad. Chris would take them out for supper once a week. Alma in her spare time would work on the broken furniture, they looked like new. The super couldn't get over how good every thing looked. It was in such poor shape the super was going to throw everything out. That is, until he saw what a nice job she had done. She said with a smile, "I'M FROM MAINE, WE DO EVERYTHING AND DO IT RIGHT."

She was saving every penny she could get her hands on. She had the hospital, the D.C.F. and she wanted to pay back the police dept., but most of all she wanted to get her little girl. The D.C.F. said she had to make so much money each week to pay all her bills. She would go see her little Blue eyed, Blond, Baby Girl every chance she got. She was growing like a weed, still smiling all the time, and would sleep all night. She would eat every thing in sight. The people were wonderful with her. She now had a name we will call her KAREN. That is my mothers name and I always loved it, KAREN...Karen...Karen.

She went looking for a second job after she got through at the courthouse. She found a job at the Outback Restaurant from 7 to II pm. The pay was small but the tips made up for it. She put this money in the bank. Things were going great. She met a trucker at the Outback; he delivered different things to the restaurant, a nice young man. After a few weeks he asked her out for coffee. At first she said no, but he kept asking. Finally she said ok, but it would have to be on a Monday night. That's the only night I have free. Monday evening would be fine. Chrissie didn't like him, and Chris didn't think too much of him either. His name was Michael Fox. He seemed like a nice enough young man. Chris had this funny feeling about him. The next day he ran a police check on him. The only thing he could find was a ticket for DWI. The report said he had just come from a party and had a few beers. That was all he could find, but he still had this funny feeling. When he came home that night Alma was there helping Chrissie with her homework. He told Alma what he had done. She was very upset to think Chris would do something like that behind her back. What right did he have to interfere with her life, and who she goes out with? She went up stairs to her own apartment. After about thirty minutes she started to calm down. He was only trying to help me, to make sure I was going with the right guy. She went down stairs, knocked on the door. Chrissie opened the door, they both ran into each others arms, and started crying. I'm so sorry for what I said, Please forgive me. I must have lost my head to say what I did. They were both crying in each others arms when Chris came into the room. They both told Alma they forgave her and they had no business interfering in her private life.

Alma was seeing Michael every Monday night. He told her he wanted to go back to school and be an RN or a Physicians assistant. He liked helping people and that was why he was saving his money. Chrissie was starting to like him and so was Chris. Things were going pretty good for ten months. Alma was still working two jobs and Michael still had his trucking job. They never went out to expensive restaurants only for their birthdays.

Michael had enrolled in day classes for some courses he would need in Pre- Med School. He would still be able to work and make money. On July 4th Michael asked Alma to marry him. She said, "YES." The wedding was held on the first Sunday in September, Labor Day. They only went to Atlantic City and stayed over night on there honeymoon. They had to be back working the next day. Michael moved into Alma's apartment the next night, this way they would save on the rent. Michael was doing well with his courses at school. He figured in six years he should be through.

Alma had paid off the Hospital, and the hospital dropped the charges. The D.C.F. said she was doing very well. Every one liked the name, "Karen. Karen Canfield. It had a good ring to it. Michael said as soon as they had a little money ahead he would like to adopt little Karen. He liked the little girl ... the D.C.F. would not let them have her because she had no one to take care of her during the day. The foster parents were willing to keep her for a few more months. She was so lovable and no bother at all. Alma quit her job at the restaurant, and found a nice day-care place for Little Karen. The D.C.F. approved and would check in every once in a while. Everything seemed to be going great. Chrissie, Chris, Michael, and Alma would take Little Karen and go on a picnic a couple of times a month during the summer. Sometimes Michael could not come because he had so much studying to do. He said, "He could get more done with no noise in the house". Michael would go to his classes during the day, and be home about 4:00. Grab a bit to eat and leave for his night job at 4:30. Alma would be home about 4:00. She had to stop and pick up Karen. She and Michael hardly had time to talk.

She was sleeping when Michael came home. Saturdays and Sundays, Michael spent most of his time with his studies. This went on for about one and a half years. Karen was getting bigger and bolder as time went on. At first she didn't like leaving her foster home. Going home with strangers was very hard on her. After a few months she got used to the new family. She liked the day-care the best. There were children there and she had someone to play with. Michael never had time and her mother was tired when she got home.

27

Michael did a lot of studying; things were getting harder and harder with the Class work. His job was getting the best of him. He was coming home later and later as time went on. One night he didn't come home at all. He said he was tired and took a nap in the truck. He had forgotten what time it was. When he woke up it was daylight. Alma felt sorry for him and did everything she could to help him. He was starting to get cross with Alma and Little Karen.

He started stopping in at a package store on his route and getting a bottle of wine. He would take a drink every few minutes, buy the time he finished his route he was feeling no pain. When he got home around two o'clock in the morning. Alma would smell the wine on his breath and wonder where it came from. This went on for about three and a half years. He would always say the same thing. His last stop was a gin mill and the owner would give him a glass of wine to help him sleep. As time went on if Alma said or asked a question he would start ranting and raving about how she was always picking on him. This was getting to be too much for her. She said one night, "We have got to have a talk, what is the problem? Is the schoolwork to much for you or maybe the job? Something is not right and I'm not going to put up with this way of living any longer. You are either going to be a good husband and father or you can get out now. If the job is too much for you, find another. If the schoolwork is what making you this way, leave it and go back to it in the fall. I do not want to smell wine on your breath again."

Michael hung his head, he didn't want to leave school after all he's gone through, and he could not afford to loss his job. He told Alma he was sorry and that he would try harder to be a good husband and father. That he loved her very much. That night they made love for the first time in ages. It seemed they just couldn't get enough of each other. The foreplay was out of this world. At times there bodies were so entwined that they themselves wondered how they got that way. He looked at her for the longest time, she finally said. "What are you looking at me like that for.? He smiled and said, "Honey I never new you had such a sexy body as he ran his finger around the rosy part of her breasts." She was getting back into seventh heaven when she heard Little Karen. She said to Michael, "Can I have a rain check on what I was thinking was going to happen." He gave her a big kiss and said, "Let's go see what our little angle wants." Michael stopped drinking wine at night and things started to turn around. He was more considerate with Alma and Karen.

The phone rang; this was about the 5th time this week. When she would pick up the receiver no one would answer, just hang up. Once a women said, "Sorry wrong number," and hung up. Alma figured there must be a new number close to theirs. She called the phone company and asked if they could trace the phone calls. They said they couldn't do that but there is a new thing the phone co. can install on her phone that would give them the phone number of the party that is calling. This was something new; she said you would be able to see the phone number of the party that was calling you... If it was a friend, you would see there phone number if it was a stranger, you wouldn't know the number so you wouldn't have to answer it. She said that would be fine. A few days later the phone company came and installed this thing on there phone, .a few days later the phone rang, the number wasn't someone that they new. She wrote the number down anyway. A few nights later the phone rang again, the call was coming from the same number as before. No answer. They would call all hours of the night. That was all Alma could take, the next time it rang she would let it ring and ring. When it stopped she called the number back. A sweet voice answered and said, "SPECIAL SERVICES."

The next day Alma called the phone company again, she asked what this "Special Service" was. They said they were sorry but they could not give out that information. She was really pissed. Then she thought of Chris, if anyone could find out, Chris could. She called downstairs, Chrissie answered the phone. They talked for a while, about boys and school and things like that. You know girl talk. She asked Chrissie if she would have her father call her when he gets home. No problem Chrissie said, and hung up. Later that evening Chris came knocking at her door. It was a long time sense he had seen her, even though they lived above or below one another. Chris could hear the arguing that was going on some times. But he didn't want to get involved. Now he was curious. She let him in and they went into the kitchen, she made a pot of tea for both of them. They talked for a while about his job and about Chrissie. She has gotten to be quit a young lady. She knows there's a difference between boys and girls now. He was going to ask her for some help with the girl-girl talk. She smiled and said she would be more then happy to help. Now came Alma's problem, she explained the trouble she's had with the phone company. Ringing and know one answered. The phone company had installed this thing on her phone so that she could see the phone numbers before she answered it. About the time she called the number back and got a woman answering the phone. "Special Services." She gave him the phone number and asked if he could find out what it's all about. He said, "It's not in his line, but he knows a detective that would be happy to look into it for me. It may take a few days, but I'll let you know just as soon as I hear."

They talked some more about little Karen, how smart she is and only 4 years old. She's still a very happy little girl. The bigger she gets the prettier she gets. I'm just worried what's going to happen when she starts to go out with boys, you know how boys are. The blond, blue-eyed well stacked happy go lucky girl. She'll be the princess of the school. They both laughed. Chris said, "That's what I'm going through now. I wish she had a mother that could talk mother, daughter stuff with her. She feels a little embarrassed talking about periods, bras, and things like that. I'm not very knowledgeable about things like that. She has told me that the girls do talk a lot but she's not sure if what they say is right. We have a good relationship and talk open with each other but, you know." Alma said, "Why don't I taken her shopping Saturday? Chris thought that would be great. Alma asked Chris if he would ask Chrissie if she would care to go with her. When Chris got down stairs, he called to Chrissie and asked her if she would like to go shopping with Alma Saturday? She said, "Would I," and ran up stairs to tell Alma. She would think about going, if she really wanted her too. Alma told her she didn't like shopping alone, but if she was going to do something else, maybe next week or two would be better. Chrissie ran over to Alma and said with a big hug, "Saturday would be great," and they both laughed.

All week long both Chrissie and Alma were in seventh heaven, just thinking about the coming Saturday. Chrissie would come up stairs every night after supper with a list of things she needed: Socks to match her dress, and jeans, four pair all different shoes, jeans and dresses, sweaters, tops, panties, six bras, and a lot of other things. When Thursday night came, Alma asked Chrissie, "Where are you getting all the money for these clothes?" Chrissie stopped talking for a minute, did some thinking, then said, "I could baby sit for you" Alma laughed, it was getting close to her birthday, now Alma new what to get her. However she is growing so fast it would be foolish to buy all the things on her list. She explained to Chrissie what she though would be the best things to buy now, and every few weeks buy something different. This way as you grow the clothes will grow with you. Chrissie came over and gave Alma a big hug and kiss. "Gee... you are one smart lady," Chrissie said with a smile. "Now all we have to do is wait till Saturday."

Friday night Alma didn't get home till late. She had to pick up Karen and go grocery shopping. When she got home there was a note under the door that said, *give me a call I would like to talk with you; Chris.* He must have some news on the phone number. She put the groceries away, made a pot of tea, put the biscuits on a plate, and called down stairs. Chris answered the phone; he told her he would be up in a minute. There was a knock at the door; Alma hollered, "Come in if you're good looking," and laughed. Chris came in, but there was no smile on this face. Alma took him into the kitchen poured the tea that she had made and sat down. Why the long face, what did you find out? She asked. What Chris found out was not going to be easy telling Alma. He didn't know where to start. She was all excited, what was the big mystery. Chris started from the beginning. The detective I talked with had been watching that house for the past two weeks. He had gotten a few complaints about crazy things going there. He would set in his car and take pictures of everyone going in and coming out of the house. The time they went in and the time they came out. Both men and women, the women would stay sometimes for a couple of hours. They didn't look like hookers, more like the average housewife, some young and some older, maybe in there mid forties. Last Wednesday night or early morning around I am, this truck pulled up in front. The driver got out of the truck and went inside. He was gone for forty minutes. He came out and got into his truck, put it in gear and smashed into a car. He didn't get hurt, but the car was pretty banged up. The detective has pictures of everything. The driver of the truck, the lady that owns the car and the marker plate numbers of both. He was wishing that a light was smashed so he could have her pulled over. No such luck.

The detective is trying to find out what is going on inside. With all the traffic going in and out he thinks it may be a house of prostitution, or possibly a dope ring. He doesn't want to barge in unless he knows for sure what he's looking for. They are trying to put an undercover detective in side. That should start this week. What they do know is the fellow that's driving the truck also delivers packages to the back door of the house. They are trying to find out where the packages are corning from. They are trying to match the pictures with some people we have on file. Drug dealers and the like. They do know the fellow that drives the truck has no police record. A paper cup fell out of his truck, it was picked up, and the fingerprints came up with a name. They are watching him twenty-four hours a day. The car he hit belongs to a man with a record for selling drugs and gambling. The truck has no signs on it but through the marker plate we know who it belongs to. I'm afraid Michael may be involved in some way. "We can't do anything until we know what's going on in there. We have stopped several people for not stopping at stop signs, one for speeding, and one for no tail light. No one would talk about the house." The officer never pushed the issue. "Please do not say anything to Michael yet." The detective didn't want me to say anything to you about what was going on. But he knows you work at the courthouse and can keep your mouth shut.

Alma was all upset; she couldn't even think that Michael would be involved in something like this. Chris broke into her thoughts. "Are you ok?" She looked up at him and in a soft voice said, "I'm ok." Then she started thinking again, are they watching our house, and were they outside watching me? Why would they be watching Michael twenty-four hours a day? Was he in some kind of danger? He wouldn't do anything out of line with the law; maybe Michael is helping the police. Again Chris broke into her thoughts. Please don't say anything to Michael. This could be very dangerous if drugs are involved. One slip of the tongue and Michael could be in real trouble, that is, if it is drugs. It could only be just prostitutes. If it's drugs they would want to know where it is coming from, and who is supplying them, and who is supplying the dealers. That would go right down the line. Michael wanting to be a nurse would know all about drugs. He did have some extra money the other day. I never gave it a thought, oh my god... he wouldn't do anything like that ...he just wouldn't.

Chris tried to comfort her; he was thinking, "Did I do the right thing telling her. Maybe I should have kept my mouth shut, but I didn't want this to come out as a shock to her if he was in trouble." After talking a little while longer he went down stairs. Michael had been acting kind of funny lately. That time a month ago when we were making love, he never acted like that before. And they hadn't made love since. The phone rang, she jumped a mile. Should she answer or not. Checking the number. She saw it was down stairs. Picking up the phone she said, "Hi." Chrissie was on the other end. "Alma what time are we leaving tomorrow?" She had forgotten about shopping with Chrissie. She thought for a minute then said, "How does ten-thirty sound? That way we can do some shopping, have lunch and do some more shopping, and if we have time take in a movie. That is if Karen is up to it." Chrissie said that sounded great, so they left it at that. Chrissie was all excited; this was the first time she was going shopping for girls stuff, big time. She had a hard time getting to sleep that night, thinking of all the things they were going to do.

Alma really didn't feel like shopping, and then she thought, maybe it would do her some good. It would take her mind of things for a while. Besides she couldn't disappoint Chrissie. She was sleeping in the chair when Michael came home from work she wanted to tell Michael she and Chrissie were going shopping in the morning, and not to worry if he didn't see her around. She turned the light on, took one look at Michael, and then looked at the clock. "Do you know what time it is? Where have you been till three-thirty in the morning?" He looked down at the floor and said, "One of his customers was having a party and asked him to stay and have a drink with them." He got talking and forgot what time it was. He said, "He was sorry and should have called and told her. He didn't have to go to work tomorrow so he could sleep a little later. He turned and went into the bedroom. That was all he had to say."

Alma slept on the bed; Michael had to sleep in the living room on the couch. The next morning Alma got up early, she went and got Karen out of the crib, fed and bathed her. Got her all dressed. She did the same for herself. She kept looking out the window, looking for a strange car or truck. She saw nothing. At least she felt a little better about that. She got the convertible stroller out and put it by the door; she looked again and saw nothing. The time was close to ten-thirty. So she took her purse, little Karen (little Karen wasn't little anymore) but she still needed guiding going down stairs and the stroller. Once she got every thing down, she knocked on the door. Hoping that maybe Chris would answer the door, but instead Chrissie came running out all excited. Daddy said, "We could use his car today, that way we don't have to take the bus." Alma was surprised that Chris would let them use his car, he was very fussy. They went down to the garage, put everything in the trunk and off they went. Today was there lucky day. They found a parking spot on the ground floor of the parking garage right next to the entrance door to the store they wanted. Off they went, and what a time they had. Everything Chrissie saw she wanted... two hundred dresses... three-hundred pairs of jeans, a thousand pair of shoes ...racks of underwear and etc. Ok Alma said, "With a big smile on her face, let's get back to earth. They picked out three dresses, two pair of jeans, and three pair of shoes. By this time they both were starving. They put all the cloths in the trunk of the car and off they went for food.

So far little Karen was an angel, there wasn't a peep out of her. It looked like she was having as much fun as Chrissie. After lunch they went back shopping. This time for underwear socks, blouses and bras. Not that Chrissie needed a bra yet, but all the girls in school were wearing them. Most were stuffed with Kleenex or cutting a rubber ball in half and putting them in there bras. Chrissie said she would wait a little longer before she started wearing one. She just wanted to be prepared. Alma was laughing to herself, as if it was going to happen over night. By the time they got through shopping it was too late for the movies. Alma promised that next week they would go have lunch, then to the movies. That sounded great with Chrissie. Two weeks in a row she could spend with Alma,

She didn't realize how tired she was till she sat down in the car. Just as she was about to start the car a horn blew. She turned around and there was Michael, he wanted to talk with Alma. She said, "It would have to wait till she got home, she was in no position or frame of mind to talk now." He said, "It was very important that he talk with her." She again said," Wait till we get home. Now would you please move so that I may get out? I have to take the children home now Chris will be worried, wondering were we are." Michael backed up, so that Alma could back out and drive off. She stopped at the gate, paid the man, and drove out. Alma was watching the rear view mirror to see if Michael was coming. Chrissie spoke up and asked, "Alma if everything was ok between them. She said she didn't like it if the two of them were fighting." Alma to make conversation started talking about what they had done today. She asked Chrissie if she was tired, and happy with all the cloths she bought. The two dresses were very pretty and the jeans went with the blouses. I don't think they will shrink but you never know. Alma was still looking in the rearview mirror. Michael was about two cars back. She told Chrissie, "When we get home take the packages and go right into your house. Later you can model your jeans, blouses, and dresses and maybe have your father come up to see how nice his daughter looks, and how big she has gotten."

I have to talk with Michael now when we get home. Chrissy was a little concerned about Alma and Michael. When they got home, Chrissie thanked Alma and gave her a big kiss and grabbed her packages and ran inside. Her father was waiting for her and gave her a big hug. Asked if she had a good time and bought the stores out? She told her father how Alma had paid for everything. She told me it was my birthday present. I told her she didn't have to do that but she insisted. She said they were from her and Michael. She told me to go right in the house when we got home. Alma drove around back and parked the car in the garage. Took the keys and locked the doors. When she got up stairs, Michael was there waiting for her.

"Please," Michael said, "I have to talk with you." After I get through talking, you can tell me what is on your mind. Maybe we can clean the air between us. First I want to apologize for staying out so late last night. I had a late delivery at this private home. A big party was going on and the owner asked me to stay and have a drink. I was tired and wanted to get home, he insisted. I swear I had no idea what this place was, I still don't know. People were coming and going all the time I was there. I would have left sooner but he asked me to take a package and send it the next morning. He gave me a twenty-dollar bill to cover the cost of sending it and I was to keep the change. I took the package, put it in the truck and left. As I started to leave the package fell off the seat. As I reached down to pick it up from the floor, the truck went forward and banged into a car. There were only some scratches so the owner said not to worry about it. I left, took the truck back to the garage and took the package into the shipping dept. weighed it and put a stamp on it and sent it out. That way it went out last night and I wouldn't have to worry about it. I had one glass of wine, that's all I had. I had to wait for the package. That's why I was so late. If you could smell tobacco on me it was because everyone was smoking. You could cut it with a knife. That's was why I was so late last night. I knew you wouldn't listen to what I had to say so I thought it better to hold off till today to tell you".

Alma never said a word; she got up from the chair... went over to Michael, put her arms around him, and gave him a sexy kiss. Then she happened to remember. She told Chrissie and her father to come up. Miss America was going to model the latest clothing line out. She backed away from Michael, told him to hold that idea for later. Then she explained, Michael said, "That's the story of my life, always too early or too late." smiled and said, "It would be hard to wait but he would try. He asked what her problem was. Like all women, she turned her back and said, "Forget it."

Later when Chris and Chrissie came up with all the boxes of clothes, Chrissie was pleased to see Alma and Michael were talking with each other. Michael got up and said, "Let the show begin." We have with us tonight the future Miss America; she will model some of the latest clothes for the teen aged girls." Chrissie went into the bedroom and put on one of the dresses and came strolling out with her hands on her hips. Turned a few times and bowed and asked, "Doesn't anyone like it? Your suppose to clap or something." Nobody did or said anything. She was very upset and started to run to the bedroom. When she got to the door, everyone clapped and said how nice she looked. She turned around and wiped a big tear from her cheek, then gave a big smile and strolled back into the bedroom. She showed all the rest of the clothes they bought, everyone thought they were great. She didn't model her underwear and her bras. She turned red when Alma asked if she was going to model them to. NO WAY she said and smiled. Chrissie was going down stairs and call her girl friend and tell her what she did today. Michael, Alma, and Chris were up stairs talking about the good time they had today. How Chrissie wanted all the dresses, shoes, jeans and blouses on the racks... Alma said how she told Chrissie that she is growing so fast she should only buy a few things every couple of weeks, that way nothing will be to small for her. Alma made them promise not to say anything to Chrissie about what she is going to tell them. Chrissie and I where walking down the isle where all the underwear was, She said she wanted to get a half dozen bras. I told her she really didn't need one yet. She said most of the girls at school are wearing them, even if they have to stuff them with Kleenex, and some have even cut some rubber balls in half and are using them. So as not to hurt her feelings, I said OK we will buy one today then maybe next week. But Chrissie said, maybe I should wait a little longer. They all were laughing, just make sure you don't say anything about this, or that I told you. Chris said, "He was going down stairs and see what Miss America was doing."

Michael and Alma sat on the couch watching TV for a while. Michael slid his hand over and it just happened to fall in Alma's lap. She didn't bother moving it because she though she new what was coming. Another five minutes went by and he happened to slide his hand down a little farther. This time he was kind of rubbing her lower extremities. She was starting to get uncomfortable in that position and moved just slightly toward him. In so doing her hand just happened to touch his belt buckle and wouldn't you know it, the buckle came apart. He paid know attention to what happened. He seamed to be more interested in the program on TV. A few minutes later, Alma got up and said she had to go to the bathroom, but she went to the bedroom to change. She took of all her clothes ...under things and all. Then she put on her housecoat with nothing underneath. She waited a few minutes, put a dab of perfume on, and then came walking out as if everything was O.K... She came over and sat down again next to Michael, only this time the flap of her housecoat just happened to be open a hair. Without looking he replaced his hand were it was before, and giving it a gentle rub. Alma was getting a little excited. He didn't look at her or where his hand was, but he knew she was about to climb all over him. She reached over and grabbed the bulge in his pants. He yelled" WHAT ARE YOU DOING TO ME?" IF YOU DON'T STOP I'll tell my mother on you." They both started laughing. The next thing you know they are feeling, pawing, rubbing, kissing, grabbing squeezing, more kissing massaging and running his fingers around the nipples of her breasts. That was one sure way of getting Alma in the mood. She loved to have her nipples caressed, nibbled on, and sucked. That just about drove her crazy. She wanted loving right then and there. Michael had all he could do to get his pants off before she was all over him. He had his pants off and was taking his

shirt off when she was removing his underwear. Her
hands and mouth were all over him, kissing, licking,
sucking, and feeling every part of his body. This went
on for a long time. There lovemaking was what they
both looked forward to; he loved to hear her groan
and moan while making love. After about two hours
of lovemaking they went to bed. Alma wanted still
more but Michael had cooled down and wanted to
sleep.

The next day was Sunday and Michael had just a little
homework to do. That meant they could take a ride in
the country. It was a sunny warm day, a picnic would
be ideal. Michael went out and got the car. He went
back to the house to see if there was anything he may
have forgotten. Alma was coming out with Karen and
Michael was about to lock the door when the phone
rang. Michael went back in to answer it. Alma stopped
to listen, Michael was talking very softly, she couldn't
hear everything that was being said, but she did get
some of it. He hung up the phone and came out the
door. Alma was there and asked who it was? He said
it was a wrong number. She asked what they wanted.
He said they were looking for someone with the last
name as ours, FOX. I told them I couldn't help them.
Come to think about it, I never have looked in the
phone book to see how many Fox's there are, if any.

That bothered Alma all the rest of the day. When she
got home, the first thing she did was to copy down
the phone number that called. Then she went and got
the phone book. She was looking through it when

Michael came in from putting the car away. He said he was going to do the same thing himself. There was about a dozen, the first was M. Fox, the second was M&A Fox, that was us, the next was M&J, and on down the line. The last one was the FOX Co. She was wondering if the phone number that called this time was the same number that's been calling all the time. She had to wait till the time was right to check it out. It was the same number.

The next night she called Chris, told him everything she knew. He said, "Thanks," and hung up. A few evenings later there was a knock at the door. A well-dressed man was standing in the doorway. "Can I help you," Alma asked? The man reached in his pocket and took out his wallet, flipped it open. There was a silver badge, Detective, Easton Pennsylvania Police Department. This took Alma by surprise. He told her he was a friend of Chris's, and was working on the phone calls that she had been getting. She felt better now, she invited him inside. He looked familiar as though she had seen him before. Then it struck her. She had seen him at the courthouse; he had been on the witness stand in a big trial not to long ago. The difference now is he has a mustache. She invited him in, and asked if maybe Chris should be there also. He said he didn't mind. As of yet he still hadn't told me his name. When she called down stairs Chris answered the phone. Alma said there was a detective up stairs and wanted to talk with her. Would he please come up? He said he would be there in a few minutes. No sooner had she hung up the phone when the door opened. There stood Chris. He looked over and said, "Hi Jim, glad to see you." Alma was a little upset; she still did not know his name. She asked and he apologized, he thought Chris had told her JIM KUZIAK. He reached in this pocket and gave her his card. She started to take it then thought better of it. She didn't want anything around that might look suspicious. She did however take his phone number. She put that under COURT. That way if anything is said, she can always say it has to do with work.

"Let's start from the beginning, when did you start receiving these phone calls, and did anybody say anything?" "The first time was about two and a half weeks ago. That first week there must have been at least six or seven calls, day and night. The only time I heard someone was about a week ago, a ladies voice said 'I'm sorry I must have gotten the wrong number.' That voice didn't sound like the same one, as the one when I called back the other day." The detective asked about the call Michael received. I told him I couldn't get all of the conversation he was talking very low. After, he told me someone was looking for another person with a last name of FOX. I should have asked him if they gave a first name. He wanted to know if Michael has been acting in any peculiar way lately. Did he seem nervous in anyway, jumping to answer the phone when it rang. Asking questions about any phone calls, coming home late, did Michael do drugs, did Michael drink, why is Michael going back to school now, what does he plan on doing when he gets out, how much longer does he have to go. Does he have any extra clothes where he works, have you ever met any of the people he goes to school with, has he ever talked about anyone in particular, male or female? She answered all the questions the best she could. He has come home with the smell of wine on his breath, and he has come home late at times and yes he stayed out all night a few times. He said he was sleeping in his truck because he was so tired. He dozed off and it was early morning when he woke up. He has been studying hard lately and was very tired. Oh yes, the other night he came in at 3:30 AM. I was waiting up for him, but dozed off; he woke me when he came in. He was surprised to see me. I asked him, "Were have you been at this hour in the morning?" He said one of his customers was having a party and asked him to stay and have a drink with them. He got to talking and forgot what time it was. He said, "He was sorry and he should have called, A few days later he told me what happened. As he was about to leave the party the owner asked Michael if he would mail a small package for him. He gave Michael a twenty-dollar bill and said keep the change. Michael had to take the truck back to the garage, so he went inside to the shipping department and weighed the package and put a stamp on it. That way it went out that night." That was about all she could say, unless she thinks of something later.

"Now tell me what's going on? Is Michael involved with any of this, and if so just what has he done? Tell me I want to know... What about this house you have been watching, what kind of a place is it?

Do they sell dope, Is it a whorehouse or what." The detective said he didn't think Michael was involved in anything that was or is going on inside the house. "That package that Michael mailed may be a problem. Only because he mailed it and he was at the house party and had a few drinks. I also have pictures of Michael delivering some packages to the rear of the house. What we need now is the address from the package, how much did it weigh, and what was inside. Our big problem is the one that can help us is the one we can't talk to. If he is a member of the gang that's in there he can tip them off and we have lost everything. If we take a chance and try to get Michael on our side and he refuses were sunk. We have to get someone inside undercover, someone that can get all the information we need for the bust. Alma I'm telling you all of this only because you work in the court system and can keep your mouth shut. If any of this leaks out your neck and mine are cut off at the shoulders. Chris would also be hung. So please not a word to anyone. If either one of you hears anything, anything at all, please call me at once. Let Michael do what he's been doing, You can holler at him but not to loud if he comes home late, or not at all some nights. Just a thought... ask Michael if there's any openings at the warehouse, a friend of yours is looking for a part time job. If we could have one of our men work in the warehouse we may be able to find out where the packages are coming from and where they are being sent to. That way we may be able to find out what's going on or at least maybe know if we are wasting our time. In the mean time I'll see if we can get a line crew to check on the telephones. Maybe tap your line and theirs. First I'll have to get a court order to do all of this."

Things were pretty quiet for almost a week, the phone only rang once, and they hung up before I could answer it, or even the machine could print the phone number. Jim was waiting for the court to say they could tap the lines. No work was needed at the warehouse, and things went along the same as before. Michael was coming home at the regular time and everything seemed normal. Jim was starting to wonder what was going on. Everything seemed to have quieted down. Did someone talk, Maybe there was nothing in the first place. The Judge didn't think there was enough to warrant a phone tap so that was out. Jim still didn't feel things were right at that house. He went to the warehouse and had a talk with the manager. I didn't feel right telling him everything, so he made up a story that a shipment of counterfeit money was being sent to this address. Someone is suppose to pick it up. What he would like to do is put a detective in here for about a week or two as a part time worker. This way we can keep our eyes open and find out where this package is coming from and who is picking it up. We think it's coming in by boat and then being mailed to someone here. Our informants in South America think it may be sent in a week or so. A ship is coming into the states soon and it might be the one. We also would like your word that this will not get out to any of your employees. The manager said he wouldn't tell. Jim made all the arrangements and left.

Karen was going to have her fifth birthday in three weeks. Alma was getting ready to give her a big birthday party. How big she has gotten, it seemed only a few years age that she had a baby in the entrance of the Easton General Hospital. Next year she will be going to kindergarten. Chrissie was all excited and pitched in to help. Chrissie was fifteen years old by now and will graduate next June. By now she is buying her own cloths, However, every time she went shopping she would always ask Alma to go with her. The big joke was always about buying bras. Chrissie had put the first bra in a box and sealed it, put it under her bed, and said some day she would open it up. Today she picks out her own bras and they are much larger then the first one.

Saturday afternoon the doorbell rang, Alma thought it was Chrissie coming up to help. She opened the door and there stood two well-dressed men. They pushed there way into the room told Alma to sit down. Alma started to holler, "What are you doing here and what do you want." She got up and they pushed her back down on the couch. One of them said, "If you don't want to get hurt you'll stay there." The other man looked in the other rooms saw that there was no one else there, came back, and wanted to know where her husband was. They wanted to have a little talk with him. Alma told them he was having the oil changed and the car greased, at the filling station. He would be awhile, because he left only a short time ago. What do you want with my husband; he hasn't done anything to you guys, so please leave. If you don't I'll call the police. They started to laugh, lady that won't do you a bit of good. We'll just wait till he comes home. You just sit there and be a good wife. Just then Karen came in the room. She looked at the two men and asked if they were her uncles? They got a big charge out of that. She went over to her mother and asked what do they want? Alma took her in her arms and held her. She started to wiggle free. And whispered" mommy I have to go to the bathroom and make pee-pee. Alma said "have Chrissie help you, don't slip on the rug" Karen ran around the corner and closed the door.

Again Alma asked, "What do you want with my husband, what could he possible have done to make two thugs like the looks of you, want with him." "Lady it's not what he has done, it's what he's going to do for us." "There's not a single thing that my husband would do for either one of you jerks, now please leave." One of them got up and went to the kitchen looking for a class of water. The other hollered to him "Bob check on the kid, she's been gone a long time just to take a leak." This Bob guy looked in the bathroom, the girl wasn't there. "What happened to the girl lady," the other guy asked? Alma said she didn't know, she may have gone down stairs to see the people down there. She was excited to think that two uncles were here to see her. She must be telling them all about you. Just then there was a knock at the door. Alma started to get up. This guy Bob said, "Get rid of them fast." She went to the door and opened it. There stood Chris, he asked if everything was OK? She winked and said everything was fine; she had Karen's uncles here. Thanks for asking and closed the door. Michael should be coming home shortly. She hoped Chris saw her wink and close the door in his face. About fifteen minutes later the phone rang. Alma started to get up to answer it. This Bob said, "No funny stuff lady or you'll be sorry." She answered the phone..."Hi Hon, do I want to go out for supper tonight"... "No... Why don't you bring home some pizza with onions we haven't had that in a long time. See you soon"... And hung up. Michael was told that there were some guys there, but they didn't know what they wanted. They wanted to know if he had done anything wrong, that some people might be after him. He said he hadn't. The only thing he remembers doing was hitting that car, but that was only a scratch. The detective said to get a pizza make it a large, but leave the onions off. Put everything else on it. Michael stopped in at the pizza place and ordered it. He waited about fifteen minutes and it was ready. He went around to the back of the house put the car in the garage. They had him come to the front and when he got to the door, he hollered to Alma to open the door. She came over and opened the door. There was Michael, carrying the pizza. Behind him were Chris and Jim coming up the rear. Alma was so glad to see them all. She was trying to tell them about the two men. They wanted to talk to Michael. When the three of them got into the room, Jim said he had a confession to make. The two men were detectives that he had sent to Michael's house to see if Michael may be in some way involved with the people in the house. When they called and unbeknownst to Alma, she had given them the answer that Michael was OK. By asking for the pizza, the onions part through him off. Michael said. She didn't like onions so something was wrong. They all laughed. She was a smart cookie all right.

The judge wouldn't help him out, and he didn't trust the manager at the place where Michael worked. He didn't think the guy would keep his mouth shut, so Michael was the only one that had an inside track to the house. But first he had to be sure he could trust Michael, that's why he sent the two detectives over. Jim felt sorry for having to do what he did, but still he had the funny feeling something was not right. But as of now ... We had better eat the pizza before it gets cold. They all started to laugh. Chris called down stairs for Chrissie to come up. She flew up the stairs in two seconds flat, ran over to Alma, and gave her a big hug. Knowing she was safe and all right was all that Chrissie needed. Alma felt relieved, the whole thing makes sense now, but before, things didn't look good at all. She wished they had warned her before hand what was happening.

After they finished eating and drinking their soda, Jim said, "We need to talk alone; I don't want anyone else involved. My men, Michael, and myself. The rest can go down stairs or we can go down to the station house, it's up to you. They decided to go down stairs, After they all had left, Jim thought it better to talk at the house, this way if anyone was watching Michael they would think they were having a party. After they had left, Jim asked Michael if he knew anything at all about this house. What did they do there? Did they smoke pot or sell drugs; did you see any money being exchanged for drugs? Did they have any girls around, had any girls gone up stairs with any guys, or other girls? What was in the packages that you delivered to the back door? Where did the packages that you mailed out go to? We want to know everything we possibly can about that house and the people that go there. Michael was confused about the whole thing. He knew nothing about what was going on inside the house. He didn't know what was inside the packages that he left there, nor did he know what was in the packages that he mailed out. He did however know the address of the packages he was sending out... But that was all. ..

Jim was satisfied with what Michael had told them, but Jim wanted more. This was where Michael came in... He wanted Michael to find out everything he could, without being nosy. In other words, he could ask some simple questions and listen to what people were talking about. Were they smoking pot and dealing in drugs or were they running a house of prostitution. Was there anyone there that you new? Maybe a customer or someone like that? If there was, get next to him; find out what he knows about the house. Tell them you think the place is great, get excited about it, but don't ask too many questions. One or both of these men will be in contact with you. Looking for all the answers you can give us. They may be bums, drunks, or Chauffeurs; they may be lost in the city asking for directions. They will always

ask one question so you will know who they are. If
they are dressed as a bum they, Will ask for food
money, If they are drunks, they would ask for money
for a drink, If they are a chauffeur they may ask for
directions to some place. They will ask a question
that fits the outfit they are wearing. You know what I
mean? It may be both or it may be only one of them.
Their names are not important; this way you won't
say Ray or Sam... If they are looking for a hand out
give them something. Maybe a couple of dollars. We
will reimburse you later. Keep talking with them,
telling them everything you have found out. Make it
seem like you are interested in what they do or where
they are from.

"Do you have any questions? But first . . . let me ask
you a question, will you do this for us? I don't think
there's any danger involved, if there was I wouldn't
ask you to do this. All we want is information as to
what is going on in that house. Do Not. And I mean
Do Not. Do anything that would endanger yourself,
do you understand? We will do that. .. What do you
think?" Michael thought for a while, and then said,
"OK when do I start." Jim said there's one more thing,
you are to talk with NO ONE about what you are
doing, Not Chris. . . Chrissie. . . Alma or anyone else,
is that understood? And you will not be paid for doing
this either. We may be able to fix a parking ticket once
in a while though. As to when do you start? You have
already. . . Keep your eyes and ears open for any little
thing.

For the next week and a half, things were pretty quiet at the house. It seamed like everything had come to a halt. Then on Friday night, Michael saw that there was a package for delivery to that house. He copied the return address down and put the package on the very bottom because that would be the last delivery. He then went inside to the men's room, came out a few minutes later, and there was his manager going through the packages. Michael went up to him and asked what he was doing? It startled him at first. Then he said, he was counting the number of packages he had, that's all. Michael noticed the package for the house was on top. That's funny. He was sure that he put it on the bottom. What was he looking for? That's something he'll have to tell the detective about. He made his rounds with no problem. The last stop was like before, the house was jumping. He went around to the back door and rang the bell. A different man came to the door and asked what he wanted. Michael was surprised to see this new man, he told him he had a package and the other man told him to make all the deliveries to the back door the man took the package scribbled something on his sheet and slammed the door in his face. This was something new. .. Before he was always invited in for a glass of wine or whatever. Now the door was slammed in his face. He went and got in his truck, checked his watch and started out the driveway, when he got to the end of the drive; a car came speeding up and almost hit him; swung into the drive way and jammed on the brakes Michael couldn't see the marker plate, and his truck was to big to park it and walk back to check it out. The time was twelve fifty-five AM. He took the truck back, got into his car, and went home. Alma or Chris never once asked any questions about what was going on. He wanted to talk with someone but there was no one to talk with. He was getting nervous.

The following week things were pretty quiet. The usual stops and pickups. Friday night he had another package for the house, same return address. Again he put the package on the bottom for his last stop. Checking the bulletin board for any pickups was a note; make pickup at such and such a house. That was the house the package was going to. It seamed strange that a pickup notice would be posted on the board. That never happened before. He made his regular deliveries and pickups. The house was his last stop, and again it was swinging. He drove around back, parked the truck, and rang the doorbell. The same man answers the door, only this time he was friendlier. Said he was sorry for slamming the door in my face and would I like a beer or a glass of wine. He said he also had a package going out and would I please mail it tonight. It was almost ready. I told him no problem. This new man and Michael got to be pretty friendly. The man was interested in the package delivery service business. Michael told him everything he knew. The conversation slowed down, witch gave Michael a chance to ask were the other guy was he seemed like a nice man? He would always stand around and we would talk like this. Waiting for the package. The guy said he was out of town for a couple of weeks. Then changed the subject. The package was brought out by the same women as before. She said, "Hi Michael, did you get your glass of wine tonight." Michael smiled and said, "Yes thank you." Picked up the package and this time he only got ten dollars for mailing it. Back in the truck he drove out of the driveway very slow, afraid that the car would come down the road again. He drove back to the garage, copied the address, went into the shipping department and weighed the package put stamps on it and sent it out.

The next day he was on his way to school when the meter reader came down the street; stopped Michael and asked if he knew where the meter was on the apartment building. Without thinking Michael said he though it was around back someplace. The meter reader asked if he would show him where. Michael said he was late for classes and go look for yourself. Just then the gas company truck pulled up to the curb. When the driver got out, Michael recognized the man. The first man had a pair of sunglasses on and Michael didn't recognize him. He took the two men around to the back of the building, telling them every thing he had seen and heard, plus what the manager at the truck garage had done. He slipped a piece of paper in the driver's hand it contained the two addresses, both coming and going. Michael left the two men in the back of the building while he went on to his classes.

The two detectives took the truck back to the gas co. garage, thanked the manager and left. When they get back to the police headquarters, they called for Jim to join them. They may have something going with the outgoing address. They called the police department in Berwick Minnesota and asked them if they had ever heard of this address. They transferred the call over to detective George Shaw. Detective Shaw had been working on this case for a long time, but it seemed to have led to no place. When Shaw got on the phone he was surprised to hear from a police department in Pennsylvania that was interested in the case he had been working on for over seven months. It seems this outfit has an inside mouthpiece somewhere that keeps them up to date on everything that goes on. Just when we got close to something, they would move on. "Now you tell me they are in Easton Pennsylvania. What are they trying to do out there, start another whore house?" Jim said, "WHORE HOUSE" you mean that's all that's been going on in that house is screwing? Here all the time I thought it was drugs. Shaw said, "That's probably part of it too, but we couldn't get into the circle. When we would try, they would catch on and either get rid of that person or move on. We haven't seen or heard from them in several months. I still have an open book on them, but that's all." Shaw said, "Besides there must be something bigger then girls. Other wise why would they be so secretive about there business. The only thing I can say is good luck and if you find out what's going on, would you let me know." Jim said, "Thanks" and hung up. Now he's really curious. That address was just a house with no wants or warrant's to it. The next package that's going to be sent out, we will have drug sniffing dogs and an x-ray machine here. We'll find out what's inside of it, and it better be something good. We'll have to do it when the garage manager is not around. I don't trust him. I'm going to see him tomorrow, just to let him know that nothing showed up with the money in it, so I canceled everything. I'll see how he acts.

Michael went about his work, the same thing day in and day out. There was nothing to report so nobody came around to talk with him. If a bum or a drunk came around he would tell them to get lost, and keep on walking. Two weeks later on a Tuesday night when he checked in to make his rounds, the garage manager boss told him there's a message for him on the bulletin board. There was a note asking him to please pick up a box for shipping Thursday night. Thursday night, that's different. Friday night's are usually the time for deliveries and pick up's, he had to get word to Jim so that he would have the dog's and x-ray machine ready for Thursday instead of Friday. He had a feeling he was being watched, this may be a test, to see if they could trust him or not. He had to be real careful from now on. He went down to the garage where he keeps his car and let out some air from one of his tires till it was almost flat. The next morning when he drove to class, he stopped at his gas station and told them to fix the slow leak in the tire and he would pick it up later. He was late so he started walking fast. At the comer this chauffeur driven limo pulled up as if to ask directions. Michael talked as if he was giving the driver the way to go, but he was really telling him to go to the gas station, look in the glove compartment for a note. If the attendant says anything, tell him you're my brother-in-law and you are picking up a map that I had in the glove compartment. He waved his arm in a couple of directions as if to say down that street turn... Etc. etc. then walked on to class. When the classes were over he walked back to the gas station and picked up his car. The service station man said that a man came in and took something from the dash. Michael said "Oh Gosh, I forgot to tell you my brother-in-law was going to pick up my map. I didn't think I was going to stop here, but that's OK. Sorry.

Thursday night after making all of his stops, he went to the house to pick up there package. He rang the bell. When it opened the first guy was back. Michael said, "What's your name? I was here a couple of weeks ago and a stranger opened the door. I asked where the other guy was, witch would be you. He said what's his name? I said I didn't know his name but he's the guy I always see. This guy was kind of pissed because I didn't know your name. He didn't even give me a class of wine and slammed the door in my face. I had to wait about fifteen minutes and he only gave me $10.00. I thought he was still here, seeing as its Thursday and not Friday. So welcome back. The guy laughed, he said he was sorry about that, but he didn't expect they would be away that long. But he had some sickness in the family. The next time then, who ever answers the door and wants my name, say you know Tony. Michael laughed, and then said he was sorry to hear about the sickness in his family. Tony said things would be all right now, and changed the subject. Tony asked Michael if he would like a glass of wine. Michael with a smile on his face said sure. He had to wait for the package, like always. Tony went and got them both a glass of wine. Tony and Michael got to be real pals. Tony wanted to know all about Michael, where he came from, any family... married... kids... what he was going to school for... did he like it... and did he like the work. Michael in turn asked... what kind of wine he got and where can he get some? Tony said any time you want some more let him know. Michael said he'd like to get a bottle soon, Tony went in another room and came out with two bottles of wine and gave them to Michael. Here he said, when you need more, let me know. Michael wanted to pay him but Tony wouldn't think of it. Michael asked if he made it. Tony laughed and said no but his family owns a grape vine, they both got a kick out of that one. Just then the same girl brought out the box, handed it to Tony. Tony checked it over to make sure it was sealed tight, and then gave it to Michael. As he was about to leave, Tony called him back, reached in his pocket and gave Michael a twenty dollar bill. Michael tried to refuse it because of the wine he had given him, but Tony wouldn't think of it. Tony said, "The wine was a present to you, the package is business, you take the money." Michael smiled, shook his head, took the twenty dollar bill and left.

This time the box had a different address on it, and was quit a bit heavier then before. Michael got the address. When he got back to the garage, all hell was going on. The place was all lit up and police cars with there lights flashing were all over the place. Michael didn't know what was going on. A man in a suite came over and talked with Michael, he said there was a box containing counterfeit money, bills in tens and twenties and they were coming from South America., and they were trying to find it. So they were X-Raying every box and package in the place. That was coming in. Michael said he had some that were going out, and if it would be all right to put them on the side and go home. The man said he would find out and left, a few minutes later a policeman came over to the truck and asked for my driver's license. Michael showed it to him; he copied it down and gave it back to Michael. The officer told him to back his truck over on the side, it would be OK, and he could go home. Michael parked the truck, took his two bottles of wine, and went to ring out. He heard someone say check all the trucks. When Michael got home he told Alma what was going on at the garage, had a sandwich and a cup of coffee and went to bed.

The next day at school he heard they found a box with a lot of money in it. Michael wasn't worried; his mail was going out, not coming in. When he got though school and was going to his car, a drunk was in the parking lot. Michael went over to him and told him to go. He even helped him to the side so he wouldn't get hit and he gave the drunk a couple of dollars for food. The drunk was pulling away and talking at the same time. Telling Michael they checked the box out and haven't gotten a report back yet. Michael kept pushing the drunk back finally the drunk took off down the street. Michael got in his car and went home. Had a bite to eat and went to the garage .everything was quite. The boss came over to Michael and told him about the big time they had last night. Michael said he saw it but was tired and didn't hang around. What happened anyway? He asked. The boss said, "How this copper came in a few days ago and said there was a package of monkey money coming in from South America, and it was going to come to our garage. Then yesterday he comes back and said they found nothing on the ship, so he said he was sorry and left. Last night all hell broke lose. At ten o'clock police cars with there lights flashing, Police dogs and everything came in to our garage," the cop said, "He was sorry but the tip was wrong .well you know what happened after that. They checked every box and package in the warehouse. Then they found it. One of the dogs sniffed something, they x-rayed the box, and what looked like newspapers was really funny money. Boy could I have had a ball with all that money." They said it was the best they had ever seen, over a million dollars in tens and twenties.

Michael was happy that nothing was disturbed on this load; at least he didn't think so. He would check with Jim later, from a private phone. He heard nothing for a week. He had left a bottle of wine behind the apartment house so they could check it out. No report on that either. The house was still having parties but no pick-ups. Michael stopped in one night, said he had a delivery near there and was checking if anything was going out. Tony came to the door, saw it was Michael and let him in. Michael was telling Tony about what happened at the garage the other night. Cops all over; checking all the incoming packages only. They found a bundle of funny money, over a million dollars worth from South America. My boss said the cops said it was the best they had ever seen. Tony just shook his head. They only checked the incoming packages though Michael said that's all. Tony said they had nothing going out and he would call when he needed something. Michael said ok and left. On his way back to the garage he stopped at a pay phone and called Jim. The first thing Jim said when he answer the phone was "Do you know what time it is." This had better be important, so lets have it. Michael didn't realize how late it was. He asked Jim if they had found anything in the box or with the wine. Jim said the wine was very good; the box was a different story... That is being traced wherever it goes. What did they find... drugs, funny money..., or what? Jim wouldn't say what was in the box, or where it went after it left the garage. He hung the phone up and got back in his truck. He started to pull onto the highway when he noticed lights behind him. He hadn't seen any cars before. Now where did he come from? Michael was getting a little worried. He started down the road, keeping an eye in the rear view mirror. The headlights seem to have dropped way back; he didn't pay any more attention to them. Just as he was about to turn onto East Street the light turned red. He stopped and as the light turned green, this car pulled up beside his truck and forced him onto the side of the road. Two men got out and walked back to the truck. Michael was scared now. What would they want at this time of the night, with him? As they approached the truck they split, one on each side of the cab the one on the driver's side asked Michael if he know where so and so street was.

Michael felt a little more at ease. They were lost, he told the man to follow him, he was going into town and would direct them right there. They said "thanks" as the man turned to go back to the car. The second man opened the passenger side door and shot Michael in the chest; he then turned and met the first man. The truck and Michael sat there till nine the next morning. An alarm had gone out to be on the lookout for the truck and driver missing since last night. A state highway patrolman happened to see the truck.

Alma had called the police around three thirty am, and told them her husband hadn't come home from work yet. She called Chris down stairs and was all upset. Chris put on a pair of pants and shirt and went right up stairs. Chris called headquarters; they hadn't heard anything as yet. When the call came in that they had found Michael and the truck, an ambulance was dispatched to the area and took Michael to the hospital He was still alive, but in serious condition. They called Alma and told her they found Michael and his truck and was taking Michael to the hospital. Nothing was said about his condition. She didn't know what to do. Chris told her to get dressed and he would take her to the hospital He was going down stairs and wake Chrissie and let her know what was going on. When he got down stars he called headquarters, he wanted to talk with the officer in charge. He told Chris... Michael had been shot and in serious condition, they didn't expect him to live. Chris found out what hospital and hung up. He woke up Chrissie and called Alma and told her to be ready, he was taking her to the hospital Chris wasted no time in getting there, he parked in the ER parking area, and they ran into the waiting room. Told the receptionist who they were, a doctor came out and told her they did everything they could, but it wasn't enough, Michael had died. Chrissie hugged Alma and Chris was holding them both from falling. A nurse came over and gave Alma a pill to help her through the hard time ahead. Chris left Alma and Chrissie and went back to headquarters to find out what happened. It was too soon to tell, the detectives were working on it now.

Chris went to the garage to talk with Michael's boss. He didn't want to talk with anyone. The detectives were already there. They towed the truck to their garage. There were so many people around the truck that they had rubbed out any footprints or tire tracks that may have been there. They were dusting the truck for fingerprints and looking for the bullet, or bullet hole. They were hoping that the bullet was still in the truck. They found nothing... By the looks of things, it must have been a mob rub out. His truck was seen a number of times at this house, so they assumed he was part of the party.

Alma felt a little better after taking the pill. She realized what had happened and was able to meet with the undertaker. Chris was a big help in arranging everything. After the funeral Chrissie stayed up stairs with Alma for several weeks. Alma finely got it together, and went back to work. Everybody was very understanding and willing to help in any way. Still no word as to what... Why and who did this dastardly thing. Nothing was missing from the truck; Money and watch were still with Michael... Jim had talked with Michael that night. It was about twelve thirty am... Michael had told Jim everything that he new. The next day the detectives went to the house, rang the doorbell. Tony answered the doorbell, the detectives asked him about Michael. "Sure he knew Michael, a nice fellow. Sure he gave Michael some wine; sure he received and sent packages by Michael." That's all they could get out of him. Tony seemed very upset about Michael's death. He liked Michael, and if there was anything he could do for the widow, please have her get in touch with him. The detectives left, they found out nothing. Everything seemed on the up and up at the house. They were getting nowhere in the case. There was no witness, no fingerprints, no tire tracks, nothing. Jim was starting to think that maybe the mob rubbed out the wrong guy. It was put in the paper that anyone knowing anything about the murder please call the police department at once, the phone number is 301-564-9000. Alma was still very upset. As time went on there was still know leads in Michael's murder. Alma couldn't bear going out in the morning and coming home at night without Michael. Chris and Chrissie where a God- sent to her, they were always at the right spot at the right time, when she needed help but she still wasn't at peace with what happened. She wanted more... someone to blame for her misery. She was forever blaming everyone at the office for things that never happened, and people were getting upset because that was not her way. Finely her boss came to her and said, "for her to lighten up with the people or she would have to do something she didn't want to do." She didn't say what but it was plain what she meant. After that Alma was more considerate with the others. She was more like her old self again. Things still bothered her; she would call Jim almost every day to see if there was anything new. Jim was very patient with her, but there was nothing to tell her. . Little Karen wanted to know where her Michael was, when was he coming home, plus a million other questions.

One day she decided she would leave Pennsylvania for good. It was a bad dream for her. She had been reading books about New York State, Connecticut, and Rhode Island. The more she thought about moving the more she liked the idea. She would wait till school was out, and then take a vacation up to the northern states. She liked the snow so maybe New York State would be the first place to look. She had saved a little money, plus Michael's insurance and they had a car. Karen was almost 7 years old now; still happy go lucky and always smiling. If she was going to make the move, now would be the right time. The first week in June came; Alma invited Chrissie and Chris up for supper. She told them she had something to tell them. After eating Alma said, "She was going on a vacation up in New York State. She told them what she had in mind. They both tried to talk her out of it, but she had made up her mind. She asked, "Chrissie if she wanted to come along with them. Chrissie had a part time job and a boyfriend and didn't want to leave either one. Chris never told her not to go, but he was very sad. He knew what she had in mind. And there wasn't much he could do about it. He told her what ever made her comfortable inside and out it was her decision. If you ever need anything he would always be there for her. Alma got her two-week vacation starting the day after school was out. She packed the car and left, waving till they were out of site. She had the map all marked out, which route to take and what towns she would go through, and what to look for. She wanted a medium size town, friendly people, and a good school for Karen. She would also want a job. The courthouse was really the only thing she had ever done so that would be the first thing to look for. They stopped in a small city called Plantsville for the night. The people were friendly, and the rate they charged for the room was not bad and they didn't charge for Karen either.

The next morning they went to a little restaurant down the street for breakfast. There was a sign in the window "waitress needed." They went inside. It was a quant restaurant. Clean tables and rugs on the floor, even the windows were clean. They ordered breakfast; Alma kept looking around, she liked what she saw. When breakfast came there was enough for two on each plate. Pancakes, eggs scrambled hash brown potatoes ...and excellent coffee, and real maple syrup. At that hour in the morning they weren't very busy. There was only the cook there, doing the cooking, waiting on tables... cleaning the counter and everything else. But the place was spotless and he didn't seem to mind. He was humming to himself and was talking with a few customers. He seemed like a real nice man. When he came over to Alma he said, "What a nice day it was going to be, not to hot and not to cold how about a refill on the coffee?" Alma said, "It was the best coffee she has had in a long time, and yes she would love a second cup. He said it was his secret blend. He makes it himself." She asked, "If he was the owner, chief cook, and bottle washer he said with a smile". He just bought the place a few months back. It was in horrible condition, dirty, you couldn't see out of the windows. It took him three weeks to clean it up. He still has more to do, like changing the light fixtures and putting some nice pictures on the walls. She asked about the waitress job. He looked at her and said, "You would be interested in witnessing?" "Maybe", she said. What are the hours? The cook asked, "Don't you want to know what the pay is first?" She said, "Not really, the tips probably would take care of the pay." "This is the first woman I ever met that wasn't interested in making a thousand dollars a week." They both laughed. He sat down in the booth across from her. He asked, "What's your name?" She said, "Alma." He said, "Hi Alma I'm Bill, and I own this here place." She asked a lot of questions about the city. What were the prime industries in the city, how was business's doing in town and a few other questions? Just then a police officer came in. "Hi Bill how ya doing...nice day it's going to be. How about a big cup of your famous brew?" Bill talked with him for a few minutes; the officer gave Bill a dollar and walked out. Bill came back to the table and sat down. Alma asked, "Did you charge that policeman for his coffee? Bill said, "Sure did, why do you ask, she said, "Back home the policeman never pays for anything." Bill said, "If they don't pay they don't eat or drink. We pay our police very good. They are no different then you or I or any other customer, besides the chief won't allow the officers to have anything free." They talked for a few more minutes. Then Alma asked for the check, paid it and started walking out, Bill followed her to the door and asked if she was really interested in the job. Alma said, "She would let him know."

She wanted to look the place over first. This was only her first stop. Karen thought Bill was pretty cool. They got in the car and started riding around, looking for other restaurants, churches, factories, courthouse and the police station also the firehouses. She liked the overall size of the city and the people were real friendly. She never asked; Bill why the other waitress quit. Maybe there wasn't enough business. The food was very good and the place including the windows was very clean. Bill seemed like a nice enough fellow. But the place had been run down and Bill only opened it a few months ago. She stayed around till noontime; she wanted to see what kind of lunch business he had. She parked her car across the street and watched. There seemed to be a steady flow of customers for about two hours then it slowed down. She didn't know how Bill handled all those people. After the rush hour was over and only a few customers left, she went over and told Bill; She had a few days off from her present job and if the waitress job is still open when she gets back, she may take the job. Said, "goodbye to Bill and left."

Alma and Karen got in the car and started looking at the map again. Went over to the gas station and filled the tank, and took off. Rt. 41 seemed to be the main route through New York State up to the Canadian boarder. She kept her eyes open all the way up to the next good-sized town. She was in no hurry but it was getting late and she was looking for a nice place to spend the night. Several signs read: *Stay in The Green Mountains of New York State... Stay At The Arrow Town Motel...3 Miles Ahead...Clean, Friendly, And Reasonable.* It was a fairly large town and a lot of new homes were being built. Construction was booming. Their must be a new factory going up some place. They got there in no time flat. The motel was on top of a large hill. It had a beautiful view and what a sunset. She pulled into the parking spot and went inside. Asked the clerk, "What the price of the room was, and if there was an extra charge for Karen.?" The desk clerk said, "The price of the room and there was an extra charge for Karen. The price was twice of what she paid last night and there was a ten-dollar charge for Karen. She said, "Thanks and left". They got in the car and she started the motor, on the windshield she noticed a ticket. She shut the motor off and went to see what it was all about. The ticket read that she was parked in a customer parking spot and that there was a ten dollar fine. Alma was furious; she took the ticket back into the motel, handed the ticket to the clerk, "And wanted to know what this was all about." He told her, "She had parked in one of the guests parking places and there was a Ten Dollar fine. Alma was really pissed. First she said, "There's no sign out there that says the spot is reserved, second this is not a legal ticket. This is a ticket distributed by the motel, and third. She could have the motel arrested for passing out fraudulent tickets." The clerk took the ticket and said, "He was sorry and walked away. "She got back in her car and drove around looking for the police station. She found it about six blocks away. She then started looking for the courthouse that was two blocks from the police station. It was getting late and they still had to find a place to sleep. She stopped at a gas station and asked if there were any motels around. He said, "Not within 10 miles. That would be up in Kingston on route 41, but the Arrow motel is only about six blocks from here." She said, "Thank you and headed north." About 9 miles up she came across the Little River Motel, it wasn't the fanciest, but it looked ok. She pulled in the driveway. They went in and asked the fat lady if they had any rooms left. The lady was very nice, she said, "She had only one left and it had a double bed, shower, and TV. The price was Twelve dollars for the night for both of them." Alma paid the lady, found cabin seventeen. It wasn't the best in the world but it was clean. And it smelled fresh. The toilet was clean as well as the shower. The towels smelled air fresh, it made her think of home. The next morning it looked cloudy as if it was going to rain. She asked a man that was mowing the lawn, "If there was a good place to eat around." He said, "Down the road apiece was a little dine," She said, "Thank you," and off they went. Karen said, "Was there something wrong with that man?" Alma smiled and said, "No that's just the way folks talk around here. They're good folks." When they got to the diner the parking lot was full. Trucks of all sizes, that meant only two things either good food or pretty girls. Alma wasn't sure if they would find a seat, that's how full the place was.

When they got inside, she found out what the big deal was at the diner. Both good food and pretty girls, and the prices were well within reason. After breakfast they went to the maps again. Karen was such a sweetheart, never a peep or a complaint out of her all the time they've been gone. Alma said, "Let's head into Vermont and see what's there." So off they went; the farther east they went, the more ski resorts and motels. They were on route 82 and it was a beautiful ride. It must be really nice in the wintertime, with all the snow and the pine trees showing green through the snow. They traveled for about three hours, as they came around a corner, there in the middle of the road stood a big buck deer. Alma had all she could do not to hit him. He didn't seem in much of a hurry, because Alma had to drive around him. Karen got all excited, that was the first live deer she had ever seen. They stopped at a diner and had a bit to eat; Karen was still talking about the deer. When they got into the car Karen hollered, look ma, what is that? Alma looked and told her, "It was a porcupine the Indians used the quills like needles." Karen wanted to know, "If we would see any Indians." I don't think so but you never know.

They did a lot of traveling that day, they stopped at the entire little gift shops along the way, and Karen kept her eyes open for more wild animals and Indians. She saw birds she never saw before, and once she thought she saw a Bear. Alma just smiled, and didn't say anything. It was getting late and they had to find a place to stay for the night. There were no signs on the road like they had in New York State, so they just kept on going. Down the road they came to a little town called Eagle Pass. Karen wanted to know, "What an Eagle was, and why would they call a town Eagle Pass? As Alma was explaining what an Eagle was they came to a bend in the road and there was a little diner. Alma decided to stop for information and something to eat. On the front of the diner was a Big Eagle carved out of a tree trunk. Karen couldn't take her eyes off it. It looks like a turkey, Alma laughed. When they went inside everybody was talking at once. Alma found a table near the window. Alma asked, "The waitress if there was a motel around, a nice, clean, and friendly." The waitress said, "Down the road was a nice place. When her folks come up they always stay there." They had something to eat and took some homemade donuts with them and drove down to the motel. It looked pretty good; they had a pool and a mini golf court. Inside it was very clean and neat. The price was a little high, but it was there busy time of the year, and if they didn't make it now, they would have to wait till it snowed. The place had a beautiful view of the mountains and the grounds were well kept up. They stayed over night and took off in the morning after breakfast. Driving down the road, they came along side of a nice brook. There were several men fishing. Alma stopped the car so that Karen could watch them fish. Karen got out of the car and went over near the edge of the brook. Alma was looking at the Map when all of a sudden Karen let out a scream. Alma looked up, one of the fisherman had caught a fish and was showing it to Karen when it started to jump around. It scared Karen at first, and then she smiled and was talking to the fisherman. As they traveled down the road Karen kept talking about the fish. The man took it off the hook and put the fish back in the brook, Karen thought that was great. Karen was talking about the trip they were on, the Deer... Porcupine... the fish and the fisherman that put the fish back into the brook. The big Eagle carved out of a tree, and the view. She had so much to tell Chrissie and Chris. It will take her forever.

Alma was doing a lot of thinking; they weren't to far from the New Hampshire state line. Maine was just on the other side. Did she dare go home? She said, "Why

Not." She would show Karen off to her grandmother. That would make everyone happy. They drove all day and got into Freeport around five in the afternoon. She new there was a motel just on the outskirts of the city, so that's where they went. She parked in the parking space and went in with Karen. They had only a few rooms left. She registered at the desk, asked about meals, and was told there was a good restaurant down the road apiece. They went to there room, it felt good to be home. They rested for a while, then Alma said, "Come on I'll show you my town. She couldn't wait to see her mother and show off Karen. They drove over to the gin mill. The only problem was the gin mill wasn't there anymore. In its place was a nice looking restaurant. A big sign on a pole said "FRIENDLY'S RESTAURANT." We serve only friendly people. Alma smiled, parked her car in the parking lot, and started to go in. She started thinking, Big Ben must have sold the place, and the new owners rebuilt this nice restaurant. She figured they might as well go in, have something to eat and maybe find out what happened to the old owners. They went inside, carpets on the floor, booths, and tables, a place for a band and clean windows. They found a booth near a window. A waitress came over with a big smile on her face, "asked if she could get them a coffee and a soda for the little girl while they looked over the menu." When the waitress came back, "She told them that all the meals are cooked to order. No fast food here." After they gave the waitress there order, Karen said, "She had to go to the bathroom." Alma had to go also, they found the ladies room. It to be spotless. As they came out of the rest room Alma saw Big Ben only he was in a suite. As they sat down in there booth, Alma was debating weather to go over to him or not Just then Big Ben came over to there table and said, " pardon me but aren't you Alma Canfield?" Alma said, "yes" she got out of the booth and gave Ben a big hug," Who mite this young good-looking girl be," she then introduced Karen. He picked up Karen and gave her a big hug, sat her back down in the booth.

Come in the back, I want to show you the place; It's changed a little since you were here last. As they walked around back of the bar they could smell food cooking. They went through the swinging doors and there was her mother, doing the cooking. He said, "Karen honey look who I have here. Karen turned around, took one look, and ran to her daughter. Alma introduced little Karen to her grandmother and Big Ben." Everybody was hugging and kissing and laughing, dancing and talking all at once. After things cooled down they all started talking at once, where, who... When... how long ago ...and so on.

Alma started, "she told how there was an accident on route ninety-five after she left here on her way to Pennsylvania. She lost her memory, had Karen in the entranceway of the hospital in Easton Penn. Met Chris in a bus station. She was confused and he helped, she had no place to sleep, he gave her his address and she went there and found his little daughter Chrissie. She got a job in an outback restaurant and met Michael, they got married. Michael was going to school to be a male nurse. Someone shot him while doing his night job. They think it was a mistake, a mob hit. She had to get away. They traveled north into New Your State then over into Vermont and now to here. Next it was mother Karen's turn to talk. "After your father died, I went to work for Ben. I paid off the bill and stayed on. I rented out the two rooms up stairs in my house. Six years ago I and Ben got married. With Ben running the front and me doing the cooking, the business really took off. We hired a band to play on Saturday nights hired more help both in the front and in the kitchen. The Gin Mill was too small, so we built this place over the old one then tore the old one down. This is what we ended up with, it was a good move. Some Saturday nights there's not enough room inside so the folks will dance outside. Ben put a window out through the side and sells drinks out there. In four and a half years we paid off the mortgage now it's ours free and clear. Ben could never have done it with out my help." Ben say's, "it was his personality that did it.' We all laughed. I think of you often, wondering if you ever got to your aunts house. How she was, "And if you had a boy or girl. I remember reading about the accident around that time but never thinking it may have been you. Thank God you made it. The paper never said how the girl made out or what happened to her after. So I didn't know. I'm so happy to see you both." She said, "Tonight we have something special." We all sat down at the table, mother Karen came out all dressed up and sat with us. We bowed our heads in a short prayer. Mother Karen clapped her hands and out came two waitresses' and a pushcart filled with food. The main course was Lobster with all the trimmings. They had four rooms above the restaurant they rent out. Karen and Alma took one room, "only with the understanding that they pay for it. The meal was on them, so we pay for the room." The next day Alma and Karen went for a drive through the country. She stopped and saw a few old friends. It seemed to her that she got older and they stayed the same. Things hadn't changed that much in eight years. Little Karen couldn't get enough of the hills and valleys and the river that seemed as if it was going up hill at times. The wild animals she had only heard about were all over. Bear, raccoons... robins... pigeons ... mice... Cats and dogs and a whole lot more. They stayed at the Friendly Restaurant for four days. The morning of the fifth day they left. They had to get back to Penn. She still had a job to go too. She would like to know what Jim had found out about Michael's death. She still cried herself to sleep nights. Why? Did that house really have something to do with Michael's death, were they prostitutes or laundering money, and was Michael involved, did he find out about it and that was why he was killed? Why? Why? Why? Why? Why?

She also wanted to stop off at Bill's place in Plantsville, on the way home. The people were friendly and the place was clean. Bill seemed like a real nice fellow, you could see he was well liked in town. When they stopped for gas, Alma looked at the map again. If she took route two south it would take them to route twelve thru New Hampshire into Vermont. They would spend the night just this side of Bridgewater. In the morning follow route twelve to route four in Vermont. They should be in Plantsville New York by late afternoon. Karen was getting excited; she had to tell someone about all the things she has seen. When they pulled into the parking lot, Alma noticed the sign was gone. Now she was curious as to whom he had working as a waitress. She herself never had done that before but you have to start someplace. She still liked this little city anyway. Maybe she would check out the courthouse tomorrow and see if they need any help. She drove around looking for a place to stay, and then she remembered the little motel they stayed at the last time they were there. She found it without any trouble. Clean reasonable rates, and friendly. After she had signed in she got to talking with the manager. He told her about the school system. Its old fashion but the kids learn. "They start off learning the ABCs,"

She asked, "About industries in the town? He told her about ten miles up the road they were putting in a large warehouse and factory. We are hoping that we get some of the people down this way. If that happens we will be a booming little town. However he did say, "He hated to see the land filled with houses. Trees cut down and people from the city where not as friendly as country folk." Alma agreed with him, "She also told him she was from Maine." That brought a smile to his face. "I thought you were one of us by the accent." She smiled and said, "She would see him later." Alma liked what she heard. The next stop was at the courthouse. She went inside and sat down, she wanted to see how they ran there operation. Each county runs there's different. After about and hour she went to the back office and, asked for the person in charge .A few minutes later this old man came out and asked, "If he could be of help, he was the one in charge." She asked, "If there was any openings for a court stenographer." She gave him a short rundown on what she has done plus the reason why she wants to move to the country. She would be happy to give him a written resume if he wants." The kindly old man said, "My name is Harvey Binder; folks around here call me Harv. What is your name?" You seem like an honest person and I haven't been wrong to many times in my life. She smiled and said, "My name is Alma, and this is my daughter Karen and it's a pleasure to meet you Harv."   "When I took this job almost sixty years ago, I took it on a handshake. If you are truly interested in living here and wanting to be one of us, this is what I want you to do.

"First I want you to live here for six months, send little Karen here to our school. Try and get a job, Bill over at the diner is looking for a waitress that would be a good place to start, and also help with the rent. This way you would get to know a lot of people in town. Then if in six months we like you and you like us come and see me. I know we can use help here in the courthouse. How does that sound to you?" Alma left the courthouse singing and swinging Karen's arms, and they both had smiles on there faces. First we have to find a place to live. But before that we need something to eat. They went over to Bill's Restaurant, there was a girl waitress waiting on tables. Bill was in the kitchen cooking. The girl came over and asked, "If she could help them." She had a smile on her face and was very friendly. "Can I get you a coffee and a soda while you look over the menu?" Alma said, "That sounded like a good idea, I'll have a decaf coffee and Karen will have a hot chocolate. I'll take mine regular." When she came back with the drinks she told, "Them it would take a few minutes because everything was made to order." In about fifteen minutes she came back with her arms and hands full. She placed each order in the right spot, as if she had been doing it for years. The crowd was just about gone when they finished there meal. She felt a tap on her shoulder, turning around she saw it was Bill standing there with a big smile on his face. "Hell-ow people" he said. Karen had a big smile on her face and said, "Howdy Partner" they all got a kick out of that. Bill sat down beside her and gave her a big hug. He called the waitress over and with a smile on his face said, "I'd like you to meet my daughter, Ruth." Ruth this is Alma and her daughter Karen. "They are the ones I was talking about a few days ago .I had a feeling you would be back so I took the sign out of the window." They all laughed. "The job is still open." Alma told them, how they went over to the courthouse and met Harvey. "What a nice man." she told them what he told her. "Find a job, a place to live, and send Karen to our school and see if the people here like you and her and you and her like us?" Alma didn't worry about Karen making friends; "she would get along with anybody." Well, "The job is yours anytime you want to start. The next thing would be to find you a place to live."

After thinking for a few minutes he said" would you like a house, Cottage apartment... or a tent? What would you like? At first she thought, I've never given it a thought as to where we would live. I guess for a few days we will stay at the motel and look around. This could be our new home so we want it to be right the first time." Bill thought, "That was a good idea, in the mean time he would keep these eyes and ears open for both." She should find a place near the school, but in the country. About a few acres of land, that way if they wanted to have a horse or something they would have plenty of room. Ruth said, "She would be happy to show them around. Karen wanted to know "If there were any Indians around?" They all laughed. Karen still wanted to see Indians. "Yes we do," said Bill, "Not to far from here we have a tribe. Nice people, minds there own business, and very friendly. Karen couldn't wait to see them. Do they do the war dance and pray for rain?" Bill with a straight face said "I think so. Ruth asked her Father, "If she could take an hour or so off and show Alma and Karen different places around the city?" (The old timers still call it town instead of city). Out where the new school is. He though, "He could handle the rush this time of day," so off they went. Karen was all excited, "So the first place they went was down into Indian country. There houses looked just like ours, there cars were like ours". Ruth knew a lot of them, so when she saw them we stopped.

They were playing basketball. We went over and were introduced to them. Karen seemed disappointed. She thought they would have bow and arrows and live in tents and ride horses. They looked just like us except there skin was a little darker then ours. They were very friendly. She never said; anything more about Indians again. We headed north of town; there was a big reservoir with pine trees all around it. That was where all the water for the town comes from. Heading East down a new country road stood the new school. They made it larger figuring growth for the next ten years. A ball field, Soccer field and an in door pool plus a Basketball court inside. Every thing was up to date. Next they turned south; a new development was going in because of the school. These homes had about seven or eight rooms each. Beautiful but not for me said Alma. They went about a mile and a half down the road, there was a for sale sign three acres FOR SALE there was a hill in the back, nothing that couldn't be leveled of Alma took the phone number down and said she would call them about it. They went about a half mile more when they saw an old house for sale. Alma stopped the car and they all got out. They looked at the front of the house and went around to the back to see what that looked like, it had an in ground pool and a nice patio with an outside fireplace. As they were looking around a car pulled up next to there's. The couple got out and started walking toward them. The man said, "Hello can I help you, my name is Charlie, and this is my wife Clare we are the owners of this place. If you would like we could show you around inside and out. Alma introduced them all and said, "They would love to see the inside". They went in the front door, the looks from outside were deceiving. Inside was ail natural and looked up to date." The outside of the house looked like it was one hundred years old. Charlie said, "That was the way they wanted it. Old looking on the outside and modem on the inside. They had just put the for sale sign up this morning. Clare has arthritis and the cold weather in the winter makes her suffer. I have a heart condition and can't keep the yard up like I want to. We have decided to sell and go down where it's warmer". Alma was very interested in the place. She asked, "How much land was with the house. Charlie said, "Four acres more or less. Down over the knoll there's a pond, it has a brook running in, and a brook running out I've never seen it go dry since I've lived here". He said, "No wet basement either." Alma asked, "Him the asking price." He said, "Eighty Thousand." That was more then what Alma wanted to spend. But the place was in move in condition. The yard was well taken care of, and there was four plus acres. She had no idea what property was going for up here. She told them, "She just drove in from Pennsylvania and stopped here for the night. Liked what she saw and would like to live in a small town like this. She would like to bring a friend she just met out to look at it, if it's ok with you." Fine Charlie said, "When do you think that would be?" Alma said, "I'll try and make it tomorrow sometime, would that be ok with you?" We have to go someplace tomorrow, but I can leave the key under the flowerpot and you can look around, if that's ok with you." Alma started to laugh, they all looked at her and Charlie said, "did I say something funny" Alma said, "heavens no, you reminded me of back home. That's where we always keep our key. Nobody ever had to break into our house, the key was always there, but nothing was ever missing." Clare said, "That's what country folks are all about, helping each other friendly ... and honest." They left it at that. She would try to make it back tomorrow. They shook hands and left.

Alma really liked the place. It had every thing she wanted, woods a pond, nice house great property. Now to see what it's worth. They went back to the restaurant and told Bill what they found. Bill knew the place very well, knows the people that own it. They are customers of mine. Bill suggested, "She go and ask old Harvey at the courthouse to look at it. He knows more about the price on land then anyone. Alma though that was a great idea. She went down to see if he was there. He was there and when she told him what she had in mind, he said, "He would be more then happy to go with them." They set a time at nine in the morning, she would pick him up at the courthouse, and they would travel on over and look at the place. Harvey went down to the town hall and checked the maps out and to see what's going on out there. The next morning Alma met him at the courthouse and off they went. Harvey showed her a short cut to the house. He hadn't been inside the house in over forty years. They checked the outside of the house, it looked weather beaten but in good condition. They then went inside; he couldn't get over the way it was fixed up. All modem, nothing like what the outside looked like. Alma asked him, "What he thought a reasonable price would be? He said, "Right now, I would say about sixty five to seventy thousand dollars". Alma told him, "They want eighty thousand. But in five years this will be worth three times the price. Harvey said, "There's a lot of building going on up the road apiece that means this place will be booming in less then five years. They both aren't feeling too good so they may take a little less. If this is what you like and want to make the offer, say sixty five thousand, you can always go up. I think they will take it. What have you got to lose?"

Two days later, Alma called Charlie and Clare and, "Asked if she could come out to see them? They said, "They would be home till four thirty that afternoon. They were going down to buy the train tickets, and if not sold before they leave, they would turn it over to a real estate broker." Alma said, "We will be there within the hour." She got Karen dressed, stopped to see Harvey about purchasing the place. Harvey said, "He would help in anyway he could. Alma and Karen arrived within the hour. Charlie and Clare were both very upset to think that they would have to leave there beautiful home to someone else. Especially to city people who don't know beans about country life. Karen took a liking to Clare and couldn't help feel sorry for her. She went over and sat next to her and held her hand. Alma had a lot of questions to ask, but seeing the condition they both were in she didn't have the heart to ask. She told them, "She was very interested in the house, and would like to buy it but, the price was a little out of her range. Could they come down any on the price?" Charlie looked at Clare then said," We have been talking it over, and if you wanted to buy this property, we would reduce the price. Would you be interested in the furniture? Alma never gave that a thought. She had nothing as far as what was in this house. Again Alma said, "The price is what I have to go by. Charlie asked, "What could you afford to pay, if you were to buy this place? Alma thought for a minute then said, "I think sixty five thousand would be my best offer. I'm sorry for taking up your time and I wish you both good health, as they were standing and about to leave Charlie called them back, "let me ask you something. What would you do with all the furniture if you were to buy the place?" Alma turned and said with out a bet of hesitation, "I would never think of selling it, that's for sure. I would use it as an heirloom." Charlie called back to Clare and said, "Honey I think we have sold our home to this very nice country lady and her daughter; Karen and Alma jumped with joy, they put there arms around Clare and Charlie and all four were crying and laughing with sorrow and joy.

Alma went back to see Harvey and told him the good news. He was happy to think. Someone as nice as Charlie and Clare would sell the house to another nice person like Alma. Harvey drew up the papers; Alma went down to the bank, met with the manager, and told him what happened. She wanted to open an account both checking and savings. Also she wanted to apply for a mortgage. The manager was happy to help with the deal. Alma said, "She would transfer all her accounts that afternoon. The bank would take a look at the property and let her know tomorrow at this time. Alma could hardly wait. Friday after noon Alma and Karen were at the bank waiting for the manager. When he came in, he said, "Hello and went directly to his office and made a phone call. He was on the phone for about five minutes hung up and came out. Well Mrs. Fox, you have now purchased a wonderful house as is, we could find nothing wrong inside or outside you are one lucky lady. Congratulations." They all shook hands, she had tears in her eyes. The manager said, "He had a message to call Charlie and Clare when he got back from lunch. They would like to see Alma as soon as possible. Alma said, "They would go right now if it was ok with him. He said," Sure go, and enjoy your new home."

Alma and Karen ran out the door to the car. It took them about two minutes and they were at their new home. Alma ran up the front steps and rang the doorbell. Clare came to the door, smiled and said, "honey you don't have to ring your doorbell, this is your home now." Alma and Karen went up to her, and held her for a long time.

Charlie came out and with tears in his eyes, "Wished them both all the luck they needed." Clare told them, "The fridge is full of food. We bought steaks and stuff this morning so it's all fresh." Charlie said, "Let me show you the cellar, you never did see that." Charlie led the way. He opened the door and said, "Here's the light switch." He flipped the switch and the basement lit up. They went down the stairs to a room as nice as all up stairs. There were three rooms and a bath all furnished. Alma just stood there; she didn't know what to say. She went over to Charlie and put her arms around him and cried. These were the two best people in the world. Alma wiped the tears off Charles shoulder. He said, "This was his room, when Clare was having a hard time sleeping, he would come down here and read or watch TV. Now that's enough of that, l just wanted you to know, there's no ghost's living down here." There car was all packed and there train tickets were in his pocket. They were driving over to Albany and taking the train with the car down to Florida. They had purchased a condo in Florida eight years ago. It has been rented out for the past five years, as a matter of fact; they were going to sell it a number of times. But never get around to it. They had a son, but he got killed in the war. There's no one left. They thank god every day they didn't sell, now it will come in handy. Taking the train will save them from driving, as it is they will spend three days and two nights on the train. Alma said,"She would back out of the deal if they didn't call or write as soon as they got to Florida. We will be worried sick till we know you arrived safe and sound. And another thing... this front door will always be open to you, if we aren't home the key will be under the flowerpot." They all laughed at that. There was one little matter they would like to ask, "Could we spend the night here and leave the first thing in the morning? Alma said, "On one condition: you have to come with Karen and I to Bill's restaurant for supper, the treat is on us. So you can't refuse." Alma called Bill, "And told him what was going on. Tonight they would all be there for supper, and you and Ruth must join us also... that's an order." Shortly after supper the place started to fill up with all there friends, some how everybody in town had heard about Clare and Charlie moving to Florida and selling there home. That's how news travels in a small town. They all came to say 'good-bye' to Charlie and Clare and to meet and welcome the new owners Alma and Karen.

The next morning Alma and Karen took off to Pennsylvania. She wanted to tell Chris and Chrissie about the house she bought and the job she had. "There was plenty of room for them to come and stay the summer". She went to the bank, "moved her accounts over to the new bank, then to the courthouse. Said," Goodbye to everyone, and went over to the city hall." Said, "Goodbye and went back to their apartment." They spent the night there. The next morning, they looked around and didn't see anything she really wanted. If Chris and Chrissie wanted anything they were welcome to it. The landlord was sorry to see them go, she really fixed the place up nice. She called, Jim; to see if there was any news on Michael's murder, and to tell him where she has moved to. They still have parties at the house, some last all night." Jim and his men never found anything wrong. Jim said, "He would never stop looking. And to this day he blames himself, For Michael's death.

There was three weeks before school started, and Alma and Karen wanted Chrissie and Chris to come up for a week before school starts. She "asked her father if he could have a week vacation time off." He asked this boss, and he said yes." They called Alma and said, "They would be up in three days." Chris had a map of New York State and would call when they got in town. Alma and Karen were so happy, they figured on hot dog parties, swimming ...fishing... walking in the woods. There was no end as to what they could do.

After their six-day visit, everything got back to almost normal. Alma started working at Bill's and she registered Karen in school. They got a note from Chrissie and Chris thanking them for the best vacation ever. Alma wrote back and told them, the key was under the flowerpot, so the front door was always open for them, Come anytime. Karen would help Alma at the restaurant after school. Things were going good. Bill and his wife Bee though everything was going so nicely that maybe they could take a vacation. They wanted to go over into Maine, and maybe see about buying some Lobsters for the restaurant. They left three weeks later, Ruth... Alma ... Karen ran the place. People would ask, "Where's Bill?" when told they were on vacation they all said, "Good for them" they needed it. When Bill and his wife got back, they had a large fish tank a pump and eight Lobsters. They had stopped in a little town called Freeport it was right on the ocean. There was a big fancy restaurant called Friendly Restaurant. They stayed there for two days. The people were very friendly and showed Bill the proper way to cook lobster, make lobster stew, and where to buy the tank and pump and the best lobsters around. Bill figured it would take him about a week to cook the lobsters just right. He had a sign made for the window. Get your lobsters here. For two days, not a single Lobster was sold. He started to wonder, did I do right, investing all that money in the tank, pump, and lobsters? Harvey came in on the third day and ordered the first Lobster, word of mouth got around about Bill's lobsters, and he couldn't keep up with the orders. He had to get a larger tank and pump plus a lot more Lobsters.

Bill's restaurant grew into a gold mine, in six months he had to hire four more waitress and two cooks. Harvey came in one day and told, "Alma she was needed at the courthouse". A steady job with more then twice the pay she was making there was waiting for her. She didn't want to leave Bill but the money sounded real good. By going over to the courthouse meant that she was accepted in the town, which made her real happy. Plus that's what she had been doing all her life. She had a talk with Bill about Harvey's job. Bill felt bad to think he was losing her. But he knew it was coming one of these days. He said, "He would always have a job for her if the court-house job didn't work out." He gave her a hug and wished her the best. Karen wanted to stay with Bill after school, Bill thought it was great.

As time went on Alma was doing good at the courthouse, and Karen was doing everything at the restaurant. She was cleaning the tables, stacking dishes, sweeping the floor etc. Alma and Karen were getting along just fine with the people. They all thought they were country people, and that made a difference. Alma had a Lawyer that was interested in her. They would go for rides, or have cookouts in the back yard. He took Alma and Karen up to his Cabin in Vermont. They learned how to ski and Karen thought that was the greatest. On Karen's tenth birthday Alma told her, "that George wanted to marry her, if it was ok with her." She liked George in a way but not like she liked Bill or Chris. She told her mother, "That if it would make her happy ...do it." The following spring they got married by one of the judges at the courthouse. George was married before and so was Alma. Everything was going pretty good for 8 months. George moved in with Alma in the beautiful old house. One day the judge asked Alma,"If she would stay over and help out on writing some legal papers." Alma was more than willing, and said, "She wouldn't mind at all." She called Karen, and told her about working late and that George would pick her up and take her home. That way she could take her time doing her homework. She wanted to stay and go home with her mother but gave in and went home with George. All the way home George was acting funny, talking funny and using dirty words.

When they arrived home Karen ran up to her room and locked the door. George was down stairs, after about half an hour, "He calls up to her and says supper is ready, come on down." She was hungry and maybe he had a bad day. She came down stairs and started to walk into the kitchen when George grabbed her from behind and said, "Let's play." As she turned around she saw that he was completely naked. She tried to fight him off. She kicked him; scratched his face and shoulder she screamed and kicked and cried. He grabbed her by the hair and through her on the floor and raped her. She cried, and kept on hitting him but he would not stop." He told her, "If she ever told her mother he would hurt her and kill her mother." Karen didn't know what to do. She didn't want her mother to get hurt and she didn't want to be blamed for anything that might happen to her. She ran up stairs to her room, locked the door, and cried. "When she heard her mother's car drive up, she ran into the bathroom and was taking a shower." She had to wash off all the dirt that George left on her. As she was drying herself she glanced in the mirror, she noticed large red bruises on both of her breasts, scratches and black and blue down near her crotch. Down between her legs was all bruises and sore and the towel was covered with blood. She got dressed and made it down stairs. Later that night when George was watching TV. Alma asked Karen, "What was the trouble, she wasn't acting right? Karen didn't know what to do, George would kill her if she talked but she couldn't go on any longer. She told her mother, "every-thing that happened." Alma went to the phone and called the police station. She talked very low and to a Detective that she knew. He said, "He would come out as if it had something to do with her work." About fifteen minutes later a knock at the door. George answered it, Hello officer what can I do for you? The detective said, "He had to see her about some work she was doing for him." The detective said, "my gosh George, where did you get all those scratches on your face." George smiled and said, "He was trimming some bushes and they went across my face," The detective told him, "To put something on it, so it doesn't get infected." Asked, "Where Alma was," he told him, she was upstairs working on his paper work go on up, it's the door at the top of the stairs." He knocked on the door, she said, "Come on in. When he got inside, Karen was there with Alma. Karen told the detective everything that happened. He asked, "If he could see some of the bruises? She hesitated at first but Alma said, "It was all right. She removed her blouse and showed the detective the bruises on her shoulders and stomach, the other bruises he didn't have to see". He asked, "If he could talk with her mother alone, Karen wanted to stay, but her mother said, "She had better go to her room." The detective said, "If he took him in tonight he'll be out on bale in a few hours. Let me go back and talk with the chief. I'd like to keep this as quiet as possible, not only for Karen's sake but you as well. I will call you back tonight. I want to throw away the key on this bastard, raping an eleven-year-old girl." But, "first we'll have to take her to the hospital for a physical examination; there also could be a lot of bad publicity on both sides." Him being a big time lawyer in town, "You may have to get an outside lawyer who doesn't know him. That will cost you a lot of money.

You being a new comer in town, and Karen so friendly with everyone she may be asking for trouble. Let me go back and talk with the chief, I'll get back to you." As he was leaving he said, so George could here, "I'll talk with the chief and see if he wants to change the language on that deposition, I'll call you back Good night." Fifteen minutes later the phone rang. It was the detective; "could you come down to the station right now, you can, we'll see you then." Alma got her shoes back on, Karen wanted to go with her, at first she didn't think she should, then said, "All right she could go with her." They went directly to the police station. The chief wants, "Karen to be examined now over at the hospital. I will call this doctor friend of mine; he will keep his mouth shut till I tell him to talk. He's a nice fellow and a very good doctor. We've used him before on another case just like this." The chief called, and asked for the Doctor, he came to the phone, "Hi Chief what can I do for you." The Chief explained what happened. The Doctor told him to send them right over.

They got to the hospital and went into the emergency room. They asked for Dr. Beckworth. He came right out, and took them into an examining room. He asked, "Them all to leave, Karen was all upset and wanted her mother to stay with her." Dr. Beckworth understood and said, "It was all right." He had Karen strip naked, "Not only did he see the bruises but he took pictures also." After the exam, He said, "He had what he wanted." He said, "It was OK to get dressed now." She got dressed fast and ran to her mother. "I'm scared mommy, I didn't mean for that to happen, I fought as hard as I could. I scratched this face and shoulders and kicked him." He told me, "He would kill you if I told on him." Look what he did to me, I hate him, I don't want to go back home while he is there. Please mommy don't make me go back home with him." Alma held Karen real tight, "She promised she would protect her and comfort her, and George would never lay another hand on her." The Chief told the detective to go and pick up George. They would hold him over night, without charges. "Let's see what he has to say. I'll put everything on tape, this way there will be no way he can say "I didn't say that." The detective took a police officer with him and they went back to Alma's house. They rang the doorbell and waited, nobody came to the door. They rang again and again. They tried the door, it was not locked. The Detective went to the car and called the Chief. "Told him about the door," the Chief asked, "Alma if it was all right for them to go inside? Alma said," Sure do whatever you have too, to get him out of there. I don't want that man around anymore." The Detective and the police officer went through the house. Room by room, down stairs and up then down in the basement. George couldn't be found in the house, he can't be to far away, his car is still here. They went out in the back yard and called for him, still no answer. The detective walked down to the pond, there was George sitting on the dock. He turned when he heard someone coming. He saw the detective and asked, "If everything was all right? Maybe he would take Alma and Karen out for a sandwich later. Alma's been working too hard lately. The detective asked, "George to come up to the house; he had something to tell him." George said "I hope everything is all right" the detective said, "I'll tell you about it when we get to the house." George came along with no trouble. When they got near the car the officer put handcuffs on him and put him in the car. George wanted to know, "what was going on." He said, "Karen would be worried that he wasn't around, and Alma would be worried because he wouldn't be with Karen." When they got to the station, officer pulled the car in the garage. Blow the horn the detective said, "When he did the doors closed." They lead George into a holding cell in the station house. They searched him again and found nothing of value on him. They had him remove his shirt and pants. They found scratches and bruises on his sides and back, plus the scratches on his face. They asked, "Him how he got them;" He said, "He fell in the back yard." George said, "He didn't have to answer any more questions. What is going on, why am I here? "I didn't do anything. What's this all about? I'll get a lawyer if you keep this up. I know my rights. You can't hold me." The detective said, "He had a few questions he wants to ask him, first he had a few things to take care of and he would be back". He left George to figure out what his next move would be. How was he going to get out of this one? They have had trouble with him before but could never prove anything on him, maybe this time would be the time.

George was left alone, the police officer went back to his desk, and the Detective went back to his to finish working on a report from another case he had. A few hours later George is getting pissed. "What the hell is going on here?" "I didn't do anything, I'm a lawyer I know my rights, let me out of here now. He's getting nervous; he's walking around his cell. He kept touching his face and holding his sides. He's mumbling to his self. That little bitch did a job on me. Wait till I get my hands on her, she has no right to do this to me. She asked for everything she got, she played up to me for the last six months. Smiling and asking questions about what the dogs were doing, I know what she was after, the little bitch." The camera and tapes were rolling the only thing was the tapes would have a hard time picking up what he was saying. He was talking more to himself them out loud. He went to bang on the bars of his cell, his ribs were so sore; they hurt whenever he picked up his arms. The Chief was watching behind a two-way mirror. Shaking his head he said, "I do believe, this time I think we have him He's really worried. "We'll let him stew for another hour or so." The phone rang, it was for the Chief. The doctor said "Chief I've got some pictures that show bruises and scratch marks, black and blue and have taken specimens from her privates. They are being tested and annualized right now. The girl and her mother should be there about now. The girl needs a lot of help. If I can be of any more help, call me. I'd like to see this bastard put behind bars for a long time. I'm hoping Karen gets over this in time, but she's pretty upset. Thank god she has a good mother. Talk with you later Chief." The Chief had just hung up the phone, when Karen and Alma came in. Karen would not pick up her head; she was too embarrassed to look at anyone. The Chief went over to her, put his hand on her shoulder, she pulled away so fast you would have thought she had had a bolt of lighting go through her. He got down on one knee, "And started talking to her in a very soft voice. Explaining to her that nobody was going to hurt her like that again. She had every right to be angry and afraid, but she also has a life to live. What happened today should not make her life a living hell. This is something that you have to put away back in your head and never think of again. You turn the switch off on this experience. There are too many good things to think about and do so as of now, you live for today and tomorrow and forget yesterday. OK? You are a very nice girl and you always will be. If you ever want to talk with me, you are always welcome. Your mother and I are good friends. I see her quite often in the courthouse. She's a wonder women and friend so if you have anything to say, say it to your best friend your mother. Do you feel better now? We will do everything in our power to put that man behind bars for a long, long time." The Chief talked with Karen for a long time, like a father would. When he got through, she came over and gave him a big hug. They both had tears in there eyes. Alma couldn't thank the Chief enough; she also had tears in her eyes. There wasn't anything more they could do at the police station and by now it was getting real late. So they got in the car and went home. When they pulled in the driveway and Alma shut the engine off. Karen put her arms around her mother and gave her a big hug. She asked do I have to go into the house; I still have bad thoughts of what happened? Alma said, "Honey you have to face it sometime so it might as well be now. Come on I'll be with you all the way, and all the time" They got out of the car and walked hand in hand into the house.

The Detective stopped in to see George once and asked him a question. George is getting real mad now; they are holding him with out cause. The Detective told him only a few more hours. The Chief had a meeting to go to, when he gets back he wants to have a talk with you, so sit tight. As the night went on the Chief let George do some more thinking.

George didn't get any sleep that night, in the morning he was mumbling to his self again. They can't pin anything on me. The next morning the Chief came in to see him, along with the detective. The first thing he said "Was please except my apology for not getting back to you last night. The meeting lasted longer then I figured. The chief wanted to know how he got all the bruises, scrapes plus the black and blue spots all over his body. George said he fell in the back yard. The chief said in a quiet tone, "Let's start from the beginning once more, you picked up Karen at the restaurant and took her home. Where were you when you fell? Was it in the back yard or side yard? I think you said the back yard, am I right? If Karen was home, did she hear you fall; did you say anything, holler, swear, or limp to the house? Did you bleed, I guess you must have there's some scabs on your back. Boy that must have been some fall, how did you get the black and blue spots and the scabs on your back? I can see the scraps and bruises on your stomach when you fell forward, but how did you get all that damage on your side and back? I think we should take you over to the hospital and have your body checked over. Maybe something might be broken, ribs or something, this way you can't say we hit you here in the jail cell. Is that O.K. with you George?" George wasn't too happy about going over to the Hospital. He told the Chief he would sign a paper saying it didn't happen here. The Chief said, "I still think we should have a doctor look him over; he turned to the Detective and asked what he thought. "It's a good idea, I'll get the car". When the Detective left, the Chief asked George, "If there was anything he wanted to say to him, you know how the law goes, if you talk now, things will go a lot easier then if we find something you did wrong later. Think about it". George didn't say a word. When the Detective came back, the Chief asked him, "If he had told George why he was brought in for questioning." The little girl Karen was raped last night and you were around the house at that time. She has been examined at the hospital, and they have taken some blood samples, you wouldn't mined if we took some blood from you, just for a sample, that way we can rule you out as the rapist. Would that be O.K. George? I'll have a nurse come right over and draw some blood. We wouldn't want to send you to prison for a long time for something you didn't do. Those boys in prison don't like child molesters. They would make you one of there girl friends in about fifteen minutes if you lived that long. Oh... Aye, that's right you had nothing to do with the rape, did you George? If you did rape her and said you did, I think there's a place they send people like you were they don't have the hardened criminals mostly child offenders. That way you get to live a little longer, which place do you want to go George, the first, or the second place? We have proof George, the first or the second. George started to cry, he didn't want to go to either one. But they had him. He said, "She made advances to him. She would pull up her dress and tease him; she would have no panties on. It drove me crazy. The Chief broke in; you mean that Karen would tease you by undressing in front of you. Is this what you will say in front of a room full of people? That she invited you to partake in a sex orgy with her. Is that what you are trying to tell us, that it was all her fault, she put you up to it, is that what your saying? How long have you two been making out, why did she resist this time. Did she like having sex with you, did she ask you, or did you ask her? Tell me all about it George, people don't like men that rape little girls. We are going to have a hard time keeping you alive. Things like this don't happen often in the country. Especially to nice little girls like Karen. Everyone that knows her knows she's a friendly girl and not a sex fiend, you are the sex fiend. How do you want to play this out? Are you going to admit it, or say she enticed you? George didn't say anything for a long time, he new they had him, no matter what he said. The townspeople would hang him. Finally he said," let me get a lawyer, and are you going to put this in the papers?

If you do, you will be responsible for my life. The chief looked at him and said," George I have everything down on tape. I don't need you around here. The tape say's it all. We can keep this quiet and have the Judge sentence you, or we can have an open court. It's up to you, I will give you twenty-four hours to get a Lawyer, you are not to leave town, and I will have the bondsman put a high bail on you. If you make it all well and good, if not in that cell you will stay. Good day George." The next morning the Judge set bail at five hundred thousand dollars. George had one phone call he could make. He knew he couldn't call his wife, and there wasn't another lawyer in town that would help him, they wouldn't even talk to him. He called the bank, asked for the president, when he got on the phone George explained the situation to him. He needs the money now. The bank president asked what he had for collateral. He thought for a minute, he doesn't own a house and the few dollars he has in the bank would no where near come close for what he would need for the bail, you have nothing to cover it with, said the bank president, I'm sorry but I can not help you, and hung up. He put his face in his hands, and said to himself, how did I ever get into this mess? The little bitch got what she deserved. Now I have to suffer.

Alma was in constant touch with the Chief. When told that he could not raze money for the bail bond, she jumped with joy... even Karen was happy about it. The Chief figured he would keep him in the cell for a few more days then present him to the judge. It would be up to him to do what ever he thought necessary. The Chief and the judge both knew if he was to go to a state prison he would last maybe a week. The other inmates would pounce on him and use him as there prostitute. They would have no mercy on him. Raping an eleven year old girl does not go in prison, he would be raped not by one but by a hundred inmates they had to figure someplace where he would be safe and yet not have life to easy. Maybe down south on a chain gang. We could say he robbed and slapped around a kid for this collage money he had been saving for. That way he would have to work his ass off in the heat, and if he screws up the guards would take care of him. They would tell the warden what he had done, but not to tell anyone else. The Chief put through a call to the prosecutor in Alabama. He had met him a few times at the police Chiefs conventions and a few other meetings. They said he was in court on a big case and they would have him call you back when he had a chance. The Chief said that would be fine. Thanked the secretary and hung up. Two days went by before the prosecutor called back, he apologized for not calling sooner but they had a big case they where working on. The prosecutor went on explaining some of the details. When he was finished he asked what can I do for you. The Chief by this time was wondering if he was doing the right thing, by calling down there. Then he thought of little Karen and said, "This is what we have up there, and went on to explain what he had in mind." The Chief almost felt sorry for George. The prosecutor told the Chief what they do with men who rape young girls down there; we have so many Blacks down here that run around half-naked that is an everyday thing. We prosecute them and put them on the chain gang, along with the rest of them. If they get out of line the guards will beat the shit out of them. Nobody says anything. Sure we can always use another hand down here. As far as telling what he did, that would be up to you guys up there. We would expect some reimbursement for lodging and so forth. When do you think he'll be ready to come down? The Chief said he would get back to him on that, as he hasn't been before the judge as yet. The prosecutor said; when you call ask for Jim Bob. They'll get in touch with me faster. Gotta go now, ya'll come down and see us, ya hear. The phone went died. The Chief went to the high court judge and told him what was going on. He looked at his calendar and said he could hear the case in two weeks. Keep him here, by his self, don't let no one in to see or talk with him, otherwise it will get in the papers, and if that happens, we could have a lynching party on our hands.

Alma went back to work in the courthouse, Karen wanted to go down and stay with Chrissie for a few days. Alma called Chris and asks if it would be O.K. maybe for a long weekend, Friday thru Sunday, after checking with Chrissie, everything would work out just fine. Alma gave Chris the details on what happened and thought, Karen with Chrissie would be good for her, by now Chrissie was a young lady. She's in her last year of school, and still didn't know what she wanted to do. Chris was promoted to the detective bureau. The only thing wrong with that was he didn't have regular hours like before. Chrissie was a sensible girl but he still worried about her. She has a boyfriend, but he's going to school to become a dentist, and is home only on weekends. When the Chief told Alma what was going on she was happy to think he would not be around any more, the state would pick up the tab, so it wouldn't cost Alma anything. The only thing left was getting a divorce. Harvey Binder said he would take care of it.

Karen and Chrissie had a nice girl-to-girl talk. When Karen came home she was much better. Then one day, headlines in the paper read, 'GIRL RAPED BY TOWN LAWYER'. Everybody was talking. They didn't put any names in the paper, but everyone knew they would come out. The Judge was livid, who told the press about this. The Chief was called into the Judges chamber, "What is the meaning of this? Who told the press about this? I want that man or woman brought in here now. Do you realize the job we have ahead of us now? There could be a hanging around here. Have the editor of the paper over here now. I want to talk with him and you are here also." The Chief left the chamber, got on the phone outside gave orders. In fifteen minutes the phone rang again, and again. People came down to the police station. The desk clerk said he new nothing about the headlines, and would hang up, only to have the phone rang again. They called every lawyer in town, nobody knew anything. Within a day or so things started to quiet down. The guard was brought before the Judge. He was a supernumerary officer and didn't know that there was a zipper on the case. The Editor was called in and the judge read him the riot act, what do you mean printing something like this without calling me first, to see if there was any truth in it. Do you know what you have started here? Everyone wants to know who did what to whom. What lawyer and who is the girl. That girl, if there was one would never be able to live it down, everyone would look at her and talk, and she's the one that got raped. If I catch you printing anything like this again with out checking with this office first, I'll have your hide. Do you understand? I don't want another word printed in any paper or said. I have enough to do around here without this type of bullshit. Now get out and print your paper with some good news for a change. The editor went out the back door; he had nobody to blame but himself. He should have checked with the Chief first. But its news and that's what sells the papers. He'll check with the police officer and see what he has to say. People were talking about George; they hadn't seen him in a long time. He's usually around the police station looking for work. Somebody said he left town in a hurry. That was why nobody cared for him, he really wasn't a bad attorney, but people just couldn't stand him. He was always down talking the cops. Karen was still putting her time in at the restaurant, and Alma was still at the courthouse. Everything looked pretty normal. The Judge had the hearing and sentenced George to ten years at hard labor in Alabama. Jim Bob put him in with a bunch of child molesters. They worked and never said a word to each other. The word went out that George moved out of town.

Alma started getting headaches again, not bad, but bad enough to make her miss a day of work once in a while. She went to the doctors; he gave her a complete checkup, and said she needed some female work done. He wasn't sure that that was the cause of the headaches but he did know there was going to be problems down there sooner then later. And it should be taken care of now. Once that was taken care of, then he would look deeper into the headache problem. The doctor wanted her to stay home for about three weeks. She went home and started figuring when would be the best time to have it done. She checked at work to see when the vacations would be over so every one would be back working. She would need about three to four weeks. She had two weeks vacation time coming, so really she would only be missing about two weeks. The first of August would be about right. That way Karen would be home and the courthouse would be slow. She asked the Judge, and he thought that would be a good time. She planed on taking four weeks off. The doctor said he would arrange everything at the hospital. Time went by fast; she had only two weeks to get everything in order. She checked with Chris and Chrissie, things were O.K. on there end, Karen was worried but didn't know why. Alma had gotten her divorce from George, and everything had quitted down about the two of them. Everything was in order Bill and Bee would take care of Karen while Alma was in the Hospital. Alma had the operation as planed, everything went according to plan. She was feeling great in two and a half weeks so she and Karen went for rides, mostly day trips. They did stay over one night at Santa's Village. They both though that was a great place. Karen was able to feed the animal and pet them. She had a lot to talk about when they got home. Alma went back to work in three weeks, and feeling fine. No headaches. For the next two and a half years things were going good. Karen was doing well in school, the job, the house everything just seamed to fall into place.

Then one day when she went to work there was a note on her desk. The top judge wanted to see her. She went to the Judges Chamber and knocked on the door, he said "come in" when she got inside she looked around, what you are doing Sir," she asked. He told her his wife was very sick and they have to move to a dry and warmer climate as soon as possible. So he will be leaving at the end of the week. The new Judge should be here tomorrow. His name is Seymour Lipton. That's all I know about him. Alma was very upset about the judge leaving. They had gotten to be real good friends. The following day, this man in his early fifties came in the courthouse, asked for the Judges chamber. Never said *hi I'm the new judge* or anything. Right off the bat no one liked him, SEYMOUR LIPTON HAS ARRIVED. Maybe after he gets used to us he'll be different, friendlier, they were all saying, give the man a chance. The two Jr. Judges were worried also, but they never said anything. He came in on Wednesday afternoon, after he found a place to stay. Thursday and Friday he sat in the courtroom, he still hadn't said a word. Saturday night all the lawyers and friends gave the Judge a farewell party at Bill's Restaurant.

SEYMOUR LIPTON did not attend. People thought, that was funny. He should have been there so that all the people could meet him. That put a sour taste in all there mouths for the new Judge.

Lipton was in the soup, they were saying. Monday came around, everyone was at there stations when the new Judge arrived. He went into his Chamber, asked for help putting his rob on, Alma happened to be walking past the chamber at the time, and stopped to help. Never once did he say thank you or even ask what her name was or what she did in the courthouse. He went right to the bench. Rapped with the gavel. It was the beginning of day one, no one will forget. Where this judge came from is a big question. Fortunately Alma wasn't in his courtroom that day. Everybody was going to walk out. Someone called the capitol to find out where this guy came from, no one would talk to her up there. They were glad to get rid of him, and we were stuck with him.

He was a strict Judge, most of the time he was fair. But he had crazy ideas sometimes. If he thought their was a chance that the defendant would turn out ok, he would give a mild sentence and a lot of community clean up time. Help clean the parks, work in the hospital, things like that. He never looked to see if they had a previous record. If there was a gay person male or female that was before him they got a very stiff sentence. He had gotten the nickname around town of Ice Lipton. The lawyers tried to talk with him, he would not listen. The Chief was the only one that he would listen to, not always but a lot of the time. Alma got a call from his Chamber. The Judge wants to see you now. She started to wonder. What would he want with me? She knocked on his door, waited a few minutes, and was about to leave when he said" come in" she opened the door and walked in, you wanted to see me Judge? He said "close the door and sit down, I've been watching you while working. I'd like you to cover my court cases, you are on the ball with your depositions, and I never have to wait. I like that. Starting Monday, you will report to my courtroom. Understood! Alma said, yes but she was in the, middle of a big hearing in Judge Weinstein's court room, when we finish in there I'd be more than happy to work in your room, but until then, I will have to stay were I am. Judge Lipton turned red in the face. Got up from his chair, put both hands on his desk, looked her straight in the face, and said "I shall repeat it one more time... Monday morning you will report to my courtroom. Alma got up from her chair, looked him in the face, and said, "I either finish the case I'm on or I quit. I will not leave a Judge hanging for a secretary. Lipton sat back down, looked back in her face again, and just looked. It made Alma nervous the way he kept staring at her. "Finely," she said, "If you have nothing more to tell me I have work to do." Judge Lipton was speechless. No one had ever talked to him that way. She got out of her chair and started for the door. "Ms. Canfield please come back and sit down." Alma was furious; who does he think he is GOD to talk that way to me or anyone else in this courthouse. She stopped at the door, waited a minute or so then turned around and went back to the chair and sat down. She looked him square in the eyes and said, "Judge Lipton, we are a loyal, hard working, honest bunch of employs working here, we try to help each other. If your attitude is going to be like it just was and, has been with me and the rest of the good people that work here. I will tell you right now, you had better start looking for all new help. We are not used to being treated and talked to like this. Do I make myself clear Your Honor? Now let's start from the beginning. If you want me to work in your court room, you will have to wait till I'm finished with this case." Alma has never been so mad except that time with her ex husband. The Judge got out of his chair and walked around in front of his desk, stood directly in front of Alma and said, "You are the first person to stand up to me in all the years I've been practicing law, and I must say it felt good, knowing someone has the balls to set me down. When you get through with Judge Weinstein, I'd like to have you come and work in my courtroom. How does that sound?" Alma smiled and said, "That's more like it. But remember the rest of us in here are human also." She got up and said "Sir if there is nothing else, I have a lot of work to do." He went over and put his arm around her, and promised to be friendlier with everyone. When she left, she went directly to the ladies room, and splashed cold water on her face and looked in the mirror. She couldn't believe she said what she said to the presiding Judge. She smiled to herself, and though, I didn't even get fired. The next morning things were different, the Judge even said good morning to every one he saw.

They all stopped, smiled, and said good morning Judge. He had to admit, it felt pretty good. When Alma got through with Judge Weinstein, she went with Judge Lipton. He was not the best of Judges but she did her job and that's what she was supposed to do. Nothing more was ever said about that day in his Chamber. He did loosen up a bit but he still could be mean. Three months later he called her into his Chambers and had her sit down. He had a file in front of him and started talking about her ex-husband George. He wants to come back up and serve his time. By the looks of this deposition, George could be in for a long time, unless he gets out on good behavior. If he comes up here, he may never get out, but we could send him to another state and not tell what he's in for. What do you think of that? Alma couldn't believe what she was hearing. Her friend the Judge would have George brought back up here and spend time in a jail close to here and maybe get him out sooner. The Judge said "now if you treat me nice, I'll see that he never comes back up here. It will be up to you." She looked at him, "What do you mean, treat you nice." Judge Lipton said "You know we could go out and have a few drinks now and then, then maybe come to my apartment for a night cap and, who knows what's next." Alma looked at him and said" you mean you would have him sent back up here if I wasn't nice to you. ? He had a silly grin on his face. "What I meant to say is I would like your company, and if it leads to something, George may stay in Alabama for the rest of his life." Alma got up from her chair, went to the door, and walked out. The next day after court he asked her what she thought of the proposition. It wouldn't be too hard to have him sent to Pennsylvania and, maybe out in two- three years. We could talk about it tonight over a drink or two. How about I pick you up at seven thirty. I hope you can get a baby sitter for little Karen for a few hours tonight, and if you tell anyone about our little party. I would just deny it, that's all. I think they would believe me first. Remember I am God. See you at seven thirty. Ruth came over and stayed with Karen, Alma told her she had some work to do with the Judge, and would only be gone a few hours. Ruth said" no problem." Lipton was there at seven thirty sharp. Blew the horn, he never bothered coming to the door. She came out and got in the car. He drove north about ten miles and stopped at a gin mill. They got out and went inside. There was a lot of smoke and not much light. There was some dancing girls up on the stage, they were strippers and had already striped down to there G-string. The waitress where all topless, and the guys were feeling there breasts when she would serve them drinks. They always gave good tips so the girls didn't mind a little feel, they rather liked it. The waitress came over to our table and asked what we wanted. She stood next to Lipton, and let her breasts hang down on his shoulder. She was well stacked with the largest nipples she had ever seen. Alma ordered a rum and coke and Lipton ordered scotch on the rocks, then he said make that a double. The waitress said no problem and left. When she came back, she bent way over and almost slapped Lipton in the face with her large breasts. She kept looking at Alma all the time she was serving the drinks, making sure she wasn't getting upset with her. Alma paid no attention to her or her big tits. The girls on stage had left, all except one, when she got down to her G-string she wanted one of the guys to come up and help her take it off. He wouldn't so, she asked for some one else. Lipton got up and volunteered, she motioned for him to come up to the stage. The music was load and playing take it off take it off. He got down on his knees and with her in front of him he started to take the G-string off. She bent over and said take your time let them get excited a little bit more. He pulled the front of her G-string out not down, looked inside raised his head and winked at the crowd. Then he lowered the other side. She bent over and put her breast, one on each side of his head, as he turned his head she put a nipple in his mouth. She said don't bite it; I have to save it for the next show. He laughed, reached his hand around back and grabbed her ass and rubbed it. She really liked it, and asked for both hands. He started rubbing them up and down the crack in her ass. Then pulled her G-string down so that it dangled down between her legs, with his other hand he reached in front pulled that down so the G-string fell to the floor. He took a bow and she told him to go back to his girlfriend and take it out on her. Everybody laughed, clapped and whistled. He came back to Alma and sat down. She had her head down and was so embarrassed she wouldn't even look at him. He ordered another round of drinks and a different waitress came this time. She was much smaller, so he didn't give her as big a tip as he gave the other girl. They stayed for about one half hour and he suggested they leave. She wanted to stay, at least. She was with people. She wasn't sure what lay ahead. He was feeling the drinks and she wanted to drive home. He wouldn't think of it. She said" I'll walk otherwise" he knew she would to, so he gave her the keys. As they were driving back, he slid over in the seat and started running his hand up and down her leg. She kept pushing it away, but he kept going farther and farther up till he came to her panties. She was trying to drive and slap his hand, and watch the road, and she was getting a little excited. She really liked the feel of his hand, but he was too rough. She didn't want to tell him to take it easy, and then he would know she liked it. He lived about four miles from her house and he wanted to go home first, he had to go to the bathroom, she wanted to go home first but he was in no condition to drive. She thought maybe she could sober him up enough to drive her home. When they got to his place, she had to help him in the house. Once inside she leads him to the couch in the living room, and put him on it. She went to the kitchen and found the coffee pot and coffee. She put the water on and went back in to see how he was doing. He had taken off his shoes and shirt and went to the bathroom. When he came out he only had his shorts on. Alma was worried he was going to try something with her. She went in the bathroom and got his pants, he was sitting on the edge of the couch. She got down on one knee with his pants in her hand and tried to put his legs in them. He grabbed her hair, pushed the pants aside and reached down and grabbed her blouse. Ripped the buttons and pulled her out of it, all this time she was trying to get away. He pulled her head down to his crouch and opened his shorts. With his other hand he had a hold of her bra. He pulled that off her shoulders and grabbed her breast. He started to squeeze till she started to cry. He then started to rub and run his fingers around her nipples. That felt good to her and she told him so. That way he would be gentler with her. By now she knew there was know way of getting out of there without doing what he wanted. She stopped struggling with him and lay back so that he could do what ever he wanted to do. He had taken off his shorts and was working on her slacks and under panties. When he looked up his face came into her breasts. He said" my god they are great." That was the first words he had said since they got home. He started to climb on top of her when all of a sudden he started yelling "I AM GOD, I AM GOD and I am fucking Mary and we will have baby JESUS." Alma didn't know what to do or say, her mind went blank... God must be nuts, she said "are you going to be Seymour or God, either way put your pants on and take me home. She rolled off the bed and started getting dressed. He just lay face up on the bed. She took one look at him, smiled, and thought to herself, he's in no mood to make Jesus that's for sure. A short time later he got up, put on his pants and shirt and shoes, and went out to the car. He never said a word to Alma when she got in the car. He drove her home, she got out, and neither said a word, no good night or anything. She went in the house and started laughing.

The next day nothing was said about the night before. Court went on as usual. Alma thought for sure he would say something but he never did. It was three weeks before he asked her out again. She said, "If I go there will be no drinking scotches on the rocks" He said" his drinking days are over." She tried to make excuses for not going, but he again mentioned George's name. He said in a passing way, "I wonder how George likes working with blacks and all that heat? I'll bet he would give anything to be back up north, what do you think Alma?" They made plans for a weeknight, that way not too many people were out. She wasn't happy about what was laying ahead that night. She knew he wanted to go to bed with her, but she was not in a lovemaking mood with him. The thought of George coming north was the only thing that made her even consider going out with him in the first place. He wanted her to drive over to his place around seven. That was fine with her. This way she had a way of getting home. When she got there, a note on the door said to walk in, no one was around, she looked in the living room, kitchen, she called his name, still no answer. She looked in the bedroom, and there he was naked, standing up on the bed. She started to turn around and walk out, he told her to turn around and come back in, she told him to put some clothes on, and' went out to the kitchen. She thought, what is this nut up to now, a minute later he came out wearing a robe. He told her he had a joyful evening planned and she was to participate as the leading lady. First he wanted a bit to eat. He had some frozen dinners in the freezer, took them out and put them in the microwave, got some glasses out and a bottle of wine. After the meal, he led her into the bedroom. He turned on the TV and disrobed. He walked over to Alma and started taking off her clothes. She just stood there, never moved an inch. He got down to her bra and panties, stood back and looked at her. He didn't say a word. Took her hand and lead her to the bed. He pushed a button on the VCR. He turned her around; when she looked at the TV it showed two people naked, making love. Lipton said tonight we are going to do what these two are doing. He looked at the TV. And saw the man moving his hands all over the girl; Lipton started doing the same thing, moving his hands all over Alma's body, just barely touching her skin. She looked to see what they were doing, he was taking off her bra and then started fondling her breasts... she was thinking of all the work she had to do back at the office tomorrow. He was kissing her nipples and running his tongue all around her tits. He slid his hands down her sides till he came to her panties. His thumbs were hooked into the sides and slid them down and off her feet. His fingers started investigating the lower parts of her body; he started gently rubbing his hand up and down. This was starting to excite her, she started moving side to side and then up and down. His head was going down past her belly button. He had spread her legs and was putting his fingers down inside her thighs and gently massaging. She was really getting excited now.

She tried to think about work at the office, and everything except what he was doing to her. But with no success. Her mind just went over to what he was doing and she couldn't stop it. His hand stopped, he started moving his head and body up. Kissing and licking her tits on the way, he brought his body up to the point of placing his penis in her mouth; she opened her mouth and accepted it with great pleasure. After working it for a few minutes he withdrew and slid back down to her private parts, there he started licking and rubbing all over. It almost drove her crazy, no longer did she think about work. She grabbed hold of him and wouldn't let go. She groaned and moaned with joy. He entered her with great force. They were both getting short of breath. She had never felt like this since Michael... Michael, how could she do something like this and now think of Michael. Lipton had just reached his climax and was pulling out when she pushed him off, jumped off the bed, and ran for her clothes. She started to cry. What had she done? She lost her head; no more would she let any man play with her mind. Quickly she got dressed and ran out of the house; never again would she let that man in her bed or her in his.

The next four weeks went by and nothing was said about that last night or any other night in the future. She felt relieved; she had enough to think about at the house. The next four weeks went by and nothing was said about that night or any future nights, which was fine with Alma. She had enough problems at home. The old slide up and down windows wouldn't slide, so washing them was a pain. She called a home improvement company; they sent a salesman out to look at the house. He introduced him self as Jay Johnson. After looking the house over and measuring the windows he said he would get back to her in a few days. He had to check the sizes and the best window that would fit. She told him that would be fine.

She had been neglecting Karen quite a bit lately, because of working late and other things. Karen was now almost in her teens. Another two weeks and she would be thirteen. She had been acting funny lately. Alma thought that she may be getting her period. She needed to have a talk with her. Tell her what's ahead in her life. The different phases her body will be going through... Karen didn't seam as happy lately. Something was wrong. Karen had gone out with some friends that afternoon. When she comes home they will have that mother daughter talk.

Things at the courthouse seemed to be going pretty good. Judge Lipton hadn't bothered her or talked to her in over a month. That made Alma curious, what had she done to him now? Then the thought left her mind. He had caused enough problems as it was. As long as George was not around, she was happy but she still didn't trust the Judge. When she got home that night there was a note on the table... The salesman Mr. Johnson called and wants you to call him back, KAREN. Then she had the phone number. She wanted new windows, the kinds that tilt in so she can wash them. She called and asked for Mr. Johnson. "Mr.

Johnson hadn't come back to the office as yet, would you care to leave a message," she said. She told the girl she was returning his call and that she would be home all evening. The girl said she would have him give her another call and hung up.

The back door slammed shut and in came Karen. Alma said, "Hi Karen how was your day?" Karen walked past her and said something like, "OK I guess." Alma asked Karen, "If she had a few minutes, she'd like to talk with her". It's been a longtime sense they had a talk. Karen said, "Later," and went up stairs. That was not the way Karen usually was, something was bothering her. She went up stairs and knocked on her door. Karen said, "She was tired and wanted to rest for a while." Now Alma was really worried; at five in the afternoon and she's tired. Alma went downstairs, just as she got to the last step the phone rang. Alma picked it up and said, "Hello," no one said anything; and then the dial tone came on...the phone went dead. Alma figured, someone had dialed the wrong number and forgot about it. She went in the kitchen and started making something for supper. She made potato salad, and there were still some cold cuts left over and a large pickle, which she cut in half. There was still a large piece of chocolate cake, and she cut that in half. She made a large pitcher of lemonade. It was hot out, and she thought they would eat outside on the patio. They hadn't done that sense last fall. It also would give her a chance to talk with Karen. As she was carrying some stuff outside, the phone started too ring then stopped. She thought that was strange but kept on doing what she was doing. She got everything outside, came to the foot of the stairs, and called up to Karen…no answer. She went up to the top step when she heard Karen say, "I won't do it again, it's not right. I don't care what the other kids think. I have got to go now, so don't call me again," and hung up the phone. Alma made out she didn't hear anything and called her again from the bottom of the stairs. Karen hollered down and said she wasn't hungry. Alma started up the stairs. Karen's door was still closed. She knocked and went in. Karen was lying on the bed. Tears were in her eyes. Alma sat on the edge of the bed, took Karen's hand and asked, "What's the matter honey, care to talk about it." Karen said she was tired. She had a fight with one of the kids today, and she was all upset. Alma said, "Come on down and have something to eat and we'll talk about it, OK". She started to pull Karen, Karen got up by herself, and they went down stairs, and outside. They sat down and started eating. The phone rang again, neither one got up to answer it. Then Alma said, "I'll bet that's the window- man calling." Buy the time she got to the phone it had stopped ringing, and she started to go back when the phone rang again. It was the window-man this time. He wanted to come out and talk with her. She said, "anytime, she will be home all evening." He said he would be there within the hour. That would give them enough time to finish eating and may be talk a little. When she got back outside, Karen wasn't there. Alma looked around for her, but could not fine her. She finely walked down to the pond; Karen was sitting on the dock. Alma sat down with her. She told Karen anytime you want to talk I'll listen. I've got all the food out, so let's go up and eat, maybe you'll feel better. The window man is coming within the hour. I would like to clean the patio off before he gets here, if passable. Karen got up and they walked back up to the house. They sat down and finished eating. Nothing was said. Karen helped her mother clear the table and, then they both sat outside, waiting for the window man.

Alma went inside and made another pitcher of lemonade and put a lot of ice in it so it would stay cold longer. They heard the car door slam shut, Alma went around front and met the window man, showing him the way to the back of the house. She asked Karen if she would go in and get another glass. When she got back he had all his papers spread out on the table and was talking with Alma. She poured some lemonade and gave it to the man. He looked at Karen and said" my name is Jay Johnson I don't think we've met." Karen said "I'm Karen and this is my mother" and sat down. Jay started going over the window sizes and the type he would recommend, and the cost. The price was a little more then she had figured on, but the windows were what she wanted. She said, "She would take them, but needed ninety days to pay for them." Jay smiled and said, "They have a twelve month interest free payment plan, if that would be better for her." She thought that would be much better. It wouldn't strap her so much. Jay said, "It would be a few weeks before they would be there if that was all right with her. He would send the sizes out tomorrow and they would start making them right away. He started to leave when she asked him if he would like another glass of lemonade. He said," it sure would go good on a hot day like this, besides this was his last stop today". They got talking about windows, and maybe a new front door. Just then the neighbor's dog came wandering in the yard. He was a nice old dog. He would come over every once in a while, he seemed to like Karen, she would scratch his back and ears and he would just stay there forever as long as she scratched him. Jay said, "He has a little Heinz 57 dog. Karen looked at Jay and asked, "What is a Heinz 57 dog, I never heard of one?" Alma had heard of the dog but didn't know nor did she ever see one. When Jay told them it was a mixed breed, they all started laughing. He stayed for an hour and half, talking about his childhood, growing up in the mid west. Memphis Tennessee, well it was a little town west of Memphis called Cross Bow, population 37 and a half people. They all started laughing again. Karen said, "What is the 1/2?" Mrs. Long Bow is expecting any day now. So they say. They talked about the weather, the house, and flowers and just about everything. Karen was getting right in the conversation with them, Jay looked at this watch and said, "He was sorry but he had to get home to his dog. He got up and started walking to his car. Alma asked, "If he was going to help installing the windows." He said, "No, but he'll be here supervising the job. I'll be here when the job is finished to inspect it" That made Alma happy, because she knew nothing about windows, or doors for that matter. They all said, good-bye and he left.

Alma and Karen went back to the patio and sat down. Alma started talking about her job, and the things that went on in court that day. After about 15 minutes, Alma asked her, "If she felt better." She said, "She did" and that was the end of the conversations. They both sat there waiting for the other to talk. The phone rang and Alma started to get up to answer it. Karen said, "She would, and almost ran in the house. Buy the time she got there the phone had stopped ringing. She came out with her head down. Alma asked, "If everything was ok." She didn't say anything, just nodded her head. They both sat in silence for a long time again. Finely Alma said, "She was going inside and read a book. She never was interested too much in TV." Karen said," Mom we have to talk." Alma said, "Any time; I'm here for you honey." She sat back down in the chair. "Mom I'm scared, the girls are all talking about there periods. I haven't gotten mine yet, I get cramps and all, but that's it. They are starting to call me a freak, could this be because of what George did to me? They are all starting to wear bras, I have nothing. I feel and look likes a freak." She started to cry, Alma told her she wasn't a freak; some girls develop later then others... She told her how she was a little over thirteen when she started to bloom. Her chest got sore and she started her period all at the same time. There's no set time, things just happen. Some girls get there periods when they are ten or eleven years old, some not till thirteen or fourteen. I think the best thing to do is we'll go to the doctors. Have the doctor give you a complete examination, you should have one anyway and so should I. I'll make an appointment for the both of us. "How's that?" Both Karen and Alma felt better now. Karen went over to her mom and gave her a big hug. The following day at the office, Alma asked one of the ladies who she likes, "who's a good female doctor? She told Alma who she goes to. Alma told her she would like her self and daughter to have a good Doctor, a good family Doctor. She told Alma that she goes to Dr. Alice Greenville. She called Dr. Greenville and made an appointment for the following Tuesday at four fifteen. Both Alma and Karen went to the Doctors. They spent about an hour talking with Dr. Greenville. She was just the type of women to be a Doctor. Very caring and listened to every thing they had to say. She asked a lot of questions and made separate files on each one. After all the questions she wanted them to come back in a few days for a complete physical. They left the Dr's office after making an appointment for Friday at three o'clock for Karen and three forty-five for Alma. They left the Drs. and went up to the restaurant for a bit to cat. Alma hadn't been there in a while and it was good seeing all the old faces, and talking about old times. Bill had done over the restaurant and it looked real homey. The food was the same, the best in town. Bill and Bee came out when she walked in; they both came over and gave her and Karen big hugs. They had a bit to eat and went home. All the way home Karen talked about how nice Doctor Greenville was. At first she was very nervous but Doctor Greenville made her feel right at home, just as if she was one of the family. After they had there examinations they had to wait for about a week before the tests came back. Alma got a call while at the courthouse the following week. It was Dr. Greenville; she wanted to see Alma at the earliest possible time when she had a few minutes. Things were fairly slow at the courthouse, and there was another reporter there so she said she could come over right now if it was ok. Dr. Greenville said she would wait for her. Fortunately she was only a few blocks away. She asked her boss. She said, "Ok, but try not to be too long." Alma told her partner were she was going and left. When she got there Dr. Greenville was waiting for her. They went into her office and sat down. She had Karen's folder in front of her. She told her what she had found.

Karen had been damaged internally, from the rape. Plus it's been on her mind all this time. By having it on her mind, this has in some ways slowed the process of having a normal period. She wants to be like all the other girls, and by not having her period has put a strain on her and her system. The damage done by the rape, I think in time she should be ok. It's her mental and physical condition we have to worry about. I believe that when her breasts start to develop, so will her mind and body. You will have to keep talking to her in a gentle and reassuring way that the time will come and everything will start popping all at once. Not having her period now is not a big deal. I have heard of females not getting there periods till there early twenty's. I want to have a talk with her, but I wanted to talk with you first It was a very trying time for both of you, but Karen has to learn to let lose, and start living a normal girls life. There nothing physically wrong, just mental worries. I would like to talk with Karen alone at first, if it's ok with you. Dr. Greenville was a peach. As Karen said, "She's like a member of the family," she talks and listens in such a way you feel comfortable with her.

Dr. Greenville asked Alma, "How she's been feeling lately. Any headaches, feel like vomiting, chest or breast soreness, stomach problems, anything out of the ordinary?" Alma "Told her how she felt a little sick in the mornings and the smell of food made her want to vomit sometimes. But she has been through a lot lately. She felt that, that was the reason for feeling like she does." Doctor Greenville looked at her for a minute or so, and then asked if she was married? Alma said, "No more," and then started to explain. Dr. Greenville asked her, "When was the last time you had sex with your husband? Alma started to think back... My gosh, it has to be three years ago. When was the last time you had your period? Alma thought for minute and said, "Come to think about it I am late. Why do you ask?" Dr. Greenville looked her in the eyes and said" YOU ARE PREGNANT" Alma got out of her chair and said, "That's not possible, it can't be", then she put her head in her hands and said, "Oh my god." She sat back down in her chair, and looked at the Doctor. She lowered her head and said in a low voice, "she was raped by Judge Lipton about five week ago." Dr. Greenville said "let's start from the beginning. What happened?" Alma told the Doctor, "About the rape, and how Judge Lipton had threatened her if she didn't do what he wanted." The Doctor asked, "What was he threatening you with?" Alma, "Started telling her all about George, How he was down in Alabama on a chain gang for raping Karen, and if I didn't do what he wanted, he would have George brought back up here and release him for good behavior. I was willing to do just about anything for that not to happen. We went out twice, the first time he got so drunk that nothing worked. The second time was about five weeks ago. He would always say how nice the weather was up here, and no black rapists to live with. And not have to worry about being raped by some big black, but things could change. He went for about three weeks without talking to me. Then as I was leaving one night he called me over. I had a headache, and told him so. I said "I would see him in the morning, A few days later he asked me again. I told him that the man was coming to look at my windows. I want to replace them with the new type. My god, how am I going to tell Karen? What will she think of me? What should I do? My god, I don't want that man's baby."

Dr. Greenville talked with Alma about other things with her health; she said, "How she found a polyp that should be taken out. I don't believe there's anything serious, but why wait until it is, or could be. I also found a lump in your Left breast. I also think it's just a fatty tumor. But I would like a biopsy done, just as a precaution. Otherwise you look very healthy. Blood pressure and heart are fine. I will want a complete blood work up on you both. I would like to make arrangements for these as soon as possible. I shall call you when we have the dates figured out.

She called Alma a few days later. "How is the 17th? She had planed on the same day surgery if it was all right with her. She would be in, in the morning and out about noon. Come back to the office in three days, we should have the reports by then, and change the bandages. If there is someone who could drive you to the hospital and home again that would be great. If not, she would make arrangements for someone to do it for her." It seemed everything was happening at once…Karen's and hers. When Alma got home, she had a talk with Karen. She told Karen what Dr. Greenville had said, "And not to worry. Nothing is wrong with her." She also told Karen, "That she was going to have a few lumps taken out," after Alma got through talking." The windows are coming in the later part of next week. Karen said, "Jay had called and gave her the news. There was a lot to do, the following week want by in a hurry. The windows should be in Monday. It should give them enough time to get things in order. Alma should have her surgery done and Karen could help with the housework. The hospital called the day before. They want Alma to be there by 6:45 in the morning. How would she get there? The phone rang, it was Dr. Greenville. "Just checking to see if the hospital called and everything is ok?" Alma told her, "She was having trouble trying to get a ride." The Doctor asked, "Where do you live." Alma started to explain to her were she lived. Dr. Greenville said, "Don't worry; I can pick you up on my way to the Hospital. She only lives about a mile down the road." The Doctor was wondering who had bought the old house. She picked up Alma at 6:30.

And a friend brought her home a little after noon. She felt pretty good, a little tired was all. She wasn't used to getting up that early. Three days later she drove to the Doctor's office with Karen. The Doctor had gotten the reports back and they were just as she had thought. Everything was fine, but she wanted Alma to come back in six months for a checkup. She also told her how she had a nice talk with Karen on the phone. When she hung the phone up she was singing. They both smiled. The only thing left now was the windows. When they got home, there was a message on their answering machine. Mrs. Fox, please call Dr. Greenville at your earliest convenience. It was too late to call her now. I'll give her a call in the morning. She started to think... Dr. Greenville said, she wanted to see me in six months. What about the pregnancy? Wasn't she going to keep track of my progress? I'll bet that's what she wants me for. She didn't want to say anything in front of Karen. The more she thought about it the more it upset her. She had to think of some way to have a miscarriage and make it look like something else. She found it hard to get to sleep. All she could think of was having the baby, plus telling Karen...And what about Chris and Chrissie?

Jay called the following Monday, the windows are in and they will deliver them Tuesday morning. They should be finished in two days. Can someone be there to let them in the house? Alma told him, "Karen would be home. If they needed anything, maybe she could help." At the end of the second day all the windows were in. Karen even had them all washed before her mother came home what a difference in the looks of the house. Alma just stood in front of the house and looked and looked. Not only did they look good, but Jay said, "It would save her about 25% on her full bill also." He said, "He would be back in a few days and see about the front door." Alma had been working on Karen's birthday party for the past couple of weeks. She had planed a big party for her. Friday evening there was a knock on the front door. Alma opened the door, and there stood a deliveryman with a box in his had. He asked if her name was Alma and she said" Yes," He said, "Then this box is for you, Have a nice evening" and left. There was a card on the top of the box, Alma opened it. The note read: For two of the nicest customers in the world, Karen thank you for cleaning the windows, and Mrs. Fox thank you for calling us...signed Jay. She opened the box and there was a bouquet of yellow roses. Karen was all excited; nobody had ever sent her roses before. She took one small rose bud and put it in their old large dictionary, along with a note with the date, time and why she got it. Alma thought that was a very nice thing she did. Karen's birthday party was planed for the coming Saturday night. Everything was in order. Jay came back the following Wednesday evening and measured the door. He asked Alma, "If she wanted a window or just a plane door." She thought for a minute. "There was a high window in the old door; let's keep it the same way!" She would like a peephole below the window, that way I can see who is outside. Jay thought that was a very good idea. He marked every thing down. As he was about to leave he turned to Alma and asked if maybe he could take her and Karen out for dinner some night. Alma thought for a minute. Then she asked "Are you going to be busy Saturday night? This took him by surprise. No, why do you ask"? Karen had gone in the house so Alma could talk, but it had to be soft. She explained the party for Karen and would like him to come. No presents, just him. He thought for a minute, and said, "He would love to go. Alma told him all about it.

Friday was Karen's birthday but nothing was said. Bill called Friday morning and asked for Karen. Karen picked up the phone. Bill asked her if she could come and help them decorate the place. One of the big shots in town was going to have a birthday party for there kid and they like my lobsters so they want to have it here, and if she's not busy Saturday afternoon would she help them out. Karen was all excited. She liked working in the Restaurant; she met a lot of nice people. This was the first big party that she's going to work, and she was all for it. Karen's thirteenth birthday party was something she'll never forget. She worked hard all day Friday and Saturday morning. The place looked great. Karen had no idea that this birthday party was for her. She worked so hard, she wanted to take a nap. Bill told her, "She could lie down in the back and he would call her when things got going." Some of the kids from school were the first to arrive. Karen was still sleeping Bill went in and called her, He told her, "people were starting to come in and he needed some help." Alma had been there for about an hour helping, getting things ready; putting up the big HAPPY BIRTHDAY KAREN sign and all that. When Karen came out, she almost fainted. All the kids from her grade in school were there, and they all sang happy birthday to her. She sat on the floor and cried.

She couldn't believe what was happening. She had forgotten about her birthday, she was so excited thinking about decorating the place for a birthday party for someone else. The rest of the evening people kept coming and going, some stayed for a long time some just long enough to give her a kiss. Chris and Chrissie came up from Pennsylvania. Dr.Greenville stopped, Harvey Binder along with about twenty-nine other friends, co-workers, and Judges from the courthouse. They said that thirty-seven school friends and teachers were there. Seven friends from the town hall stopped in to wish Karen a happy birthday. The biggest thrill of all was when Alma's mother and her husband came down. Alma had invited them, never thinking that they would travel all that way for Karen's birthday. Alma introduced Bill and Bee to her mother and big Ben. Bill took one look at Big Ben and Big Ben took one look at Bill and they both let out a howl. Would you believe Bill said, "This is the gentleman that showed me everything there is to know about lobsters? They are the couple that made this restaurant what it is today. We stopped in at there place one night for supper. We ordered Lobsters, It was the best we had ever had. We asked the waitress if the cook was around that make this lobster, she smiled and said sure. She went in the kitchen, was gone a few minutes, and out came this here guy. We ordered a drink for all of us, he sat down, and we started talking about the proper way to cook lobsters. We told him we had a restaurant down in New York State and there was no one around that sold Lobsters on their menu. I would like to give it a try. We told him we would pay him whatever he wanted, if he would show us how to cook lobsters. He asked us how long we where going to stay. I told him however long it took. From that minute on we became good friends. I worked in the kitchen with him and his wife for almost a week. I never saw so many Lobsters in my life. He had two large tanks that were filled each day with fresh Lobsters. That place kept two Lobster boats in business. He showed me how to make everything you could make out of Lobsters. He told me where to buy the tanks, the pumps and how to treat the water to keep it fresh. My next problem was buying the Lobsters. I had to be able buy at a good price and I didn't know anyone down our way that sold them. He gave me a phone number to call when we got back home. This company deals a lot with fish; I've known them for years. Tell them I told you too call. Let's see if they could help you out. The rest is history. And to think, all this time it was Alma's mother and her husband. Big Ben and Bill took of by themselves; they were gone for a good long time, when they came back nothing was said about what they had talked about. Shrimp and Lobster was the two things that seemed to have moved that night. Salads and Swedish meatballs .and spaghetti and scalloped potatoes home made bread cookies and ice cream. At seven o'clock Karen cut the cake. There must have been about fifty people there. Alma and her mother cut the cake into pieces and every one had a piece. Chris and Chrissie were going to stay at Alma's house, now with Alma's mother and husband there; they too were going to stay. That was no problem there was two bedrooms up stairs and the basement could sleep a dozen if they wanted to sleep on the floor. There was a fold out couch and a single bed in the basement. That was no problem. Besides everyone was so tired they didn't care where they slept. The first thing Sunday morning, they all got up, had breakfast, and went over to the restaurant and helped clean up. Bill was surprised to see everyone come in to work. They cleaned the tables, washed the floor, and even washed the windows as well. They did all the dishes, pots, and pans. They used paper-plates and paper cups which was a big help. There wasn't too much left to do. When they got through, the place was spotless.

Alma called Bill to one side and asked, "What the bill was; he said he hadn't had time to figure it up yet. They went back to where all the help was. He said, "He had something to say, "First I want to say thank you all for coming today. This place looks like a million dollars; again I want to thank you all. The second thing I want to say is, "It's easy to tell that Karen and Alma are one of us, with all the people here last night it was amazing." If they didn't think that you were great, there wouldn't have been one person here. That's country folks, they stick together good times or bad. Today is a good example; the ladies came over from the courthouse. People came from Maine and Pennsylvania plus everyone else, to help out. Again I want to thank you all and God bless each and every one of you." When they got back home Chris and Chrissie said, "They should be getting back." After saying good-bye to everyone and giving Karen and Alma a big hug and kiss, they left for home. Alma's mother and Big Ben were the next to leave. Alma wanted them to stay a few days but Ben wanted to get back to his restaurant. Alma and her mother had taken a walk around the property. Ben was the best thing that ever happened to her, he's such a sweet man, always willing to help. She told Alma that they would be back down to see them. I think Bill and Ben have something up there sleeve. They said good-bye to everyone, and left. Alma's head was still hurting; she thought it was because of all the excitement, everyone one coming and going. She was just exhausted. She was getting ready for bed when the phone rang. Karen answered it, and let out a scream. It was Charlie and Clare in Florida wanting to wish Karen a Happy Birthday. They talked for quite a while; Alma was telling them what they had done to the house and all. They agreed that there was a draft that came in around the windows once in a while. They wanted to talk with Karen once more to wish her a Happy Birthday and hung up. Karen and Alma both had tears in there eyes, thinking that these two people they hardly knew would call them all the way from Florida to wish Karen a Happy Birthday.

The next day when Alma got to work, that's all they talked about, Karen's party. The number of people that came, the food was out of this world. The lobster and shrimp were something else. One girl said she never ate so many shrimp, and that sauce was something. Another thought the lobster bisque was made in heaven. As she was leaving Judge Lipton asked, "Her to come over. He wanted to talk with her." She said, "She had a splitting headache and could it wait till morning. She was very tired from Saturday and Sunday." She started to think, she didn't see Judge Lipton at the party. She was just as happy. He said, "Tomorrow would be fine," and she went home. She thought that was strange, he hadn't said two words since that night, now what would he want. She had made up her mind. She wasn't going to go out with him again. Nothing was said the next morning and Alma forgot about it. Wednesday night the phone rang and it was Jay. A door had come in, but was a little different then the one that was ordered. He was wondering if she would take a look at it. If she liked it, they would install it on Saturday. He would come over and pick up both her and Karen so they could take a look at it, and take them back. If she didn't like it, they would have the other one sent. She asked Karen if she would want to go and she said yes, they would look at it together. He came over and picked them up. They looked at the door and both thought it would look ok. Jay thought it would look ok also. He would be there Saturday to make sure it was installed right.

The carpenters were there bright and early Saturday morning. The weather was great, sunny and a little cool but just right for working outside. The new door took most of the day. They finished up around three thirty. Standing back out near the road looking at the front door and the rest of the house, Alma was thinking to herself, I've got to take a picture and send it to Charlie and Clare. I'm sure they would appreciate it. Thinking to herself; she did not hear Jay come up behind her, Jay asked, "Well what you think of it?" She turned around and said, "I don't like it, would you please take it out and put the old one back in." At first he just looked at her, and then they both started laughing. She told him what she was thinking, "Wait a minute, I have my camera in the truck, let me take your picture standing in front of the house, better yet lets get Karen out here also." Jay went up to the door and rang the bell, Karen answered the door. Jay said, "Come on out, I want to take your picture so we can send it down to Charlie and Clare." Karen said, "Let me comb my hair and change into something nice." Jay asked if she had an evening gown. Alma said, "Come as you are, Clare wouldn't know you all dressed up." They all laughed. Jay took about four or five pictures. He said, "He was going to send them in to the contractor's newspaper, Maybe they will print one, who knows." Jay looked at his watch, it was a little past four. He asked Alma, "If her and Karen liked barbecued food. He knows of a place that has the best spare ribs around. "If you're not doing anything, would you care to get some?" They both said, "They liked ribs. But they would have to get cleaned up first.

Jay said, "That would be fine, that way he would go home and get cleaned up himself."

He was back in about an hour. They were ready when he got back, this time he brought his car. He drove north for about thirty-five minutes, as they rounded a bend in the road; right in front of them was the bar that Judge Lipton took her to. They went past that for about a mile. A big sign say's THE- OX-PIT. STOP HERE FOR THE BEST RIBS AROUND. They got there just in time to get a table outside. You could stay and eat all night if you wanted to. You paid one price at the door, and that took care of the evening. They felt real comfortable with one another. Jay was telling stories about the different jobs that he worked on. Some were real funny, others were not. Karen and Jay made about a half dozen trips to the pit. Alma still had that headache and didn't feel like eating too much. After the first date, things just seemed to catch on. Every Saturday night they would go out someplace different.

Karen got a job babysitting for some people down the road; they liked to go out Saturday nights also. That meant Alma and Jay would have to go it alone. Karen was making money for the first time, and was happy as a lark. Now she could by her own clothes, and things. Jay liked sports of all kinds, and Alma was a sports fan also. Karen liked to go also when she wasn't working. As time went on Jay and Alma got to be real chummy. They would go to a ball game or some sporting event and then have dinner and go to either Jay's house or

Alma's and watch TV. Alma found out that Jay's wife had died of cancer five years ago. He worked for this company, and then bought shares in it right after his wife died. He never had dated till he met Alma. He started loosening up and was more fun to be around, type of guy. After them going out for about a month Jay started making advances. Alma was wondering when that would happen. She was getting a little impatient, and was about to start something herself. The most so far that he had done was take her arm when they crossed the street. Now he was giving her a good night kiss and hug.

She often wondered what it would be like in his arms. One night at Alma's house they where watching TV. A commercial came on showing ladies underwear. Jay said to himself, "Looks just like what my wife use to wear." Alma asked him, "If that excited him?" He said, "At the time but he hadn't thought much about it any more. She said, "What would happen if I wore something like that?" He didn't say anything for a long while. He finely said, "With clothes on it wouldn't make any difference. He couldn't see it anyway." She started to tease him. She unbuttoned the top four or five buttons on her blouse. Enough to show her bra, it too had lace all around. She looked at him and said "does this do anything to you? He dropped his eyes down to the valley in her chest. It's been a long time sense I even thought about it, but things may be different now. He reached over and pulled her to him. He gave her a mouth open kiss. He put his arms around her and drew her close. She came to him willingly. She started to unbutton his shirt, when the phone rang. It was Karen, the people she was baby-sitting for called and asked if she could stay the night. They wanted to go to a party and wouldn't be home till sometime in the morning. Karen wanted to know if it would be all right. So she could call the people back. Alma said she could stay, but she was to get a phone number as to where they would be, just be careful. She came back to Jay with a smile on her face. She asked, "If he had anything to do with the people down the road staying out all night, so Karen wouldn't be home." He said, "No but it worked out all right anyway. She took his hand and led him up stairs." She was going to ask him, "How she could improve the bedroom," but she didn't have to. He already had plans in his head. She turned to face him; he still had that smile on his face. His hands started to wander over the backside of her. She was hoping he didn't stop because it was feeling real good. He moved around behind her and with one hand slid it under her arm; she raised her arm up enough so that he could reach around and put his hand on one of her breasts. He started to massage it very lightly. He then unbuttoned the rest of the buttons and gently removed it from her shoulders. The slacks she was wearing had an elastic belt. With his hands on her hips, he slowly pulled them down and dropped them around her ankles. She was wearing pink panties with a lot of lace around the top. The bra matched perfect. He turned her around so that he could face her. It seemed to her that everything he did was in slow motion, but each move did something to excite her a little more. He picked her up and gently lifted her on the bed, as he was ready to let go of her, she pulled him down next to her. He was removing his shirt and she was working on his pants. She reached down and pulled the pants off his legs. Looking back up, she saw this large bulge in his under shorts. She was getting inquisitive but she decided to do like he did to her; go slow and see what happens. She moved her hands up his legs real slow and very lightly. She could see that he was ready to grab her, but she backed away just far enough so that he couldn't reach her. They both started to laugh. She grabbed hold of his under shorts and gave them a good pull. The snaps popped and the shorts stood straight up in the air. He felt a little embarrassed for a second, but she was massaging this thing that seemed to be getting larger and larger the more she stroked it. Thank God she stopped when she did, otherwise, who knows what would have happened. He was taking her bra off with one hand and her panties off with the other. It seemed that they both came off at the same time. She rolled over on top of him and just laid there while he gently moved his hands over the two moons. That gave her so much pleasure. He started kissing her and moving his hands over the rest of her naked body. She moaned and groaned with pleasure. For once she thought she could really enjoy this lovemaking without being pressured into it, like she did with the Judge. They continued into the wee hours of the night. Laying in each others arms, feeling different parts of each others body, getting to know each curve and bump. Pinching and pulling her hair, teasing, kissing, and sucking on her breasts. That's one thing that really drove her crazy. She loved having her tits kissed, sucked and his tongue rolling around the nipples. There was no intercourse that night. Foreplay was all that was needed. That went on for hours. Intercourse would have meant only a few minutes of pleasure, Foreplay can give you pleasure for hours. Alma never had anything like that before in her life. She was totally exhausted and released tension. She just lay there with a big smile on her face. That was the best night of lovemaking she has ever had, and they didn't have intercourse. It was sun up when Jay woke up. He got dressed and very quietly went down stairs, wrote a note and left it on the table. He went out to his car and went home. The time was 6:30 am. Alma woke up at 8:30 am and felt around for Jay. He was no place in the bed. She got up and put her housecoat on and went down stairs. Thinking he may have made coffee. On the table was his note... "It was a great evening; we will have to do it again soon," Love Jay. She went to the phone and called him. He answered the phone on the first ring. With a song in his voice he said Good morning. She smiled and said, "What a night, did I miss anything?" Did I go to sleep before the show was over? Did you have a good time? I dreamt we had a night of love making like I never had before. Is that true, did you have the same, or was I really dreaming? He started to say something but stopped. His mind was on what happened last night. It was a long time sense he had a night as good as that. He told her he didn't want to leave but he didn't want Karen to come home and find us together in bed. I don't know how she would take it. Alma never gave it a thought, but he was right. She didn't know how Karen would take it. She made coffee and toast and put jelly on it sat down and started thinking about last night.

The phone rang, it was Karen. "The people just got home; they want me to stay for a few more hours while they get some sleep. That is, if it's all right with you? Alma asked if she got any sleep last night. She said yes, she went to bed at 10:00 o'clock and slept till 7:30 this morning. The children were very good. They like her so they mind her. Alma said, "OK. But I want you home by 3:00." They talked for a few minutes and hung up. What Karen didn't tell her mother was these people have HBO On there TV. There was a movie on and it was a dirty one. Karen took it all in; curiosity got the better of her. First it showed a couple making love, they were both naked. That was the first time she had ever seen a man with out clothes on, and what they were doing to each other. She started getting this strange feeling in her groin. She put her hand down there and sure enough it was all moist. As she watched the show, two girls came together. They to were naked, and there breasts were firm and they were playing with each other. Karen was taking off her blouse and started rubbing her chest. They felt sore but she couldn't stop rolling her fingers around the nipples. That was giving her the most pleasure. Between watching what the two girls were doing and what her one hand was doing in the groin and the other playing with her nipples, she couldn't stop herself. A few minutes later she had the most thrilling experience of her life while still watching the movie. She sat back and sighed; now she is confused. What had she done? When George raped her, she never saw what he had in his hand. All she knew was that it hurt; whatever he put into her. This time when she did it, it felt good. She had this guilty feeling now. Should she tell her mother and Dr. Greenville what she had done, or keep it to herself till school starts and hear what the other girls had to say? Her train of though was interrupted when the children came bounding down the stairs. She ran to them and asked them to be quite. Their mother and father were trying to get a few hours sleep. They tiptoed into the kitchen, Karen smiled and whispered, what do you want for breakfast? Jamie, the boy, was eight and Janie, the girl, was seven, they were two great kids and they though Karen was the best. Maybe it was because Karen was closer to there age. They would ask some crazy questions. Like why do skunks have white strips down there back and not yellow or red? How come girls have too squat and boys can stand up to pee, do all married people have kids so they can holler at them, etc. After breakfast she took them outside to play. They had kites and wanted to fly them, but there wasn't enough wind to get them up in the air. They put them on the back porch too save for a windy day. Karen went in the house to get a book; she was going to read a story to them. She went to the living room and stopped short. The people up stairs were having an argument or something. She wanted to do it this way and he wanted it done the other way. Finely they got together and nothing more was said. At least what she could hear. She got two books and went out side. She gave each a book and said they have to read aloud a paragraph from each book one at a time, that way you will know what each story is about. They thought that it was going to be fun. It kept them quiet for a long time. They really enjoyed it. At lunchtime they went in the house, Karen told them they still had to talk softly otherwise they would wake their parents up. She made them some cereal and peanut butter sandwiches. They liked it when Karen was there, she made good stuff. At 3:00 their father came down to take Karen home. When she got home, he gave her two twenty-dollar bills. She thanked him and ran in the house. "Mom, mom look what I've got. I earned forty dollars, that's two dollars an hour." She was jumping with joy. Now she could buy that dress she wanted, with her own money.

Things went very well for the next few months. Jay and Alma and Karen were all happy. Judge Lipton spoke to Alma, only when he had to. Karen was confused about her body. When school started Karen, found out a lot of things about her body from the older girls. She felt better knowing that what she did was what most all the girls did. She started to get her period and her chest was starting to swell, just like Dr. Greenville had said. Most of the other girls her ages were already well developed by now. That didn't bother Karen, she thought, I'll get even with them all. Just wait and see. Karen was a bright student and very popular amongst her classmates. She was a whiz at basketball and she loved to swim. When winter came all her thoughts were of skiing, Ice skating was fun but it's not like skiing. She tried to get her mother to take her up north for a weekend. Where they have the ski trails and ski jumps. One day she said something to Jay like, "How come you never took up skiing?" He said, "He never had the time, but he was thinking about it now." That would be great; we could get Mom and go north for the weekend, how about that?" Jay thought it was a good idea, and he was going to talk with her mother about it. Two days later he came over to the house for supper, at the table he casually said how he was thinking about learning how to ski. He thought that he would go up north for a few days and try it. Nothing more was said. The first of December they had a big snowstorm. After the roads were cleared, he decided to go north. Just to see if he would like it. He mentioned to Karen if she would like to go for the day. She was all excited, and said, "SURE." You didn't have to ask her twice. Alma looked at both of them and said," What am I suppose to do, sit home and knit sweaters." They both laughed and told her what colors they wanted. She said, "Nuts to you two; go buy your own sweaters. I want to go skiing also." At one time she was a very good skier. That was when George had the cabin in Vermont. She had forgotten about that place. It's just as well; she wanted nothing to do with him.

The following week on Thursday, Jay called and said he wanted to go skiing Friday. Then he changed his mind. Alma had to work, so Saturday would have to do. They left early Saturday morning. They only had to travel for about an hour and a half to get there. The place was mobbed. They had to wait for over an hour to rent the skis; then another hour to get to the slopes. By now Jay and the rest was not a happy bunch. They got up at four in the morning, had breakfast and left. They got up here at six-thirty and now it's ten, and they still haven't skied. What a business, they were all set to go when the instructor said he was all filled up. It would be another hour. They went inside for some hot chocolate and some pastry. Jay looked around and saw some people he knew, he went over to say "hello" to them. She turned to see who it was, she almost fainted. It was George- what in the world was he doing there, and how did Jay know him? George kept eyeing Alma with that silly grin. She went outside with Karen. A few minutes later Jay came out. He didn't know about George, Karen, and Alma. He was starting to tell Alma what a nice guy George was. He even suggested using his cabin up in Vermont if they wanted. Alma pulled Jay one side. She told him George was the one that raped Karen three years ago. She wants nothing to do with him. He was not supposed to be out of prison for another ten years. How did he get out now? Then she started to think. "JUDGE LIPTON". He shortened his sentence. She would check with the secretary Monday morning and find out what happened. She was also going to talk with Chief Rose. Alma was wild; it was hard for Jay to believe George would do something like that to a ten-year-old girl. Alma had Jay take them home at once. Alma hadn't told Karen yet that George was out of prison. She would be scared to death to go out of the house. They got home at four in the afternoon Alma got on the phone and called the police station. She asked for the chief. The officer asked who it was that wanted to speak to the Chief. "Alma told him who she was;" the officer said, "hold on a minute". They knew each other pretty well, When Alma got through telling the Chief that she saw George today he was fit to be tied; Because it was Saturday the Judge would not be around. We'll have to wait till Monday. I'll call my friend in Alabama. Chief Rose went back in his files and took out George's file. He read it over real carefully to see if there as a loophole about an early parole. As far as he could see there was nothing. It said, He was sentenced to ten years in Alabama state prison

Sunday evening Alma had Karen sit down in the living room. She told her about seeing George at the ski shack. She also said how Chief Rose was going to see Judge Lipton Monday morning and find out how George got out of prison in Alabama. The Chief was going to have an unmarked car at the school both in the morning and at night when school let out. The teachers were told to watch for anyone, man, or women that didn't belong around the school. If spotted call the police dept. at once. If in a car, try and get the marker number. Monday morning the chief went over to see Judge Lipton. Lipton Said, "He was to busy to talk with anyone. Have him call later and set up an appointment." The Chief was furious. He went back to his office and had the officer at the desk call to make an appointment with the Judge. It would be two days before the Judge would have time to see him. The officer said, "That was all right and hung up. He went to the Chief and told him. The Chief had him write down the time the call was made, the conversation and what time the appointment was made for and the time the call ended. He had him make a new file with the heading" God Lipton". And make sure you put that in the file. He also told the officer to call the prosecutor in Alabama. He wanted to talk with him personally, as soon as possable.The Chief also said, "He wanted everything on tape, and put in the Lipton file". The prosecutor was in court and would call him back. The Chief also said "if one word ever gets out about what I'm doing, I swear to god, you will never get another job anywhere, is that understood." the officer said "yes sir" and went back out to his desk.

He called Alma back and told her what was happening. Now she was worried. They could do something to Karen because her name was never used in the papers. She could be kidnapped or run over by a truck and people would thing it was only an accident. She called the Chief back and explained what her feelings were. The Chief understood but there wasn't much he could do, unless the law was broken. He would have a car drive by there house once in a while. That's about all he could do. She asked if there was a good lawyer he knew that would give her some good advice as to what to do. He thought for a while, and then said, "I think you would be better off getting an out of town lawyer, someone that has never been before Lipton in court." She thought it's too bad she's so far away from Pennsylvania. There were two or three good lawyers that would love to take the case. Jay was staying away; he didn't want to be in the middle of this. George was his friend, and Alma was his girl friend. He called her on the phone and explained everything to her. George handled all the legal matters when his wife died and never charged him.

Alma felt alone. She started looking in the phone book for a good lawyer from the courthouse. One she could talk to, someone to give her advice. Maybe he could give her a name of a good lawyer from another district. She found one that was well known in Plantsville. She called and made an appointment. He could give her fifteen minutes on Wednesday at four thirty, if that would be all right with her. That was fine with her. Tuesday dragged by, Karen was in school, Alma was working in court. The chief had an unmarked car outside the school watching for Karen. Nothing happened. Karen came straight home from school. She stayed in the house the rest of the day. Wednesday Alma had a hard time concentrating on her work. Four o'clock finely came and Alma ran out of the courthouse and drove five blocks to the lawyer's office. She made it just in time, and went right in to his office. He knew her from the courthouse, by site not by name. He was very nice and easy to talk to. She knew she only had fifteen minutes so it was hard to tell and explain everything in that short of time. He called his secretary, "And told her he didn't want to be disturbed for the next half-hour." Now he started asking questions. The more he heard the more interested he became. He said, "He would like a few days to look into this, as this was a very serious matter."

He got her home phone number and said, "He would call her in a day or so. He wanted to talk with the Police Chief." He also wanted to look at the files the Chief had and the ones at the courthouse Alma left the Lawyers office feeling pretty good now we will see how smart Mr. Judge Lipton is. Attorney Steven Ryan may be just the man I'm looking for, she thought to herself. Let's see what he comes up with. Two days later Attorney Ryan called, "And asked if she could come to his office today at four thirty," she said, "Yes she would be there." Now she was really getting excited. She called Karen from the Court House and told her she was going to be late, and stay in the house. Don't answer the door unless you know who it is and don't answer the phone till I get home. Poor Karen was beginning to feel like a prisoner her self. She would see different cars parked on the street at school. These must be unmarked police cars. At least she hoped they were, and that made her feel better thinking that someone was watching over her.

That night after work Alma went right down to Attorney Ryan's office. He led her in to his office and they both sat down. He had a stack of papers in front of him. He told her he had made copies of every thing that was written about Mr. Lipton and George Hewitt. Lipton had been made a Judge in 1965. His father and brother are both Lawyers. He came from the Midwest and was sent out here. Why I don't know yet. We do know he's not well liked at the different Court Houses he's been serving in, and he has moved around quite a bit. We haven't found out why but we will. He was married for eight months. His wife left him for another man. They got an annulment. He has never remarried…that we know of. He is a very clever man. I checked the files the Chief has and it states that George Hewitt is to serve ten years in the Alabama State Prison for child rape. There is nothing that says he can be let out on good behavior, but there's nothing that say's he can't. The Judge up here says there's a clause that says he's eligible for parole after serving one third of his sentence on good behavior, and seven years probation with the understanding that if he should be charged with any arrest of any kind he would be sent back to the Alabama State Prison. To serve out the balance of his sentence… Attorney Ryan himself went over to the courthouse to check the files over there. They must have filed them away, because there was nothing regarding this case at all. That seems strange to me, there should have been something there. I'm going over again tomorrow and have the janitor look in the old file-rack. I'm glad the Chief still has his. Attorney Ryan wanted Alma to start from the very beginning. This was a very serious charge that Alma was going to bring up against the Judge. Not only would there be a charge to get George out of prison, but forcing you to have sex with him in order to keep George in jail, and then letting George out without a hearing. This would make the front page of every paper in the country, especially if he wants to fight it. He may want to keep this hushed up, being a top judge and all. Even if he wins the publicity would go bad for him.

Alma started from the day George raped Karen. How they took her to the hospital and the doctor even took pictures of the bruises on Karen. George even had scratches and black and blue marks all over his body. George's blood matched the blood found on Karen. He was brought to the jail house and locked up for the night. Karen fought him off the best she could but he still raped her-- his semen was found on her clothes and on her. She told him how they handled George, and why he was sent down to Alabama. If he went to jail here the guys would use him as a prostitute for raping a ten-year-old girl. He would have been lucky to last a week up here. The old Judge had to take his wife to a warmer climate. That's when Judge Seymour Lipton came on the scene. How he found out about George I don't know. The only thing I can think of is when he came here, he never talked with anyone. One day, I lit into him about his manners and attitude. He thanked me and was a little more human from then on. One day he called me into his Chamber and on his desk was a file on George. He said, "If I didn't do what he wanted, he would have George brought up here and set him free," He said, "He was God and could do whatever he wanted." The following week he called me to go out with him. I told him I didn't want to. He brought up George again. He was forcing me to have sex with him or else. We went to that Strip Joint just north of town on route 41. He got pretty drunk. He even got up on the stage and danced with one of the strippers. We went to his house I was thinking I could sober him up enough to drive me home; instead he tried to rape me. He took off his clothes and jumped on the bed. I was trying to find the coffee pot and coffee. He called me in the bedroom and ripped my clothes off. Threw me on the bed and jumped on top of me naked and shouted, "I AM GOD, I AM GOD I AM GOING TO FUCK MARY AND WE WILL HAVE BABY JESUS." Then he passed out. I got dressed in a hurry I turned around to see what he was doing. I can tell you this; he was in no condition to do what he had in mind. The last time, he said that if I didn't do what he wanted he would bring George up and George would help him do what he wanted.

Karen was having some troubles and so was I, I asked one of the women at work who a good female Doctor was. She told me Dr. Greenville. I called her and made an appointment for the coming week. Karen and I went to see her. We liked her right off the bat. We spent about an hour with her just talking about our problems. We made another appointment for the following week for complete physicals. She called me about a week later and said she wanted to see me. She told me about Karen and then she hit me with a bomb, she told me I was pregnant. That I also had a polyp that should be taken out before it got any larger. There also was a lump in my breast that needed to be tested to see if it was cancerous. She didn't think so but she wanted to be sure. She made an appointment for the same day surgery. The hospital called me and I went for the surgery. The polyp was removed. And in doing so the fetus had to be removed, which meant I had an abortion. This was something I had no control over, thank God. A blood sample was taken and it turned out that Judge Lipton was the father. To this day he doesn't know. He had asked me out a number of times after that. One time I had a splitting headache and told him so, another time I was having new windows put in my house and was going to meet the salesman that night. I told him what I was going to do. I think he figured I didn't want to go out with him. He never asked me out again. I don't know what I would have done if he did ask me out.

Attorney Ryan had been taking notes, the things that he wanted checked to make sure she was telling the truth: *(1) Proof that she was raped, and the Judge was the father, (2) Get the stripper at the strip club... the one he danced on the stage with and the waitress that was serving them drinks, (3) Where did the files go on this case in the court house, (4) Call the prosecutor in Alabama, find out who, when and why he was let out of prison.* Alma left the Attorneys office and went over to the Chiefs office. The Chief was with some people but should be finished in a few minutes. She said, "She would wait and sat down. The people came out and Alma was told she could go in. The Chief stood up when she came in; then they both sat down. Alma asked the Chief what he thought of Attorney Ryan. The Chief sat and thought for a long time. Then he said, "I have gone over just about all the attorneys in town, the one that I would have if I needed one, would be Steve Ryan. He is a fair, hard working man. I don't ever remember him coming into court without knowing what was going on. He has a good crew working for him. They really dig into the case. Alma wanted someone in town that she could trust and call or see when she had to. From what she had seen of him in court, she thought he was about the best. She said, "By the way, has that prosecutor from Alabama called you yet? I would like to know how George got out of jail." The Chief said, "No, he has not heard from him at all." It was to late today to call him but the first thing tomorrow he would call down there again.

That Saturday that Alma saw George, George got on the phone and called Seymour. He told him that Alma had seen him at the ski shack. She was with Jay Johnson and the girl. They were going skiing. He was a good friend of Jay Johnson, had been for years. He owed George a favor or two. What's going on now? Lipton didn't like it, he had to do some thinking, how was he going to get out of this one. First he had to go over to the Court House and get all the files he could find on George. Then he had to change the wording on a few papers. This way it would look like his time for parole was up now. That's what he told the prosecutor down in Alabama. They didn't even want the papers sent down. The Judges word was good enough over the phone. They gave George twenty dollars and a bus ticket back to New York State. They also told him that if he was to get in any kind of trouble, the next seven years. He could end up right back down here with the black boys. George was going to make sure not to get in any trouble. He wasn't going near Plantsville that's for sure. Now she has seen him, she will tell the Chief and everyone else. He thought he had better call Lipton. At least let him know what the story is. Lipton was trying to figure out what he was going to tell the Chief if he should ask. If he could fix the paper work showing the serve time to be ten years less seven for good behavior. With the understanding at any arrest would send him back to Alabama for the balance of his term. Monday all day he worked on the files, trying to make it look like he had done the right thing. The Chief wanted to see him... Why? Was it about this matter or something else? He was getting a headache trying to keep things straight. Working all day, he was sure he had it down right. Now he had to get it into the dead file section; this way if someone wanted it they would have to go digging for it. He spent the next two days in court. He didn't know that someone had gotten hold of the janitor and went looking through the dead files for this particular one. They told him not to say a word about what they were doing. They would have the file back the next day. Little did Judge Lipton know that the chief had the same file papers.

Monday morning the Chief got the call from Alabama. The prosecutor with a smile on his face said, "Hi Chief, got another one for me?" Chief Rose was not a happy camper. First he wanted to know how come he let George Hewitt out of jail. Nothing was ever said to him about Hewitt's release. Jim Bob said, "Hold on now Chief, you had better talk with your Judge up there first. The other day I got a call from Judge Seymour Lipton, circuit court Judge of the county 221 in New York State saying the time was up for George Hewitt and he was to be released at once." He told me he had served three years of his ten-year sentence. The balance of seven years, he was to be on parole. If, at any time he should break the law, and get arrested. He would be returned to the Alabama state penitentiary and serve out the balance of his sentence. The Chief asked "if there were any papers saying that he was to be released on that day, or any other day". The prosecutor Jim Bob was wondering what was going on. The Judge called, and that was good enough for me. We gave the man twenty dollars that he had earned working on the chain gang, and a ticket to New York State and sent him on his way. Oh yea, we gave him a suit from the Goodwill box. We didn't even charge him for that, Chief. "It was good talking to ya, you'll come down and see us some day", and he hung up.

They needed a picture of the Judge to show the girls at the strip joint. The Chief said, "How about having his picture in the paper as the new preceding Judge, taking the former Judge Webster's place. Maybe having him shaking Chief Rose's hand." It sounded good to all. The next day they took the picture and it was on the front page two days later. The picture was real good, it made the Judge feel more at home and secure in Plantsville. What he didn't know was, that picture may hang him. The attorney got one of his men to go up to the strip joint with the paper. He asked around if any of the girls remembered dancing or serving this man drinks? One big-busted girl said she served him a number of drinks, and he was a very good tipper. Another girl said she had served him some drinks and he was a lousy tipper. Another said she danced with him on the stage floor. He took all the names and phone numbers and left. When he got back to Attorney Ryan's office, they filed the pictures away. They would show them to Alma the next time she came in. Just to verify that these were the same girls that served the judge. That was another flag in our favor.

What they wanted to know was; what was the connection between George Hewitt and Seymour Lipton? Things went along for about two weeks waiting for something to happen. Nothing did. Attorney Ryan was getting nervous. He thought he had enough on the judge, but he didn't know how much influence he had up at the capital. This he had to find out somehow. He had a few friends up there. They both came from the same school and helped his brother through law school. So he had a lot of pull at the Capital level. Attorney Ryan started thinking, with all that at the capital, how about the previous jobs he's had... what can we find out there? While they were trying to find out what he had been doing, Ryan started drawing up a map, starting with rape. What proof did they have that he raped Alma? It was her word. The doctor said he removed a polyp. If that's what he's going to stick with, and not say she was pregnant, what then? The strippers at the nightclub can talk all they want about him, he had a date with him, and that date was Alma. He had a few drinks and danced with a few strippers. So what? She didn't complain. She didn't want to leave. She was enjoying herself. What about the files at the courthouse? They found them; they were put in the complete file-rack. There was a note saying after serving three years of a ten-year sentence. He could be paroled on good behavior. Besides a lot of other stuff; you know, if he should get into trouble, he is to be sent back to Alabama etc... He is not to go near the girl and so on. The prosecutor in Alabama did call the Judge to verify himself and said he would send the paper work down, but he said that wasn't necessary. Now what do we have on the judge? Nothing we can take to the courthouse. We would look like fools. The only thing in our favor is the copy of the case that the Chief has. If Alma was raped, why didn't she tell the Chief? The Chief could have called the Prosecutor in Alabama and tell him not to let George out. Attorney Ryan was thinking... I don't have enough yet, I need more concrete evidence.

Things seemed to be at a standstill, unless we can find out more about his past positions. Why did he leave? Was he relieved or did he quit? As time went on Alma could do nothing. She saw the pictures and she thought they were the girls that served those drinks, but it was dark and she couldn't be positive. Attorney Ryan would call Alma every once in awhile to fill her in on what they were doing. There wasn't much to report, they were still working on it.

Alma got a call from Bill at the restaurant one day. He wanted her to stop over and see him. Nobody was home when he called, but he left a message. She was thinking about stopping over anyway. They gave each other a hug. Bill had her set down in a back booth so they wouldn't be disturbed. He had some things he wanted to talk over with her. He told her how he had heard from Big Ben. Ben wanted to open some seafood restaurants along the Rt. 95 corridor from Maine to New York. He wanted to know what Bill thought of the idea. And would he be interested in a partnership. Bills daughter Ruth was old enough to be an overseer, watch the business, and things like that. Bill was pretty excited about the deal. He wanted Alma's thoughts also. Bill said, he could see the signs now... B & B's FRIENDLY SEAFOOD RESTAURANT...or a name like that. Alma was getting a little excited as they talked. Ben thought eight or ten places. The managers of each place would work on a commission and salary. That way if they pushed there place they could make a dam good living. If he was interested they could meet and discuss the pros and cons of the idea. Bill had already talked it over with Bee and Ruth, they were raring to go. They could see what the shrimp and lobster business has done for Bill, and just think of having eight or ten places. We could sell those lobsters and shrimp, and all the fixings. Maybe get a few more lobster boats. Everything had to be fresh, neat, and clean. Alma thought it would be a great idea,...however... who's going to see that these places are run right, and that you are not being ripped off by the managers. There are a lot of things to be discussed before going ahead. Maybe start off small, open another one in Connecticut. Then the next year open a few more. These are things that need talking about, maybe sell franchises like McDonalds does. You sell them the Lobsters and the shrimp, napkins, cups, plates, the sign for there place maybe little toy Lobsters for the kids to play with. There are a lot of things that you could do without working your butt off, Bill liked the idea a lot. He made a note of a lot of the things we were talking about. That way he wouldn't forget. For the next month, bill would ask his customers where they were from. He wanted to get an idea, were they from the south, north, or from around Plantsville. How did they hear about this place? What if anything would they like us to add to the menu? Have you told your friends about us? How often do you come here? This should give him an idea of what and where, maybe another place would go. Bill kept in contact with Ben, and Ben was doing the same thing at there restaurant. After a month, they would get together and compare notes. Karen was all excited; she wanted to work in all of them. Alma hadn't said anything to Jay. He wasn't around to much, she didn't understand why? She was getting too really like him and maybe... who knows. She would talk with him on the phone and once in a while he would come over for supper. She never mentioned George. If Jay wanted him as a friend, there was nothing she could do about it. He knew what George had done, and he knew how Alma felt about him. Karen was starting to fill out like all thirteen or fourteen-year-old girls do. She was mixing with the gang as they say. Every once in a while she would try that bra on. She was patient and didn't say anything to her mother. She started hanging around with this boy from down the road. He had a car and was graduating this year. Alma was getting a little worried, Karen... she thought... was a sensible girl and could take care of herself. Besides, she knows what she went through with George. She hadn't met him and didn't even know his name. When Karen came home Alma said, "She wanted to have a talk with her." Karin said, "She had a lot of homework and would talk later," and went right up stairs and closed her door.

Karen had been baby-sitting for this couple for about three months. She was very happy to stay with the kids, first they liked Karen and minded her when she told them to do something, and second she could watch HBO Movies. She got so HBO came before anything else. One Friday night while she was baby-sitting a knock came at the door. When she opened it, she was surprised to see Carl. He asked "If it would be all right to come in for a while." She thought for a minute and said, "Only for a little while." The people were coming home around midnight, and she didn't want him there when they came home. They went in the living room to watch TV. Karen forgot to change channels when she went to answer the door, so when they went in the living room there on TV were two people making love. She ran over fast and changed to a different program. She told Carl, "She just turned the TV on and hadn't watched it yet. Carl was curious as to what the program was all about, and wanted Karen to switch it back. Karen was too embarrassed and said no. Carl got up and switched to that channel. Karen ran to the kitchen, she didn't want to watch it with anyone. Not even Carl of all people. She told Carl to go home. She was upset. He got up and left. She didn't talk to him for a week. He called and she wouldn't talk. Alma finely told him not to call anymore. Cool it for a while. Two weeks went bye, she finely talked with him in school briefly. He wanted to take her to the basket ball game Saturday night. His buddy and his girl friend would go with them. She said, "She would let him know." When she got home from school there was three messages on the phone, but know one left anything. This worried both Karen and Alma. Who would call and not leave a message? They checked with some of their friends. No one called; maybe it was the wrong number.

Attorney Ryan called and wanted to know if Alma new what Judge Webster's address was. He wanted to check on that parole business. She didn't know, but she would check at the courthouse and see if he left a forwarding address. The Chief had taken the unmarked cars away from the school, but he still had them patrolling the road by Alma's house. He had a feeling thing's were not what they seamed to be. He couldn't put his finger on it, he had this feeling, and it wouldn't leave him. Alma called him, "And asked if he had Judge Webster's address." The Chief said, "He didn't think so, but he would check with the officer on the desk. She held on while he went to ask the officer. He came back and said the Judge had left a forwarding address with them, but they couldn't find it right off, but they would keep looking." When Alma got to work Monday, she looked all over for the Judge's address but could not find it. This made Alma suspicious; what would anyone want with the Judge's address? She went down to the post office and asked for the postmaster. He knew who she was and came out to see her. She explained that it was his birthday coming up and everyone was going to sign a giant birthday card and send it to him, but they couldn't find his address. The postmaster said he would check it out and get back to her. She left her phone number at the courthouse and went back to work. A few days went by and still no word on the Judges address. She started asking around. She called the Chief to see what he found out. The desk officer wasn't able to find anything. The Chief had the officer call all the general practitioners in town and if that didn't work, he was to call every Doctor in town. What started out as a simple thing has turned into a major investigation? What the heck is going on around here? They thought that maybe the payroll department in Albany would have it. The Chief called there himself and asked for the person in charge. A miss Butler got on the phone. The Chief told her that he needed the Address of Judge Webster. The woman let the Chief explain and then said, "I'm sorry but I cannot give that information over the phone." He would have to send a written request on the police stationary and mail it to her, with his signature on it. Not one of his officers, but HIS. She was very busy so it would probably be a few weeks before she could get to it. The Chief said it was very important that he get it as soon as possible. If she could please hurry it up, it would save a lot problems. She said she would do her best and hung up. The Chief had the desk officer write on Police stationary a request for the address of Judge Webster. Stamp it and I will sign it right above. It was sent out Special Delivery at the post office, on the envelope was written *ATT Miss Butler*.

When Alma got home that night, she thought, "I still would like to talk with Karen. I'll do that tonight for sure." When Karen came home, she was very upset. Her mother wanted to talk with her. Why now, of all times, she had enough problems at school. She said to her, "What shall I do? Tell mom what's going around at school or shall I keep my mouth shut and not say anything." The story at school is she's the one that had sex with George, and George is the one that got put into jail. This is going around now, but the rape took place three years ago. Why now, who started it? Lucky for her, she was a popular girl and everyone liked her, but now they're starting to talk behind her back. She decided to tell her mother everything. How the boys are talking about her. Even Carl was not as friendly as before. He hasn't asked her out only that one time to the Basket Ball game. They had a good time, the four of them. Now things seem different. Nothing was said about the TV Show that Carl saw. Karen was a little standoffish, but they seemed ok. That night Karen told her mother everything, except how she watched HBO every chance she got, and that would get her all excited and she would fantasize.

Her thoughts would travel; she and a famous movie star were making love, doing what they were doing in the movie. She didn't tell her mother that part, but she did tell her how she turned on the TV. When there was a knock at the door and it was Carl. When they went into the living room, this movie was on and she turned to a different channel. She didn't see the movie except when she walked into the living room. Carl wanted to see it but she told him to leave, which he did. The rest is what she told her mother; the stories that were going around in school, and how the kids were treating her now. Alma wanted to have a talk with Carl. Could he be starting rumors? If so, where did he get his information? Could George be sending messages to someone and were they spreading it around? Alma was getting real upset. She thought of calling the Chief: Maybe he could find out. First, she wanted to talk with Carl. What kind of a boy was he? She asked Karen if she would bring Carl around so she could meet him. She said she would try. Carl was not too happy about going, but said he would. They made plans for Wednesday night at 7 o'clock. Carl was staying away from Karen at school. However, when Wednesday came he said he couldn't make it. He had to do some things for his mother. When Karen got home, she cried her eyes out. When her mother got home and Karen told her Carl couldn't make it, she was mad. She wanted to know what his last name and his phone number were. She was going to call his mother and have a talk with her. Karen gave her all the information. Alma called and told her who she was and that she would like to meet her, after all her son was going out with my daughter. The woman said she would like to meet her. Alma asked if she would come up for coffee. The woman said she would love to. They set a time and date, and then hung up. When the day came, Mrs. Gates did not come. Alma thought that maybe she may have forgotten, so she called and Mrs. Gates answered the phone, Alma told her who she was and asked if she had forgotten about there meeting date. The woman told Alma she was not interested in meeting with her or her daughter, and she didn't want her son going out with a tramp. Alma was all upset, she said that was not true and asked, "Where did you get that from? Your son has been going out with Karen for quite a while. Now all of a sudden she's a tramp? Your son is the first boy she has ever gone out with, and for that matter, ever talked about. She has told me what a nice boy he was. I think there's a mistake here somewhere and it's not with my daughter or your son. Someone must be spreading stories that are not true. I do wish we could meet and find out about each other." There was a long poise, and then Mrs. Gates said she would like to meet Karen and see what kind of a girl she really is. They set up a time for the following night. Carl still would not talk with Karen. Carl must have told his mother about the stories at school, and she didn't want her son to associate with that type of girl. When Mrs. Gates drove in the yard, Alma went out to meet her. They went into the living room and sat down. The two of them talked for about twenty minutes. Mrs. Gates still hadn't met Karen. When they got through talking, Alma called up stairs and asked Karen to come down. She introduced her to Mrs. Gates, and then asked Karen if she would pour some coffee and bring some cookies. After working at Bill's Restaurant, this was no big deal. She brought everything in and put it on the coffee table. The three of them sat and talked. Carl had heard rumors about Karen and didn't want to get involved. If he started going out with her, all the kids would think he was doing it for one reason. Karen was two and a half years younger then Carl and they were saying he was robbing the cradle. That was another reason.

Karen said the only time she went with Carl that you would call a date, was last Saturday night, when we went to the basket ball game. Then there was another couple with them. She had rode in his car, going to the store or to school, but never had she ever kissed him. She thought Carl as a good friend. Maybe in a few years she would go out with him, but as for now, she wanted to be just friends. If that didn't suit him then he was welcome to go with whom ever he wants. By the end of the evening, Mrs. Gates was calling my mother Alma, and my mother was calling Mrs. Gates Shirley. They both hugged each other and said they should meet more often. She also said she would have a talk with Carl. Carl stopped in to see Karen a few days later. They went down stairs and talked. Karen wanted to know who was spreading a rumor about her, and would he try to find out, and why would they do that to her. When they came up stairs, Alma was in the kitchen making supper. She met Carl for the first time. Karen told her what she asked Carl to do, and he said he would try. Alma asked him if he would stay and have supper with them, but Carl said he had to get home.

Carl was a little friendlier with Karen, even at school he would talk with her a little more. It went on for over two weeks before Carl had any idea as to who was spreading the rumor about Karen. Word was that a couple of boys had gotten in trouble and arrested. When they went before the Judge ...who just happened to be Judge Lipton? He told them that Karen was the one that should have been put in jail, instead of George Hewitt. The Judge said, "If he were the judge, things would have been different." The Judge "Told the boys that he was God, and therefore what he says goes." The boys got off scout free. The word was The Judge let them off so they could spread the word about Karen at school. The boys didn't want to, but if they didn't the Judge would give them both a hard time. He kept telling them he was God and nobody can go against him. Carl does not know who the two boys are yet. This is only what he has been able to piece together. The other kids haven't talked too much. That's why he has not been around Karen too much. He doesn't want them to think they are still friends. He said, "He hopes Karen understands and doesn't get mad at him. He likes Karen, and said if he had a sister, he would want her to be just like Karen. He thinks of her as a good friend."

Alma was curious if Carl was telling the truth. She was going to go through Judge Lipton's case files and see what they have to say. She has not been in his courtroom for several months so she wouldn't know about this. What she did do, was check with Chief Rose about the two boys. He said he had arrested two youths about two months ago. They were smoking on school grounds. He wanted to give them warnings, but the teacher said to have them go before a Judge and maybe they wouldn't do it again, or maybe give up smoking altogether. That's the only thing I remember arresting two boys for. My officers have not arrested any youths either, that I have heard or seen of. When I told him about what Carl said and what was spread around the school, he shook his head. The Judge is the judge and there's not much I can do. It would have to come from the high Judges in Albany, but it seems he has a lot of power there. If I were to arrest him for something like that. Look what he did to you and we couldn't do a damn thing. If we could only get something on the Judge, something positive, it would make me a laughing stock of the police department and I would probably loose my job. I'm not old enough to retire yet. Alma asked the Chief, if she could talk with the boys. The Chief said, "Because of their age he could not give her their names, but if Carl finds out, that's a different story" Then you can have a talk with them. That night after the courthouse closed, and just the janitor was there, she went into the Judge's chamber. She was looking through the files. She came across the one she was looking for. It read that the Judge had given them a good lecture for smoking on the school grounds, and let them off with a warning. That was all; she put the file back, took it out again, and looked at the names of the boys. She put the files back again and left. A week and a half went by and Carl still didn't know who the two boys were. They had an idea but nothing positive. He still kept his distance from Karen at school.

The Judge was collecting information on Alma, without her knowledge. He was also making up a lot of things that were not true. One of the secretaries that didn't like Lipton told her, "To watch her step. Lipton was asking a lot of questions. He even had a few lawyers on his side. He would do them favors, just so they would think he was a nice guy and a fair judge. He would also make notes on the Lawyers, just in case they should turn on him. When the word got around what the Judge was doing, everyone was afraid to talk with one another. They didn't know whom to trust. One day about a month later, Alma found a note in her box at the courthouse. It read... *There will be a hearing on your conduct in my chambers at four o'clock Tuesday P.M. BE THERE.* Alma could not figure out what this was all about. She hadn't done anything wrong that she new of. She was getting worried. On the way home, she stopped at the Radio Shack Store and bought a small tape recorder and tape, one that would tape for about an hour. When she got home, she looked through her clothes for a blouse that would hold the recorder, yet not noticed. She found a Brown striped short sleeved one with large pockets. She wanted this conversation with the Judge on tape. This whole courthouse was going crazy. Nobody wanted to talk with anyone.

Some were blaming Alma, some didn't know whom to blame. The Judge was very nice to them all. Before he would holler if something wasn't done the way he wanted it. Right or Wrong. It had to be done the way the Judge wanted it. The other three Junior Judges kept out of his way. They didn't want to get involved. Even they were worried. One of the Judges did ask Alma what she had done. Alma said, "She didn't or hasn't done anything wrong." This Judge seemed like he believed her, but nobody trusted anyone anymore. Before they would go out and have lunch or a picnic after hours. They'd have a grand time. Now nobody is talking, only because of Judge Lipton.

Tuesday night at four o'clock sharp, she knocked on the Judge's chamber door. She turned the recorder on and waited. She was about to leave when he told her to come in. She was a little worried wondering what this was all about. He told her to sit down. There was a stack of papers on his desk, and he was thumbing through them as if he was looking for one in particular. It was near the bottom. He took it out and started reading it to himself. He looked up and stared at Alma. Mrs. Hewitt, I have here some complaints that were left under my door. Number one, that you were seen taking certain files from my office without my permission. Is that true or false? Alma looked him straight in the eyes and said, "I have never taken any file from your office. As far as I know there's nothing in here I would want." He then said, "On August 3rd you did not take anything from my file box?" Alma said, "I have never taken anything from this Chamber without you knowing about it or you asking for something while I worked in your courtroom. " "That's a lie," the Judge hollered, I have witness that say you did. Alma again looked the Judge in the eyes and said, "If I took anything from your files, have me arrested. What else do you want from me? Are you going to blackmail me for sex like you have done before, is this what it's all about. Or, you can trump up some phony charges and send me to jail. But I will never-never be seen with you again. I don't care what kind of charges you have. By the way, what do you know about the stories that are going around the school about my daughter? How dare you let George Hewitt out of jail for raping my daughter after serving only three years of a ten-year sentence? Now what other problems do you want to discuss with me." "Mrs. Hewitt I have a whole page of complaints that were left here. I will not go through each and every one today, but if I receive any more I will have you arrested. By the way, if you think you can use sex against me as you did before; trying to get on the good side of me when I first came here, think again." "I only did what Judge Webster ordered. Having sex with me would not have kept me from doing my job." That was not what Alma wanted on the tape recorder. But he didn't say he didn't have sex with me. (She had to find Judge Webster.) She stood up and said, "If you have no more trumped up charges against me, I shall go home. As she started for the door, he made one remark that puzzled her. By the way I do not have Judge Webster's address. How would he know she was looking for Judge Webster's address? Attorney

Ryan, Chief Rose, or Albany was the only one's that knew we were looking for Judge Webster. Oh yes, the Postmaster. Someone is telling the Judge everything. But Who? Thinking back... the only one that saw her go into the Judge's chamber, was the janitor. He must have told the Judge. But why? Did the judge have something on him? Let me do some thinking. Number one: the janitor wouldn't know what she was looking for. Now what, should she tell the Chief, or talk with attorney Ryan. Number two: Attorney Ryan...one of the top lawyers in town, why would he be so friendly with the Judge? Did the Judge bend a bit on a case that Attorney Ryan was working on, or maybe the Judge has something on Ryan? Number three: the Chief, I thought he had no feelings for the Judge. Did the Chief ask Judge Lipton if he had Judge Webster's address? Is that what Lipton meant? Alma didn't think he and Lipton were buddies. However, for the time being she had to watch her backside. She thought she would ask the Chief if he had heard from Albany yet. She also wants to know, who in Albany, has the Judge got under his thumb. Who can she ask, or better yet, whom can she trust to find out? She started to think again. That Judge that asked if she was in trouble. I wonder what they have on him. The next day she ran into him in the hall just as he was leaving. She came right up to him and asked him what he thought of Judge Lipton? The Judge asked Alma how she made out with Lipton. She told him how the Judge was saying how she was causing a problem in the courthouse and that she may be arrested if there are any more complaints. The Judge introduced himself. His name was Clarence Hawter. Alma had seen him around for a number of years but never had the opportunity to talk with him. Besides, he was a Judge and you just don't go up to them and start talking. He had worked in this courthouse for twelve years as a Judge and never had seen a more mixed up place as it is now. He said he would like to talk with her away from the courthouse. He asked if they could meet some place.

She invited him to her house. They would have a dog roast in the back yard. No one would see them from the road. He said that would be fine. They set the date and time for Friday night at six o'clock. Nothing is to be said about this meeting to anyone. She didn't know what this meeting would lead to, but she had to start some place and a judge would be the one to talk to. If he was a friend of Judge Lipton she would get fired. She had a feeling that Judge Lipton would never fire her. She could make headlines, and Lipton would not like that, especially after the write up in the paper with the Police Chief. She could see the headlines now. EXTRA EXTRA READ ALL ABOUT IT. OUR NEW CHIEF JUSTICE ACCUSED OF HAVING AN AFFAIR WITH ONE SECRETARY, JUDGE LIPTON ALSO SEEN AT STRIP BAR DANCING WITH NUDE DANCER BLOND WOMEN WITH HIM HAD TO DRIVE HIM HOME. HE WAS TO DRUNK TO DRIVE. If that's what he wants, that's what he'll get. Alma's thoughts now were how to get Judge Webster's address. Nobody here wants to help, plus she doesn't know who to trust anymore. Alma got to thinking; maybe Chris could give her some ideas as to what to do. That night she called Chris. Chrissie answered the phone; she jumped with joy when she heard Alma's voice. Chrissie asked about a million questions. Then she started telling Alma all about herself. She has a boyfriend. He gets a little fresh once in awhile, but she said she doesn't let him go to far. School was getting to be a problem, she knows more than the teacher. She doesn't know why they just don't give her the diploma now and be done with it. Alma thought she must be running out of gas, because she was slowing down. Alma asked if her father was home. She said, "No not yet. He has no regular hours any more, she will have him call her when he does come home." Before they hung up Alma told her, "We always have an extra bed or two for you guys, so anytime you want to come up, you're more then welcome." They talked for a few minutes more and said good-bye. A few hours later the phone rang, it was Chris. Alma told him what has happened, and was wondering how she could get Judge Webster's address or phone number. Everyone in this town has lost it. The Courthouse... The Police Chief... The Post Office... They all had it but somehow they seemed to have lost it. Now nobody has it. Chris asked a lot of questions: full name, age, state he was born in, and what state was he moving to. What kind of car did he own, what was the marker number, and so on? He said he would call her just as soon as he had the information. They talked for a while and hung up.

Alma got home early Friday night, so she would have everything ready when the Judge came. At five forty-five, she lit the barbecue so it would be hot when the Judge came. She made potato salad, coleslaw, and a nice punch in the blender. At six sharp, he pulled into her driveway. She went out to meet him. They went to the back of the house. Karen was there ready to put the dogs and hamburgers on the grill. Alma introduced Karen to Judge Clarence Hawter. Karen looked at the Judge and said "I know this man; he eats supper at Bill's Restaurant every night. He always comes in alone. We call him Mr. C.H. We never knew what he did for a living, but he always was so neat. Karen looked down at the fire and said" he's always been a very nice man. I haven't seen him in a very long time; I think you have stopped going there, didn't you? The Judge smiled and said he has a friend that cooks for him now. They have been keeping company now for about eight months. After the meal, Karen cleaned the table and went up stairs so that her mother and Judge Hawter could talk. Alma still wasn't sure weather she could trust him, or was he trying to get information to bring back to Lipton. She was hesitant to tell him everything. She told him about the conversation she had with Lipton. He accused her of taking some files from his Chamber. She told him that she didn't remove any files from his office...she told Judge Hawter that she did look at a file in his office but never took it out; she put it right back when she was through with it. The Judge smiled. She also told him about George Hewitt. He knew about the case, but didn't know that he was set free. He also didn't know that Judge Webster's address was missing from the bulletin board. She asked him if he knew were Judge Webster went, or what state they were going to. Did he have their address by any chance? Judge Hawter said he didn't have his address, but he thought they might be going to Utah or Wyoming. I believe his wife was from there someplace. He mentioned it to me a long time ago, that they would like to go back. I'll check just to make sure, but I don't think I have his address. She asked him what would be the best way to handle this problem. He said he would like to look into this a little more closely. He asked if she mentioned it to anyone else. She told him only the one's that know were the Police Chief Rose and Attorney Ryan. And now you. She didn't mention the janitor or the postmaster. He said for the time being let's leave it at that. She also said that story's are going around that Lipton was getting things on everyone and was holding that over their heads. If they didn't play ball with him, he would fire them. That means everyone. Everyone is afraid to even talk or say good morning any more. It's a shame, because this was once the friendliest courthouses I have ever worked in. The story that is going around in school now about my daughter is ridiculous. They are saying that Karen, age ten, was the cause of George Hewitt raping her, and he was the one being in jail. She had no idea at that age what sex was all about, but the kids are wondering if it's true or not. A lot of the kids are not talking to her.

The Judge was taking this all in, but not saying much. He was trying to peace it all together. What is George living on? Is he working? Who is he staying with? Have Judge Lipton and George been in contact with each other? Why would the Judge want to cause trouble now? What does Alma have on the Judge that makes him so worried? Is there a relationship between him and George? What did Lipton do before he came here? Did he ask to be sent here or was he appointed? Judge Hawter has friends in Albany that he thinks may help him. There has to be a connection here someplace. Alma was getting a little worried because Judge Hawter wasn't talking much. Did he find out all he could and was going back and tell Lipton? She sat back in her chair and started wondering, what kind of a job she would look for? Maybe she would work for Bill running his restaurants; she thought that wouldn't be such a bad job, as long as she gets paid enough to cover the mortgage. They could always eat on the job. The judge broke her thought by saying he was going to look into this at once. Then he said a strange thing. "I have been a Judge here for about twelve years. Next to Judge Webster, I was in line for the senior Judgeship job. Then they sent this idiot here and he has everything screwed up. If we can move Judge Lipton out, I may have a chance again, and maybe we can get this place back to normal. I must say, it's getting late and I have work to do. I will keep you posted on everything I learn. I can either slip you a note or send you a letter. If we meet, it must be some place out side of the city. There is to be no meeting in court or any place near it. It may take me some time to get the information I'm looking for, so don't be impatient." He said when everything is straightened out they could be friends in the open again. She walked him to his car and he left. As he was driving out of the driveway, a car came by driving very slow. This worried Alma. Could it be one of the Chief's cars, or was Judge Lipton having the Judge followed. Then again, it could be someone looking at this old house and scenery. She was getting nervous and jittery. Maybe this is what the Judge wanted. She would try and control herself. It was hard waiting for answers from Chris and the Judge, but she had no choice. Things didn't get any better at school or at work. She went to see Chief Rose to find out if he had heard anything from Albany. He said he had received no word. He asked her if she found out anything. She told him how Judge Lipton had her in his chambers, accusing her of taking files from his office. She did not take any files and she told him so. She also said how he had witness and any more complaints he was going to have me arrested. He said there were a lot more complaints that had been slid under his door on me. I have done nothing wrong, so all of these complaints are just made up. Everyone at the courthouse is on pins and needles. They are afraid to even say good morning to anyone now. They may lose there job for being friendly with someone, especially with me. How did we ever get this Judge in the first place? I guess we'll have to wait till we hear from Albany. She said she had to get home and make supper and left.

Carl called Karen and told her that things were quieting down at school. He still didn't have proof that they were the boys. They were caught smoking, but that was all. Karen asked what there names were. Maybe she could hear something, he didn't want to tell her, but when she mentioned two boys' names he said they could be the ones. She said, "That she had heard from a few that were still talking to her that they were the first to start talking about her." The next morning she told her mother who she thought were the boys. The names matched those on the file. What should she do now? If she said anything to them, the Judge would yell, see I told you she was in my chamber, looking in my files. How else would she know? They would have to do something that would make them talk. How the Judge told them to spread the word around about Karen. About half the kids in school would talk with Karen and the other half would pay no attention to her or they would call her names. Some were her best friends. One day when she was walking into school, one of her old friends came by. Karen stopped her and asked why she wasn't talking to her. She said, "She was told not to talk or associate with Karen because her grades would go down if she did. Then she ran away. Karen wanted to talk with her alone, to find out what was going on. Who told her not to talk with me, was it a teacher or someone else. Did the boys have anything to do with it? Why would anyone say anything like that? That night she called this girl, at first she didn't want to talk about it. Then she started crying. She told Karen that she always liked her but she was told not to talk to her. Karen asked who would do something like that. Tell me, I promise I will never tell on you. There is a club that was just formed and only certain people were allowed to join. If there were problems with any of the kids, these members would not have anything to do with them. That's why half of the kids don't talk to her. The RIGHTEOUS GUARDIANS are what they are called. Karen asked who started it, and how did you get involved? The girl said her friend joined and wanted her to, so she did. Little did she know what it was all about? It seems that a couple of boys started it. They have a friend that's a Judge or something and they meet once a week with him. He tells them what to do. Your name came up quit a few times, that's why they started stories about you, I know they weren't true but I couldn't say anything and still be a member. Now I want to quit ... get out, because I don't like what they are doing. I thought it was going to be a fun club, not a nasty club that hurt people. Karen asked if she knew who the Judge was, she said his name was Judge Lipton. They meet in his Chambers. He has cameras all over the courthouse and tapes everything. He listens to everything that is said. We even saw your mother take the file from his office... He showed you that tape? The girl said yes. Please don't tell anyone I told you all these things. Karen again promised. I know you and you wouldn't do what they said you did. You were only ten years old at that time. But that's way the Righteous Guardians work. The Judge thinks he's God. I think the Judge has something on the boy's and that's why they have to go along with him. Karen asked if he ever had anyone else speak at the meetings. May be a lawyer or a policeman, or even another Judge? She said, "She's only been a member for about six weeks, she missed one meeting because she had to baby-sit while her folks went out." They don't like it when you miss a meeting. They practically demand that you be there. The club is about two and a half months old, and they are very strict. She said she has not seen any speakers except the Judge. He was not the friendliest person either. The members are not allowed to talk about what goes on at the meetings outside of the meeting room... If they are caught doing so they are expelled from the club and stories will start about there reputation. In school or out side they can talk all they want as long as it's not bout the club. Karen told her she had to go baby-sit with the neighbor's kids. She would talk with her later on the phone. She thanked the girl and again promised she wouldn't tell anyone who told her, and hung up.

Saturday morning Karen was up bright and early. They had breakfast together for the first time in months. With Karen baby-sitting, and not getting home till late, on Friday nights, Alma always let her sleep late. But this morning she was up early. They sat at the kitchen and Karen told her mother everything she learned from her friend. Alma wanted to know what the girls name was, but Karen would not tell her. She promised she wouldn't tell, even her mother... Alma didn't know what to do at first. She wanted to go see Chief Rose and ask if it was legal to have all these cameras around the courthouse. She said she heard that they were in the rest rooms also. What can he do and would he check it out, maybe go in after hours, and look for his self. Making sure no one is there, including the janitor. Then she was going to Attorney Ryan. She was going to ask him if it was legal to have microphones through out the building. She heard that there was, and wanted to know before she made a stink about it. She was told that private conversations where on tape in the judge's chamber. Was that against the law? Then she was going to send Judge Hawter a note, asking to see him. If this doesn't stir up a hornet's nest, nothing will. The Judge will probably call her into his Chambers and want to know who told her about the camera's, and why wasn't he told about them first. He must have the tapes in his chamber someplace. But where? That is the next question. She had everything figured out as to what to do Monday morning when she went to work. First she was going to find all the cameras that she could. The first place was in the hall where she and the Judge were talking. If there is one there, then that car was maybe one of Judge Lipton's spies. This isn't funny anymore. She wondered if there was one in the ladies rest room also. In the mean time, Karen was talking with Carl. She wanted to know if he was a member of the R.G.s. He said they were after him to join but so far he hasn't. She did want to know all about The Club. How many members, where did they meet, was the Judge at every meeting, did they have guest speakers, if so who have they had? He wanted to know how she knew so much about the R.G.s. He told her, she new more about the club then he did.

She pleaded with him not to join, it was a bad club, and it would only cause problems for good kids. He said he would try and find out all he could about it and let her know.

She talked with Chief Rose Monday after work. She asked him if it was legal to have hidden cameras through out the courthouse. He said he didn't know but he would look into it. Then she called Attorney Ryan, she asked him if it was legal to have hidden microphones through out the courthouse, possibly even in the restrooms? He never was asked that question before, but he would look into it and get back to her. She also asked if he had heard anything from Albany yet. He said no but he would check again. Two days later Judge Hawter sent Alma a note asking to meet him at seven o'clock at Indian Point State Park near the water, on Wednesday night. That was ok with her... Maybe either the Chief or Attorney Ryan would have had a chance to talk with Judge Lipton and he would call her into his Chambers. But no luck. She kept her eyes open for little cameras. She found two; one was in the hall and one was in the anteroom. She didn't see any microphones, but they could very well be with the cameras.

Wednesday night, Alma was at the pond in Indian Point Park. At seven sharp Judge Hawter pulled up. No one else was in the Park. He looked around and finely saw her down by the water He walked down and greeted her with a big smile. They started walking she told him how she had heard about a new club that was forming. The name was the Righteous Guardians, or for short, the R.G.'s. She told Judge Hawter everything she knew about it. He told Alma that he had never heard about it. He wanted to know who started it and who the people were, that was running it. When she told him Judge Lipton was the founder, and two boys were in charge. She also told him she thought that the two boys were the ones that were caught smoking and this was hanging over there heads. If they didn't do what the Judge said... They would be punished. He was surprised that Judge Lipton would do something like that. She asked if he had heard anything about George Hewitt. The judge said it was too soon. His people were working on it now. These things take time to check out. She also told him about the cameras she found in the courthouse. She told him how she spoke with the Chief about it. He said he would look into it. I'll bet he will go and ask Judge Lipton if it's legal, I never thought about telling him not to say anything to him. Judge Hawter said that's the first place I would go if I didn't know the circumstances. Because of the way Judge Lipton was handling the case with the boys, Judge Hawter suggested using numbers for meeting places. This place would be number 101 and the time would be the numbers after that today would have been 101700. That way nobody could be there before us, and spy on us. This was getting real deep. There was a lot involved. There should be several other places to meet also. They both did some thinking. Judge Hawter suggested a restaurant up the road called Miranda's. It was a spaghetti house. Good food, we will call that place 102-.plus the time.

If we are here, they will think we are on a date. Is that OK with you? Alma thought it was a good idea. They left it at that. They stayed for over an hour, he was very interested in this R.G. Club. He thought it was a good idea, but not the way Judge Lipton was using it. He wanted it to be more of a social club. Maybe a place they could play games, things like that. Maybe a basketball and baseball teams he was getting real excited about the idea. How about chess and checkers, he could go on for hours. Then he stopped. He looked at Alma and said, "Maybe we should start our own club... something that would counter act the R.G.s. First, we would need a welcoming name. 'Start thinking he said.'" He seamed sincere in what he was saying. The next thing she knew, she was thinking of a name, and this kind of a club would be great.

The first thing that came into her head was P.G.s Plantsville Guardians. She spoke softly when she said it. He said, "What did you just say?" She said never mind I was thinking out loud. He said no, no, it sounded good say it again. She said the P.G.s, Plantsville Guardians. He looked at her and said think no more, that's it. Now we need a logo. She said we could run a contest for the logo. He thought that was a great idea also. The idea for the club was all they talked about for the next hour. Without thinking of where they were, she looked up and said, we have walked all the way around the pond, and it's getting dark. Judge Hawter said, we should think more about this club. How would it be if we met here again next week at this same spot? Maybe by then I'll have some information on this George Hewitt person. As they got near there cars she turned and said, Judge Hawter this evening has been more, and then I ever could have thought possible. This will make the kids stop and think before joining the other club. It will put pride not shame in there lives. Look what it has done to my daughter. Now with this good club, she will be the first to join. Not only that, but I'll bet the rest of the kids will join also. Judge Hawter had only one thing to say. When we are not in the courthouse, would you please call me Clarence? She said, are you sure that's what you want, being a Judge is an honor, you worked hard for that Judgeship and if you don't mind. I will only call you Clarence when the two of us are alone. He smiled and said very well. Days went by, the Chief heard nothing and attorney Ryan found nothing out. Judge Hawter found a few things out. The place George Hewitt is staying is eight miles north of Plantsville. He is working for a lawyer as a chaser. He looks for leads in different cases. Being a past lawyer, he knows what to look for. They have him tailed now. Wherever he goes, he is being watched. He has met with Judge Lipton twice in the past two weeks. They are trying to find out what they talk about. They want to make some movie pictures so they can read there lips. If it has anything to do with the R.G.s, they will watch him closer. That's all they have now...

Oh yes, I almost forgot, Judge Lipton got George the job but nothing yet on the address of Judge Webster. Two days later Chief Rose called Alma. He had talked with a few other Judges he new and they said it was against the law to have hidden cameras or microphones in a courthouse. If they are labeled and in full view that's one thing; But if they were hidden that's a no-no. Alma was excited to hear that, now she was almost sure that the Chief was on her side. Now all they have to do is prove he put them there. Chris called, "They have found Judge Webster." His wife died two and a half years ago. He is in a convalescent home and can hardly get around. He is in Utah, a little town called Arrow Head. Chris talked with the Chief of Police out there and they are willing to help us. They will send a police officer out to talk with him if you like. Alma said she would like to go herself. She has to check on her vacation time. Attorney Ryan said the same thing as the other Judges. Microphone were illegal unless in clear view and for court purposes. Things were starting to take shape. When she met with Judge Hawter the following week, she told him everything. She checked with her boss, as far as the vacation time, it was O.K. she didn't tell anyone what was going on, or why she wanted that special time off. She could have the other week off in the fall. She made plans to leave the following Tuesday. She would leave on the ten forty Flight from Albany to Salt Lake City, then Rent a car and drive for about two and a half hours to Arrow Head. Once in Arrow Head she would go to the Police Station and have a police officer go with her to verify what the Judge was saying. She was also taking a tape recorder along. This way she would have his voice on tape as well. She called the airlines and made all the arraignments, she called Chris again and thanked him for all he had done. She told him what the story was and he was more then happy to help. She asked Bill if Karen could stay with them till she gets back. He was more then happy to help. He said he would put her to work to cover the room and board. They all laughed.

When Monday came, Alma was all packed. She left around two in the afternoon. She drove and stayed in Albany over night. That way she wouldn't be too tired when she got there. She figured about a four-hour plane ride, which would bring her into Salt Lake City around three our time but only twelve o'clock there time. Then three hour drive to Arrowhead. That would be three o'clock and a half hour at the Police Station. She didn't know how long the drive was to wear Judge Webster was. She figured she should be there before supper. Everything went according to plan, when she got to Salt Lake City they had a car ready and waiting, the rental agency had mapped out the route for Arrow Head and left it on the front seat. They figured two hours and twenty minutes. Going the speed limit, Alma figured two hours by the looks of the map. What Alma didn't figure on was the mountains. She made it in just two hours and twenty minutes. She found the police station and went in. She asked for the Chief and introduced herself. They call him roper, he could throw a rope and catch anything that walked, ran, crawled or stood still. He was a big tall man but the nicest man you ever would want to meet. He said, "If I didn't mind he would like to go with me." I was shocked to think the sheriff would like to take a ride with me to a convalescent home.

On the way out the sheriff was telling Alma how the Judge used to live here, when he was a kid. They say he had the fastest draw and best shooter around here. His wife was from a little town called Rocky Ridge, about ten miles north of here. I know for a fact that he was a good shooter because he had a room full of ribbons. I didn't really know him; he moved out and went to collage. He went to law school to become a lawyer; he was a darn good one too. About twenty-five years ago, he was appointed to the bench as a judge. After about six years, he was elevated to the Supreme Court. He was a likable man, but strict and fair. I know he was a judge in New York State somewhere. I think it was Albany or something like that. Alma said, "Would it be Albany?" "I do believe that was the name, Roper said. Alma started telling him the problem they're having back home. Roper said, "Out here I'm the sheriff, judge, and jury." What I say goes." "He would have been sent to jail for life if he was back here, George that is." Then he stopped talking. He said this place is just over the next rise, you'll see in a minute. Sure enough, it was a grand old house with modern fixtures. Swimming pool, tennis courts, mini golf, and a lot of other things. They parked near the entrance. When they walked in the front door, no knocking, no lock just open the door and walked in. This reminded Alma of back home, everybody trusted everyone. When they got inside it was like a king's palace. Wood carvings all hand done. The floors were at a high polish but not slippery There was a kindly looking elderly woman sitting over in the comer with a big smile on her face.

After they got through looking around, this woman said "Hi Roper, what brings you out to our village?" He said he was just looking around, but he wasn't quit ready to move in yet. They all smiled. They walked over to where she is sitting. Roper introduced her to Alma. She told her what a beautiful place this was. The woman's name was Miss Bessie. She's the owner of this place. She calls it her ranch house. They sat and talked for a while. Alma asked about Judge Webster. Her face lit up. He wouldn't have a chance of being single again if I was thirty years younger. I remember the day he was born. That's more than seventy-five years ago. Alma looked at her and said, "You have to be kidding, you're not that old." She looked at Alma and said, "Honey I'll be one hundred on my next birthday. I own this place free and clear, I do all the cooking, and most of the cleaning. I do have some help with the rooms, but she's slowing down some, she's in her eighties. We have five residences here. They each have a job to do every day. I charge only for lights, heat, the telephone, and water. The rest of the place is taken care of by us." She smiled and said, "That's what keeps us young," then she said, "Lets see if we can find the Judge." I wouldn't have believed it. There the Judge was on his hands and knees working in the garden. Miss Bessie told us they raise most of their food. They have twelve cows, but they're only milking ten, two are in a family way. We have two members of our family that takes care of the cows. They are milked morning and night, all by hand. We have one member that takes care of the few pigs, and the few horses we have. Another feeds the chickens and collects the eggs from our twenty-five chickens. In the fall we do get some help from the kids around, some have worked here for forty years, cutting wood, plowing the fields, and getting hay in for the winter. In the winter, all our neighbors come and help keep the road open, just in case we have to get out. Some times the snow will get to three feet on the level and twelve feet in the drifts. That's in a mild storm. When we get a little low on cash, we sell some corn or potatoes to carry us through. If the snows to deep we watch TV or make crafts. These we sell also. As they walked over to where the Judge was working, he looked up. He couldn't believe his eyes. He looked again, he got up off the ground and came over too her. He stopped about four feet from her and just looked again.

She just looked at him, she smiled and ran the four feet and gave him a big hug. She pulled back a bit and said Judge Webster, Judge Webster you look marvelous, and hugged him again. Miss Bessie said, "Now one hug was enough," she was getting jealous. The Judge asked Miss Bessie if it was all right to stop working for a while. She said only for a few minutes, any longer and I'll get Roper after you. They all laughed at that. While the Judge went to clean up, they had a tour of the grounds. There were about six hundred acres, a well-preserved barn, two chicken houses, and a large pigpen. On the way back to the house two elderly men in overalls came to meet them. One of them said, "What are you doing with my barn?" He gave them a big smile and said his name was Scottie and the other said his name White. They were the cowhands, Scottie was only seventy-nine, and Whyte was seventy-eight. That made Scottie the boss because he was one year older. They milk ten cows morning and night. Two are calf in, clean the barn, and send them out to pasture. Fix anything that needs fix in, or paint in. Miss Bessie said we had better go in. Supper will be ready soon. Tuesday nights were barbecue nights. The pit would be ready soon, when they were red hot it was time to put the steaks on, the veggies wrapped in leaves. Wine in a keg was brought out and the night was fit for a king.

After supper Roper said, "He had to get back to the jailhouse" he called from his two-way radio to have some one come and pick him up." After every thing was cleaned up, the three of them sat on the porch. Alma asked first if he had his address removed from the courthouse or any other place. The police Chief had no idea where you went. The postmaster wouldn't talk with me. Nobody knew my friend who is a detective in Easton Penn. tracked you down here through your driver's license. That's how we were able to find you. The Judge said he wondered why nobody sent cards or anything. He left his address in several places at the courthouse. The postmaster had my forwarding address. He should have been able to give it to you. It seemed as if you never where there at all. I wish you could come back and see the mess that town is in. We have tried to contact someone in Albany but no one will answer us. The new Judge must have removed them all. Her next question was the reason she came out here. Did you state in your deposition that George Hewitt the lawyer could be released after serving only three years in jail for raping my daughter Karin from a ten-year sentence? The Judge looked Alma straight in the eyes and said, "I most certainly did not." Hewitt was to serve the full ten years in the Alabama correctional institution. Why do you ask? The Judge wanted to know. Alma explained the whole thing to him. How Judge Lipton has cameras all over the court house and everyone is afraid to talk with one another. He is starting a club called the Righteous Guardians. This club is run by two boys who were caught smoking on school grounds. Judge Lipton is the ringleader; he tells them what to do and who to do it to. The court system is so screwed up it's not fun to go to work anymore. Judge Hawter was disappointed that he wasn't promoted to the senior Judges job. Judge Webster said he was too. He asked that Judge Hawter be given the job. Instead they send this idiot, I'm only sorry I couldn't stay there longer. My wife was very sick and the doctor said I had to get her to a better climate right away. She pasted away two and a half years ago you know. I sent a card to the courthouse to let you all know. Alma said there never was a card or a notice put up on the bulletin board. For that matter, I don't remember the bulletin board being there any more.

Alma asked what she could do now. The Judge asked, "How long are you planning to stay here?" She had made plans to go back the following day. The Judge said he would look into it tomorrow. He's not sure when he'll have an answer, but if she could stay an extra day or two, he would try and find out what is going on back there. Alma also said how there was a separate sheet of paper that you were suppose to have written to give George the time off. The Judge again looked Alma straight in the eyes and said, "I did no such thing." He also said Chief Rose has a copy that I wrote. She said they didn't want to use it just yet because of this release letter that Judge Lipton said you wrote. She and the judge and sheriff Roper were up half the night. Miss Bessie said she could sleep in the spare guest room. The following morning after breakfast which was at six a.m. Judge Webster and Alma were at it again. She told him how Lipton forced her to have sex with him or he would let Hewitt out. He got him out anyway. Judge Webster said, "I don't know weather you know it or not, but a Judge is never retired. As long as I live I can go back on the bench. Getting George back in jail may be another thing. I think it would be easier to put Judge Lipton in jail then it would George now. First, we will have to see what Albany is doing. What got Judge Lipton as far up the ladder as being Judge? That is something you work hard for, it's not something that's given to you because you know someone. At least in my day it wasn't. I have friends in Albany; let me check with them tomorrow." Judge Webster was thoroughly disgusted to think a Judge would do something like that.

Wednesday morning everybody was up at five-thirty. Breakfast was served between six and six- thirty am. Whyte and Scottie were out in the barn before six thirty getting things ready for milking. Alma was still sleeping when the last call for breakfast came. She came down in her bathrobe; she was still half-asleep from the busy day yesterday, plus last night. They were up till the wee hours in the morning. Judge Webster was there fully dressed and ready to go. Sheriff Roper's man came and picked him up around one o'clock in the morning. One of there police cars broke down so they only had one till they can get it fixed. Alma had only coffee and toast, then went back up stairs, took a shower and got dressed. Judge Webster was going over some books that he brought with him. When Alma came down, she went to see the Judge. He was busy and told her not to bother him. At ten o'clock he came out of the study. Went over to the phone and placed a person-to-person call to a certain Judge. He waited for a long time. Then he started talking using big words she had never heard before. When he got through talking, he gave who ever he was talking to his phone number and address. He also said he wanted it as soon as possible. When he got off the phone he came out on the porch were Alma was rocking. He told her what he was doing. He was having someone pick up the paper from Lipton's Deposition file that said he could be released in three years, and didn't have to serve the full ten years if he didn't cause trouble. Judge Webster had about twenty questions he wanted answers to. Now they just had to wait. Alma made a phone call to Chief Rose and told him a little of what was going on. Then she called Bill and asked to speak with Karen. He told her she had gone out with some of the kids from school; they were going to the amusement park for the day. She asked Bill to please have her call me when she gets home; she gave him the phone number. She said she'd be out here a few extra days, maybe two or three. She also asked about the new Fish House Restaurant. He gave her a little information then they hung up. That was the longest day she had ever spent.

Back in Plantsville that afternoon, two men who said they were from Alabama went to the courthouse looking for Judge Lipton. They asked at the reception's desk for Judge Lipton. She called and told him there were two men there that wanted to see him. He told her he would be busy the rest of the day and all day tomorrow, he was working on a big case and didn't have time. The two men looked at each other and said that was O.K. Then asked where the janitor was, she was getting nervous now. She said she would try and locate him. She called several places but could not find him. They said they would be back at four o'clock and would see him then. They went over to Chief Rose's office and had a talk with the Chief. At four o'clock they went back to the courthouse. The janitor was there waiting for them. He took them to an empty room and closed the door. They sat down and started asking him questions. He didn't want to get involved in Judge Lipton's affairs and he could not give them any deposition files without the Judge's permission. They asked if he knew there were hidden cameras through out the courthouse. He said yes he put them there. The Judge told him to, he said there might be times when they would come in handy.

"Did you know that was against the law regardless of what the Judge told you to do? You could be charged for doing so. Cameras and microphones are allowed only after they are registered and listed." They asked if he knew where the tapes were. He said he did not, and had never seen any around. One of the men was writing all this down. He asked if he'd be willing to take a lie detector test as to what was just asked, and would he be willing to go before a grand jury and tell the truth to all the questions asked. In addition, "Have you done anything wrong, where Judge Lipton could hold anything over your head?" He would not answer. He was getting real nervous now. He said he wanted to talk with his lawyer before any more questions. He saw the man write that down also. One of the men asked him if he was answering these entire question's willingly and with out couching from anyone. The janitor said yes, as the men were about to leave, the one that was writing everything down, turned and reached in his suit coat breast pocket and brought out a small tape recorder. He told the janitor that not only had he written everything down, but also just to make sure it was right, it also was on tape. Again, the janitor said he wanted his lawyer handy. They both at the same time asked" who's your lawyer"? The janitor said he didn't have one yet, and hung his head. I never thought I would ever need one. He was real nervous now. The two men left, the janitor sat there and started whimpering. He had never done anything wrong before, why now, what is going on? He had to see the Judge, find out what was going on. Just as he was getting up, one of the men came back and said, "I don't think it would be wise to talk with the Judge now. He's very busy. I would stay away if I were you, then he left. It was getting late and he was all up set, he got in his car and went home. His wife took one look at him and asked, "What in the world is the matter...you look terrible?" He sat down and asked his wife for a drink... a stiff one. When she came back with the drink, she sat down beside him; she said tell me what on earth happened? He told his wife everything that happened that day. These two men mean business, what ever they are doing. Just then the phone rang and it was Judge Lipton. He was very nice; he wanted to know what these men wanted from Alabama. Did you tell them anything? Are they coming back, and who sent them up here? Little did the janitor no that everything that went on in that empty courtroom was taped by the Judge. The janitor told him he knew nothing, about what they wanted or who sent them. The Judge hung up the phone without saying good-bye.

That evening two men went into Bill's restaurant for a late supper and some small talk. It was past suppertime and things were getting slow, Bill was starting to get worried. Karen hadn't come back yet, nor had she called. That wasn't like Karen. They overheard Bill ask his daughter if she knew who the gang of kids was that she went with. Ruth told him Carl was with them. She was sure. He was Karen's best friend. He asked if she new what Carl's last name was. She told him Gates. Bill went over to the phone book to get his phone number. He couldn't find any Gates that lives in that part of town. Now he was really getting worried. He asked Ruth if she knew where he lived. He new the street but didn't know what house. She told him, he asked if she would close up. He was going out to Carl's house and find out what happened to Karen. Bill was gone in a flash. The two men were talking between themselves. Ruth came over and asked if they wanted anything else? They said just coffee would do it. She left and came back with the coffee pot and poured. One of the men asked if everything was OK. She told them her father was worried because Karen wasn't back yet. They said they weren't from around here, but if they could help, they would be more then willing to do what ever they could. Ruth was worried, what if something goes wrong, and Karen was in an accident or something. These two men were the last ones in the restaurant. Now she was getting nervous. She hadn't checked the register out and there was a lot of money in it. She didn't want to open it with just them there. All different thoughts were running through her head, now she was worried. Just then the door opened and in came one of the police officers. She thought, does he want something or is he bringing bad news. The officer walked over to the counter and asked in a very low voice, "Is everything all right?" She said her father had gone over to the Gates house to see if Carl had come home yet. Karen was late and we were worried. He looked in the mirror and saw the two men setting in the booth. He asked if she new them, she said no. closing time was in fifteen minutes. The officer said he would wait till she locked the doors.

That made her feel relieved. The men were talking between themselves; one of them got up and went to the men's room. After he came out, they both went up to the cash register and asked for the bill. She gave it to them, one went back to the table and left the tip, and the other paid the bill. They looked at the officer and started a conversation about the town. Neither the officer nor Ruth felt like talking, one of the men reached inside his coat, the officer already had his hand on the butt of his gun. The man pulled out his wallet and showed his badge. Everyone sighed with relief. They apologized if they scared them. If they had a few minutes they'd like to talk with both of them. "This conversation must be and has to be private. Is that understood? If not we will leave now." They both looked at each other and said, "We've never seen either one of you gentleman." The two men said they would not give there names. That way if they do make a slip no names could be said.

What they wanted to know is, what do you know or have you heard about Judge Lipton. We are looking into a complaint about his judgment in a case. This is not something new for us we do this all the time. What we want to know is, how he participates in any organizations, boy scouts, church, and social clubs things like that. Is he well liked, in the courthouse, and around town? Is he well liked as a Judge, does he use good judgment, that you have heard of. Ruth said she never has heard that he belongs to any clubs, except one. He has never made any speeches, and he keeps pretty much to his self. The officer said he heard the Judge was forming some sort of club called the Righteous Guardians. If a kid did something wrong, they would have the rest of the kids talk down or not talk at all with that person. I don't know for how long or anything more. Karen could tell you more; she's going through a bad time with them now. What did she do, was it bad? Ruth said, she thinks it has to do with something that happened about three years ago. Karen was only about ten or eleven at the time, and her stepfather raped her. Now the kids are saying she teased him into raping her. Which is false, what would a girl that age know about or want sex. One of the men asked who brought this up three years later, and why? Was it in the papers or on the news, something, or someone must have started it? Judge Webster sent him to the jail in Alabama for ten years, Judge Lipton had him released after serving only three years. Karen's mother Alma should be back from vacation in a few days. One of the men asked if anyone can join this club. And how did it get started. Does the Judge come to the meeting, if not who runs them? The officer said he heard that two boys were caught smoking on school grounds. Judge Lipton told them to run this club or they would get fined, or put on work detail for a month. This is not the right kind of club these kids need. Alma and a few others are trying to start a kids club. A place to have fun in, form ball teams, baseball, basketball play games inside not look down on kids, get the parents involved. The officer said he heard the new club was going to be named the Plantsville Guardians, better known as the PG'S. That's all I can tell you right now. They said they were sticking around for a few days, and if they heard anything more, to let them know. They would be in for supper every night. If they weren't around leave a note with Ruth and they would pick it up and meet them later.

They left the restaurant and walked down the street toward the courthouse. When they got near the courthouse they saw a dim light on. They tried the door, and found it not locked. They went in very quietly, the light seemed to be coming from the back of the bench, near the Judge's chamber. Court is usually over and the janitor is all cleaned up by six or six thirty. Maybe he forgot to turn the lights out. Just to be on the safe side they went down very quietly. They heard voices, only the same voices they the janitor used when they were asking him questions. This time the Judge was playing the tapes from this afternoon. They stayed outside for a long time. When that tape was finished, he put another one in the recorder. This one was a tape that was used in the hallway. He then put on another one. This one was with a lawyer and his client; they were talking about how the Judge was so unfair that they would take it to a higher court. They spent about an hour listening to the private tapes that were made in different parts of the courthouse. After they got out side, one said to the other, we have got to get those tapes. They mean everything in this case. Let's talk with the janitor, outside of the courthouse. We know it's bugged now, so everything that was said the other night between us was taped and recorded. That's why the janitor wouldn't say anything. He has his job to look after. As they were walking down the street, this kindly old man stopped them. He said his name was Harvey Binder and he had worked in the court house for over fifty years, but when Judge Webster retired and this Judge Lipton came here, Lipton fired him, no reason, just said your through, good bye. I've been watching you two gentlemen since yesterday when you came into the courthouse. You both didn't look like lawyers going to try a case, but more like detectives.

So I have been following you around. Now I know I was right, I was in the courthouse just now when you were listening to the tapes the judge had. I want to help if I can. They looked at each other, the taller one said lets go someplace for a coffee. They walked over to the car and got in. Harvey told them to drive down to the third light and turn left, that's Route 41. Follow it down for about two miles, there's a dinner on your left. They have pretty good coffee in there. They went inside and sat in a booth in the back. The waitress came over and asked what they wanted; they all said coffee and a donut. Harvey told them how everything had changed at the courthouse. Nobody was talking with each other anymore, and he wasn't allowed in the courthouse anymore. Judge Lipton said, "If I came again he would have me arrested. The tall man asked if he had done anything wrong, that the Judge could hold against him. Harvey said, not that he knows of. He helped a lot of people out. He said, "I even got a mortgage for Alma when she bought her house; she didn't even have a job at the time either." Everyone in this town knows me, it hurts to think after all these years some jerk of a Judge comes into town and fires me and screws everything up in town. They talked for well over an hour. The two men asked all kinds of questions. They got his name, address and phone number in case they needed him for something. When they got back, they saw that the light was still on at the restaurant. They knocked on the door; Ruth looked out and saw it was the same two men. She came to the door and let them in. They wanted to know if they had found Karen yet. Bill came out and introduced himself. They told him they would give fictitious names, they didn't want anyone to know what was going on. The tall one we will call Andy and the shorter one will be Jack. They were curious about Karen; did they find her, was she OK? Bill said, "Yes they found them. Carl had a flat tire, and the batteries were low in her cell phone. They put the spare wheel on and came right home. They pulled into the yard the same time that Bill got there." He explained everything, and said he was sorry for being so late. Bill was just glad that everything was OK with them. He told Carl that he would take Karen home if it was all right with him. Carl said sure. Karen never stopped talking about the rides and games and everything else all the way home. She'll still be talking tomorrow morning. Bill let them all know how worried he was, and he hoped nothing like this would ever happen again. Bill asked them what they were doing in Plantsville. The shorter one Jack first said anything that was said tonight is forgotten at once when they leave. They all agreed.

Andy told them how they had gotten orders from Albany to check out this Judge Lipton. It seems there have been complaints about him. Judge Lipton had left word not to give out any information about him to anyone. He was checking out some stories about old Judge Webster, and it was his job to see if things were true. We could not find anyone that would want to have Judge Webster checked out. What we did find was that Judge Webster's address was nowhere around, and no one knew were he went. We also had a complaint that a person named George Hewitt was released from the Alabama State Prison with out justification. We were told to find out all we could, but not to say anything to anybody about what we were doing. When we got here, all we heard was bad things about this Judge Lipton. That's why we are asking questions now, and asking you all not to say anything. I believe we have enough information now, so we will be leaving sometime tomorrow. We do want to talk with Karen, if it's possible. We would need someone with us when we do talk with her because she is a miner. We are interested in this club, Judge Lipton is forming. We would like to talk with Karen's mother also. Bill told them that Alma needed a rest so she has taken a short vacation.

The next day they talked with Karen about what happened and how things had started up about George raping her and all. How did anyone know it was you, when it wasn't in the papers or on TV? Or radio? Karen told them the only way that anyone would know is if they went through the court papers.

They were supposed to have been put away in the basement of the courthouse. The case was closed and they were only taking up room up stairs. Someone had to be looking for them special, other wise they would never know what to look for or where to find them. They still wanted to talk with the janitor. That night they sat in there car in the parking lot waiting for the janitor to come out and get in his car. When he came out, they went over to his car. The tall man got in the car with the janitor, the short man went back to his car. The janitor was told to drive down a few streets and park. The short man followed in his car, when they stopped the short man parked and got in the back seat of the janitor's car. The short man started asking questions. We know the judge has something on you and we know you couldn't talk because the room was bugged and everything was taped. That's why we are here now. What does the judge have on you that are so strong that you couldn't talk with us? The janitor hung his head and said, "Harvey Binder was the king around here. He knew everyone and everyone knew him and though the world of Harvey. Judge Lipton had me make up a story about Harvey, how he was drunk and shot his mouth off about everything that was going on in the courthouse. The tall man asked "did Harvey drink? The janitor said he would have a glass of wine once in a while that's all. He would never talk about the courthouse, and I never saw him drunk either. He knew everything that went on in the courthouse and never once did he ever talk about anything. "If I didn't say these things, the judge would have fired me." I would loose my pension and everything else. I only have a few more years before I retire and I didn't want to lose it. Harvey was only part time and on pension so I didn't think it would matter with him. People thought he had retired, that's why he wasn't around anymore. Judge Lipton would make sure I would, lose everything if I didn't and don't cooperate. I feel sorry for poor Harvey, he was one nice man. Always a gentleman, and if he could help you he would. I worked with Harvey for about ten years, now he won't even talk with me. If there was anyway I could help Harvey get his job back, I would do it now. The problem now is the Judge has this hanging over my head...how I lied about Harvey just so I could have his job...which is not true. Since this Judge Lipton came into town, everything, and I mean everything, has been screwed up. People were friendly before, now they pass you by like your not there. I can't understand him; he thinks he's God and can do no wrong. We need Judge Webster back; he was a fine man, and a gentleman in every way.

Things were piling up against Judge Lipton, but... would they hold up in court...him being a senior Judge and all. It would depend on who the sitting Judges are when all of this comes up. Jack and Andy decided to stay a few more days. This would give them time to go all through there notes, and put them in proper order. Besides, maybe Alma would be back by then also. They also would like to talk with Karen one more time. Had she ever talked with Judge Lipton? What does he have against her and her mother, would he even talk with her? What they didn't know was that Alma was with Judge Webster, and they were waiting for their reports. Judge Webster called Chief Rose and wanted to know if he still had a copy of the deposition that he had given him. The Chief said yes he still had the copy. "Was it still in the sealed envelope the way I gave it to you?" The Chief said, "Yes, as far as I know." The Judge wanted to know for sure. "If it has never been opened, don't open it now. Send me the envelope first class mail." Judge Webster gave him a P.O. Box number and a Town and State. The Chief wanted to know what was going on, the Judge told him he would get back to him and hung up.

Andy and Jack worked most of the night filling in the details of what they had found about Judge Lipton. It wasn't a pretty picture, but if the Judge lied and gave a different version of what happened. He may be able to get away with most of the crap he's pulled. They still would like to talk with Karen again. But after talking it over decided to send the report as is and see what happens. The report was sent out the next morning. It was sent to a P.O. Box in Arrow Head Utah. This must be a sending address, you mail it out there and they foreword it to another address. It could be right here in Plantsville.

They packed up everything and were ready to move out when a knock came at the door. Andy went over and opened the door. It was a policeman with a message from Chief Rose. They found the janitor's body hanging from his garage ceiling this morning.

His wife found him when he wasn't in bed this morning. She called the ambulance and Chief Rose. They are out there now and the Chief would like you to come out. Jack and Andy looked at each other, and then asked the officer if he would show them how to get to his house. They followed the police car just outside of town. There was a lot of activity around the house. They had it all roped off, Chief Rose saw them coming and went to meet them. What in the world happened? Jack asked. The chief had no idea. His wife found him in the garage this morning. Andy asked if there were any windows broken. The Chief said not that he could see. Why do you ask? They told the Chief how they had talked with the janitor last night. He was pretty upset about having Harvey fired from the courthouse. Is his car still here') The Chief said yes, why do you ask. Could you have the car taken down to the station and put in your garage? We would like to go over it, if it's O.K. with you. Please have them keep there fingers off the car and don't rub against it. The Chief was more then willing, and called one of the detectives over. The chief introduced the detective to Andy and Jack. The detective's name was Sonny Cloud. He was half-Indian, but very smart. People just call him Sunny; they used a "U" instead of the "O". He was the head detective. They explained what they wanted with the car. He went and got hold of one of his men and gave him the order. The car was then taken to the garage and a patrolman stayed with it. Sonny told the Chief he was going back to the station to check the car over. He said this maybe more then just a suicide. He also asked the Chief if he could go along with the idea that it was more then just suicide. The Chief gave his OK, but before they left, they went over to the backdoor to see if anything was damaged, a window broken, door pried open or something like that. They could find nothing, except the lock on the doorframe was jammed full of paper, so that the lock would not work. They would check with the wife later. Some don't lock their doors.

In the garage, you can see where the stepladder is. It would be very hard for anyone to stand on the ladder, put the rope around there neck, get down and move the ladder over there. Sunny asked the coroner to please check every inch of the janitor's body. Look for anything black and blue or scratches and marks of any kind. Could he have been dead before he was put up there? We are not sure what happened. We will go down and check the car out for footprints outside of the car, and finger prints all over inside and out. His wife said he came home late. She was in bed already. She thought she heard him making a cup of tea. Sunny asked her if she knew where he was till ten o'clock. She said he called her and said he had a meeting to go to. He said he would be a little late. "That's all I know. Did you hear any voices, and are you sure he was making tea? Did you talk with him? Did you hear anything in the background, music, voices, talking anything?" She said she's not sure it was him; she just figured it had to be. She didn't talk with him and she didn't hear any voices. There were no background noises when he called. Do you know where he called from Sunny asked? She wasn't sure but she thought it was from the courthouse. What time was it when he called, she wasn't sure but it had to be around six or six-fifteen? She had a headache and went to bed early. Once in awhile he would stop at the Misty Cloud Grill and have a drink before he came home. Sunny said, Years ago, my family use to own that place. My father and his brother started the business, when my father died, my uncle could not keep the place so he sold it. He gave my mother half. Misty was my mother's maiden name, and of course my fathers name was cloud. That was fifteen years ago that the place was sold. Let's go over and see if anybody remembers seeing him last night.

They checked with the Chief, then got in the car and went down to the Misty Cloud Grill. Sunny knew most of the people there so when they went in, everybody wanted to buy us a drink. Sunny told them this was police business... Has anybody seen the janitor with anyone last night? It's very important, so please tell me. A few said no, they hadn't seen him at all last night. He was in here a few nights ago. He would stop in for a drink and then go home. Was he with someone or was he alone? Sunny asked. The bartender said he came in alone and a few minutes later a man came in, they were talking at the bar. He didn't pay any attention to them after he served them there drinks. The man paid for the drinks and they both left. That's the last we have seen of him. Is he in trouble, or did he leave his wife. They all started laughing. Sunny, Andy, and Jack left and went over to the police station garage. The car was put over on the side under the flood light. Has anyone touched this car Sunny asked? The officer said, not sense he's been watching it. They checked for foot and fingerprints on the outside of the car. There was one print of a shoe or something. It looked as if someone had stood on the fender and turned around, it was hard too tell what it was. They dusted the complete car outside. They found a lot of fingerprints. When they got through with the outside, they went in the trunk, and then to the inside of the car. They dusted everything for prints. Then they vacuumed the complete inside. They then put it up on the lift and checked the tires, and all underneath. Then they went inside and gave the prints to a policewoman and told her to check every print. He wanted a name and address on every print...and wanted it as soon as possible. They took pictures of the scuff and asked the Serge. To have someone look at the fender and see what they thought. By now it was getting close to suppertime. They were not sure this hanging had anything to do with the Judge, but they would stay around a little longer. They went over to Bills Restaurant for Supper. They asked Bill and Ruth if they had seen the Janitor last night. They thought for a minute. Ruth said she remembers him and another man stopped in for a coffee about one thirty in the afternoon. They sat in a booth and talked for a while. The man paid the bill and they left. Sunny asked if she had ever seen this man before. Ruth said, not that she can remember.

Back in Utah Judge Webster had gotten the mail he was looking for. He read it over about three or four times. Then he handed it to Alma to read over. Her face brightened up with what she read. However, the Judge wasn't too happy. They discussed each paragraph, line by line. The Judge was taking notes all the time Alma was talking. With what she had told the Judge and what he just received, she thought for sure they had something on him. The Judge looked at Alma and said" by hearing what you told me and reading all of this, you would think there would be enough to have him thrown in jail for life. However, I can see him now lying to every question. Twisting them around, making you and everyone else look bad." Maybe there were a few things that he shouldn't have done, like forming that club. It was only to have the bad kids feel ashamed. I would say, he didn't mean anything by it. I just wanted to show the other kids what could happen to them if they did something wrong. The cameras in the courthouse were put there because he had been threatened and he wanted it on tape and pictures. Alma said "What about letting George out of prison early? That was not in the agreement, but he did it. The Judge said, "That was his decision to make." but you said nothing about being released after serving only three years. How would he have known about this case, without someone telling him? Maybe George heard that I had left and wanted a new trial. If that was the case, and he got my file out and read them, and thought that ten years was too long for raping a child, then he could use his own Judgment in the case; which is apparently what may have happened here. Even going to a strip club, on his time is not worth talking about in court. The papers would say that you suggested going there... Just then the phone rang, Roper wanted to know who this man named Judge Clarence Hawter was. He said you had given him my phone number years ago and wondered if I knew you. I told him I wasn't Roper, but I would have Roper call him back. Do you know him Judge? The Judge said, "Yes, If he left a phone number I'll call him back myself." The Judge marked down a number, thanked Roper, and hung up. The judge started to like this job. He was really getting involved. He looked at his watch. There was three hours difference. It was almost noontime here, so it should be about three back east. He should be out of court by now, I think I'll give him a call and see what he wants.

Judge Webster called the old courthouse. The operator asked who was calling. The Judge asked if this was Pearl? She said yes, and who might this be. The Judge told her, and she got all excited. He said to her, "Keep your voice down. I don't want anyone to know I called. Would you please pass me on to Judge Hawter?" She said, "With pleasure." She put him on hold, a few minutes later Judge Hawter came on the line. Hello Judge Webster, how are you? The two Judges talked for a few minutes, and then Judge Hawter started telling him how the Janitor hung himself. There were two men here asking questions about Judge Lipton. They were leaving today but when they heard about the janitor hanging himself and all, they decided to stay an extra day and see what it was all about, mainly to see if Judge Lipton could have had anything to do with it. I think he did. The janitor I believe had a few things on Judge Lipton that could cause a problem for him. By having him hung, it would eliminate a lot of his troubles. Who would ever think that a Judge would do anything like that? People will think he had other problems, maybe with his wife, or drinking...he always stopped at the Misty Cloud Grill on the way home. We sure do miss you around here Judge. I happened to find this phone number you gave me years ago. When you went on vacation, and I took a chance that you might still be going there. I hope you don't mind, but I know you liked the janitor and all. By the way, how is your wife? We know she was pretty sick when you left. We hope she's feeling better. Judge Webster told him that she died two and a half years ago. Judge Hawter was stunned, I'm so sorry to hear that, I didn't know. They talked for a long time. Then Judge Webster said He would call later on in the week. Don't call me; I don't want this phone number on the phone bill. Please find out all you can, without getting nosey. Talk with you later. Oh Judge... by the way I put you in for the senior Judgeship but some how they sent this thing. Talk with you later and hung up.

Now the judge was getting really interested in what was going on back in Plantsville. At first he thought Alma was overreacting, but the more he looked into it the more he wanted to know what was really going on. He was making notes, as they were talking. He hadn't heard from Albany as yet and wanted to know why. He called his friend in Albany and asked how he made out. He told the Judge that this was a strange case. There are a lot of pieces to this puzzle that are left out. That's what we are trying to put together. The Judge thanked the person on the other end of the line and hung up. He looked at Alma and told her what the person had said. Alma was counting the days. She has to be back by Sunday. That would only give her three days more to stay out here. She will have to call Bill and Karen and let them know. She called the airport for the time the next plane would leave for Albany N. Y. the closest one to Sunday would be Saturday at six p.m. That would be our time. You would arrive in Albany around midnight Saturday night. The only other plane would be at ten twenty our time, but that one goes to Kennedy. She had no way of getting from Kennedy to Plantsville at three thirty in the morning. She booked a ticket for the six PM plane. She would have Sunday to rest up, and spend a little time with Karen. Karen would tell her what was going on in town. Everybody knows everything in the eating-places. She would maybe have time to go over to the janitor's house and give his wife her condolences. She would find out when and what time the funeral would be, and see if there was anything she could do to help. She told the Judge what her plans were, and what time she was leaving. He was sorry she had to leave. He liked talking to her and she was good company for him. Friday afternoon he called Judge Hawter again. They had found two needle marks, but haven't been able to fine out what they were from. There were no black and blue spots, not even around the neck. That seems to make them think he may have been dead before he was hung. There was very little air in his lungs and one wrist had a red band 3/4 way around.

They released the body for burial this morning. That's all they could find. We will have to wait and see what they find on those needle marks. That could take days or even weeks. They where able to make out a footprint on the car fender, and there were a lot of fingerprints also. She's checking them all out now. The Chief is keeping me informed. He calls me every night around ten o'clock. No word yet from Albany, everything was closed on Saturday, so there was no need in hanging around. Alma packed her thing and was ready to leave when the phone rang. It was for Judge Webster. His friend in Albany was on the line. He told the Judge he wanted to wait till Saturday to make this call. Judge, wait till you hear this. He said Judge Lipton was married for four months; his wife left him and took everything he had with her. He had a lawyer named George Hewitt. Hewitt was married to Lipton's wife's sister. She was a lesbian. She only made love to other girls. Poor George was left out, no sex for George. She teamed up with her sister and they left town. George got a divorce on grounds of incompatible. Judge Lipton to this day I can't find out if he ever got a divorce. He was picked up one time for propositioning a teenage girl. When they found out he was a Judge, they let him go and told him not to step foot in that town again. If he should come back, they would put him in jail. He asked for a transfer and moved out. He was moved to Easton Pennsylvania for a short time. He was a standby judge because they were overloaded and needed help. He kept in contact with his brother-in-law George. We guess that when he heard Judge Webster was retiring, he would like the job...and got it...they where glad to get rid of him. Judge Webster was taking everything down. He had a big smile on his face. The party at the other end of the line said they would get back to him just as soon as they got more information, and then hung up.

Judge Webster said out loud, Lipton must have some pull in Albany. I'd like to know with who and how he got it. We will keep digging till we find out. Alma asked Judge Webster if he thought Judge Hawter could be trusted with all this information. He said without a bit of hesitation absolutely. Alma said that made her feel better, she needed someone she could trust back home. Alma called Roper and wanted to say Good Bye but he was out on a call. She had to go back that way so if she had time, she would stop. She had a lot of traveling to do. She wanted to get an early start. She went to everyone at the ranch and gave them a big hug and kiss. Miss Bessie had tears in her eyes when she found out Alma was leaving. This was one big happy family, and she loved them all. Judge Webster was sad, but he understood that she had to get back for work at the courthouse Monday. She told Judge Webster she would call him direct the first day of the week and the last day of the week. She gave him her phone number at home and told him to call collect anytime. She also told him she had a spare bedroom if he cared to come out anytime and stay as long as he wishes. She left Miss Bessie's ranch; stopped and said good-bye to Roper and the rest of the deputies, got to the airport, returned the rental car, had a cup of coffee, and boarded the plane. As she gazed out the window, tears came to her eyes. She had such fond memories of this place and this past week. If only she could have stayed longer.

She arrived in Albany on time, picked up her car, and drove home. Karen was waiting for her and gave her some big hugs and a lot of kisses. She missed her so much. Alma was exhausted. She unpacked. Karen made them both a cup of hot tea. They talked for a bit, till she couldn't keep her eyes open any longer, and went to bed. She slept till ten in morning. When she got up and took a shower, she felt much better. Karen had made breakfast for her. She was starved, and ate everything Karen made. Karen filled-in her mother on everything that was going on in town...at least everything she knew or heard about. Now it was her mothers turn, Karen started asking a million questions. Alma laughed and said, one at a time. The weather was great; the ranch where she stayed was out of this world. It was run by Miss Bessie who is 100 years old. Her maid has slowed down a bit; she's only in her 80's. They both laughed. Karen thought she was kidding, but Alma said, "It's no lie." She has six boarders who all work around there, and each has his own job. They pay a few dollars a week for board that covers lights, water, and phone. If there's out of area phone calls you have to pay the charges yourself. If there's any money left over, that would go for paint, or repairs to equipment. She has six hundred acres, some cows, horses, a few pigs, chickens, and a garden as big as our whole place here. Karen wanted to know all about Judge Webster, how is he, is he half-dead, did he work at the ranch, and Alma said "hold it, one at a time." The Judge is fine, he misses back here. He's not half-dead, as a matter of fact, he's healthier then I'll ever be. He takes care of the large garden, plants, weeds, and collects the veggies. He does everything except dig it up in the fall. The neighbors came in with there big equipment and does that. But he misses his wife very much. Miss Bessie says that if she was 25 years younger she'd make a play for him. She say's she was there when he was born. Her and her husband had just bought the ranch and was up to their necks in debt. They owed $2,000.00 on it. The only good thing about the deal was the 300 head of cattle came with it. The garden help's him to forget. Karen wanted to know what she found out. Alma didn't want to tell her too much, she said they were getting more information and they would call her when they knew more. Monday after work, Alma sent a note to Judge Hawter, wanting to meet at his convenience. He in return sent a note back with only 102600. No name address or anything else on it. If it should get into the wrong hands, they wouldn't know what it was all about. Alma felt relieved, knowing that she had someone she could trust, and talk with. She also wanted to know if she should tell Karen all she knows, or just keep her out of it as much as possible. That night she drove up to Miranda's Pizza Restaurant. She sat in her car deep in thought when someone knocked on the window. She jumped and looked around. There stood Judge Hawter with a smile on his face. He opened the car door and helped her out. He looked down at her and said, "You should keep your car doors locked." She said, "I know, but I forgot." They walked in and sat at a booth in the back. The waitress came over and took there order. He started asking a lot of questions. She told him everything. How Judge Webster now was trying to find out who Judge Lipton had ties with in Albany. He must have something on somebody to have that much power in the State Capital. She told "Clarence" how Lipton had been married and that George Hewitt was his brother-in-law. How Hewitt's ex-wife was a lesbian and only slept with other females. And Lipton's wife and Hewitt's wife were sisters. When Lipton's wife left him she took everything that he had. Hewitt got a divorce, but there's no record of Lipton's wife getting one. Judge Hawter said, "Maybe that's why Lipton is the way he is. He's down on everyone. The waitress came with the food and drinks. She told Clarence how happy Judge Webster was to hear your voice. He was disappointed that nobody knew about his wife dying, and no one sent him a card. When you asked how she was, and he told you she had died two and a half years ago, made him feel better. He really liked the people here. If things go right and when all of this is over, I'll put it in the paper that she pasted away. After they got through eating, Alma asked if he had heard anything from Albany. He said theirs is a big silent mess over there. Nobody wants to talk; even my friends are on the quite side. When I told him Judge Webster was working on it also, this made him happy. Two men were in town asking questions about Lipton. They must be the one's Judge Webster had sent over to find out. I don't think Lipton would have any ideas as who would send them. They were from Alabama. They are digging real hard into the cause of the janitor's death. They are doing it on the Q.T., so it's harder for them. The Chief has given them all the help he can. She told him how she will call Judge Webster every Monday and Friday. If he needs anything he can call her collect, anytime. What they are interested in now are the two needle marks. What could they be from? He's not a diabetic and he's certainly not a druggie, what would they be from or for? They sat and talked for quite a while. When they left, she wanted to pay the bill, but he wouldn't hear of it. He did let her leave the tip. She told him the next time is on her and, "Don't you forget it." He didn't say a word, just smiled. They got in there cars and left. When she got home, Karen had a few notes for her. One was from Jack and the other from Chief Rose. She called Jack at the motel first. He told what happened and what they had found so far. They think the janitor's death may be tied in with this case, but they are waiting for the lab reports back. The hour was getting late and she wanted to see the janitor's wife. She hung up, got in her car, and drove to the other side of town. When she got to the janitor's house, there were two cars in the yard, but only one light in the house. She thought that was strange. The wake was over at eight o'clock and it was almost nine now. She went up to the house and was about to ring the doorbell when she heard noises coming from inside. She went back to her car, parked it so the other two cars couldn't get out. Took there marker numbers and ran to the neighbors home down the street. She rang the doorbell and waited, no one came to the door. She then ran across the street and rang that doorbell. An old lady came to the door and asked if she could help, was she lost or something? When Alma told her about somebody in the janitor's house she said she would call the police department right away and slammed the door. She waited for about fifteen minutes and no police car showed up. She rang the bell again and again but the lady would not answer the door. She was all upset now, she wanted to get out of there and find someone with a phone. It was getting pretty dark out now. She walked back to her car. When she got there, there were two boys trying to move Alma's car. She walked right on by, not saying a word. Glanced over to see if she recognized either one, but she didn't. She walked down the street to the next house and went up the steps. She rang the doorbell and waited. The door opened and an elderly man came to the door. Alma explained in a few words what was going on and would he please call the police dept., he invited her in and called the police. He gave Alma the phone so that she could tell them what was going on. They said they would have a car there in a few minutes. Just stay away and hung up. She thanked the man and went outside, and waited for the police to come. They were there in about four minutes. She watched as the boys started to run. One of the officers had a dog and let him loose. The dog took off after one boy and cornered him. The other officer grabbed the other boy and both were brought back to the house. They said they didn't do anything, they didn't steal anything. Nobody was home so nobody got hurt. The two were handcuffed and placed in the police car. Just then two more police cars pulled up. The officers looked in the window at the boys. One officer recognized both boys. They go to the same school as my kids. They play on the same ball team. He was shocked to think that these two boys would do something like that. The officer opened the front door and looked at the boys, never saying a word. One of the boys said, they didn't mean anything. They were just looking for some tapes the janitor took from school. The officer waved to one of the other officers to come over and listen to what these boys had to say. The officer then asked, who told you to come over and get them? The first officer again asked, "Who sent you over to get some tapes?" The boys locked at each other. The officer said, you don't have to tell us, but we caught you red handed and it would go a lot easier if you told us who sent you. The second officer asked if they were members of the Righteous Guardians. Again they looked at each other. They never said a word. The first officer called one of the other officers over and told him to get his partner and take both these boys to jail. Call their parents and have them come down to the police station with there lawyers. They will also have to make bond, or they will stay in jail till the case comes up in court. That could be sometime in the next couple of weeks or maybe longer. The boys were really getting worried now. If there parents wouldn't pay the bond, then they would be lost. One of the boys said to the other, don't worry we have the law on our side. Remember that's what they said at the meeting. The second officer said, "So you do belong to the R.G.'s." I thought so. Do you really think the Judge is going to get you off free? I don't know what this R.G. Club is all about but it sure isn't going to help you guys out this time. I can promise you that, and we will make sure that Judge Lipton is not the Judge seated on the bench when you go before the court. Now the boys were really worried, Judge Lipton was supposed to take care of them. If Judge Lipton wasn't the Judge, they could be in real trouble.

Two officers came over; they took the boys out of the car and walked them over to their car. By now there were a lot of people around; some were saying throw away the key on them. "These no good kids today, I hope they rot in jail." They were robbing a house, a house where they found a man hanging in the garage. I'll bet they had something to do with the hanging. The boys got into the other police car and started crying. They said, "We didn't mean anything, we'll pay for all the damage and broken stuff. Please let us go. We'll come down to the courthouse with our parents, please." The officer said, "You should have thought about the trouble you would be in if you got caught. It's to late now, so you got caught and did the crime and now you have to serve the time. I hope they throw the book at both of you." Wait till the papers write this one up. I can see it now in the headlines... two youths caught in a house where a man is found hung. Your names will be plastered all over the front page." One of the officers said they didn't have to say anything till there lawyer got there unless they wanted to. One of the boys asked if it would go any easier if they talked now. The officer said, "Wait till we get to the police station." Then they can take it all down and you can sign it. One officer asked how old are you boys? One said he was sixteen and the other said he was fifteen. The officers started talking between them selves. The sixteen year old will stand in the adult courtroom, and the fifteen year old will go to juvenile court. It's a shame... two young people getting jail time; this is going to screw up their whole adult life. When they go to get a job and are asked if they have a police record, and they say yes. Can you imagine what kind of work they will be doing, dirty work all because some jerk told them to rob the house for some tapes, and you know what, maybe they were involved in the murder of the janitor? Boy... I wouldn't want to be in there shoes. They took off for the police station. The boys said they didn't know anything about the murder of the janitor. The officer said, don't say anything more till you get a lawyer, and your parents are there. They pulled into the police station; the officers got out and went inside. They talked with the desk Sergeant, telling him what happened. All this time the boys are out in the back of the police car in handcuffs. Finely they went out and brought them in.

They stood before the Sergeant with their heads down. Each was given a plastic bag and was told to empty their pockets, and put what ever they have in the bags. After they emptied there pockets, one of the officers patted them down to make sure they didn't forget something. They then were brought before the bench. Each bag was emptied and everything was marked down as to what was in the bag. Then the boy looked over the slip to make sure it was right, and then signed the paper with the officer as a witness. The Sergeant asked them questions, "How old are you, who was driving the car, what were you after", and a lot of other questions. The Sergeant asked if the sixteen year old had a driver's license. The boy said yes, it was in the bag. The Sergeant took out the wallet and gave it to the boy. He in turn got his license out and handed it to the Sergeant. He copied everything down and gave it back to the boy. He put it back in his wallet and returned it back in the bag. The bag was then sealed. The Sergeant went through the same thing with the other boy. Only this boy had nothing to say. He wouldn't tell his name. He had a comb, a broken pencil, and seventy cents in change, also a broken pack of gum. The Sergeant asked, "What's your name son?" The Sergeant again asked what his name was. He still wouldn't talk. The Sergeant asked him if he wanted to call his family. He shook his head and said," No." The Sergeant took the older boy into a small room and had him stand against the wall and look straight ahead, he took two pictures, then he had him face the wall to his right took pictures and had him turn the other way and took more pictures. He asked him what his friends name was, but he wouldn't talk. The Sergeant took him out and brought the other boy in. He again took his pictures front and sides. Then the Sergeant sat him down at the table. "Look son we don't want to cause you any harm. You are in enough trouble as it is. I'm asking you nice, what is your name? I want to call your family. They must be worried, it's late and your not home yet. I'll help you out all I can, but you have to help me also." He told the Sergeant his father would kill him for what he had done. The R.G.'s were supposed to help them out when and if they got in trouble. He gave the Sergeant his name, address, and phone number. The Sergeant said he would talk with his folks and explain things to them. The kid felt a little better but was still all upset. After all the information was taken, they let the boys call there parents. Within the hour both parents were there. By now it was past eleven o'clock at night and the parents were in bed sleeping. They weren't too happy to think they had to get dressed and go down to the police station. The Sergeant went over and had a talk with the parents. He explained to them the seriousness of the crimes that they had committed. He did however think that they were told to do just what they were doing. They wouldn't have known about the Janitor unless someone had told them to go. Who would that someone be? That was going to be the next question. As the Sergeant was talking, the bonds man came in. He asked for the officer in charge and also asked for the deposition that the Sergeant had written. The bondsman went into another room to read the report... someplace where he wouldn't be disturbed. When he came out, he asked the Sergeant if he could speak with him for a minute. The Sergeant went into the backroom and sat down. The bondsman walked around the table, not saying anything, just thinking.

He finely looked up at the Sergeant and said" these kids are in serious trouble. If it was not for there ages I would put a bail of $150,000.00 each on then. But because they have never been in trouble before, and in your report you think that someone put them up to it. I'm setting bond at $ 25,000.00 each. If nothing more it may scare the living hell out of them if they have to stay in jail for a few days." when they get there lawyers here, and you think it would be O.K. I could see reducing it to around $1,500.00. How would that be? The Sergeant thought that was a very good idea. He would explain it to the parent that was the way it was going to be. Maybe it would make them think twice before they broke the law again. He asked the parents to come into the room. The bondsman was still there. He wanted to get there opinion as to what was going on. The Sergeant explained every thing to the parents. He then asked what they thought of the idea. They wanted to think it over for a few minutes; the first thing they asked was "Was this going on the report of each child that he spent time in jail? The Sergeant said that the kids are in enough trouble, serious trouble as it is, but he would try and keep it out of the papers. He would try to have it put in that they are out on bail. How would that be? He was also going to try and keep there names out of the papers. They were too young. I can't promise but I'll try.

The youngest boy's father started hollering and cursing, my son wouldn't do anything like that; somebody must have put him up to it. Somebody was trying to frame him, and on and on he went. The older boys parents just hung there heads, trying to figure out where they went wrong. Why would he do something like this, that club that he joined... that's a bad club we didn't want him to join it in the first place. He said that it was a cool club ran by Judge Lipton. It was suppose to straighten wayward kids out by shaming them in front of all there friends. They finely said that maybe this would teach them a lesson. Go ahead with the bond; I'm sure the lawyers will want it reduced. They thanked the bondsman and the Sergeant for being so understanding. When they got back out in the outer office, the bondsman told the boys that bond was set at $25,000.00 each, because they broke into a house, smashing things, ran from the police, looking for tapes. They knew no one would be home; they would be at the funeral parlor. So they figure now was a good time to get the tapes. What tapes? Neither boys parents were to happy about them to say the least. During the night neither boy could sleep. The 15 year old asked, what kind of tapes where we looking for, and how many. Who did they belong to? The sixteen- year old said the leader called him and said" go over to such and suche's house and look for some tapes he stole from the Judge. No one will be home. The janitor hung himself yesterday. His wife will be at the funeral parlor this evening. Make sure you look good. Take a member with you. If you don't see them in the house, check the garage. They must be there someplace. I saw you walking down the street and asked you if you wanted to come, you said sure and here we are. The fifteen-year old asked, are you going to tell them, what you just told me? The older boy said he didn't think so. They wouldn't believe him anyway. The Judge said he would take care of any problems, and boy do we have problems now. I hope he can help us out.

Alma was going over to ask the boys some questions but as she got closer to the police car, they were taking them out to transport them to the police station. She talked with the Sergeant that was in charge. He wouldn't tell her anything because the boys were under age. She looked around and saw one of the newspaper reporters she knew from the courthouse. She went over and started asking him questions. He gave her the answers she was looking for; only because he knew she had problems with the R.G.'s, with her daughter. He new that she wouldn't say anything about where the information came from. She left and asked if it was all right to take her car out of there. The cop said it was OK. They had her marker number, name, and address.

She drove home wondering what's going to happen to the boys. They didn't look like troublemakers. When she gets home she'll ask Karen if she knows the boy's. If so are they good or bad boys. They belong to the R.G. Club, she knows that much. As she started to pull into her driveway there was a strange car there. She pulled in right behind it. This way the car couldn't get out unless she moved her car. She went around back of the house and went in the back door. She heard voices and went around to the living room. She was surprised to see Carl. She said, "Carl what did you do get a new car?" He said, "No it belongs to my mother. I didn't want my car seen. I heard about what happened today. Then I got a call from one of the members of the R.G.s. they wanted me to say something that would put the two boys in another area of the city. I said I wouldn't; now they say they'll get me. I was worried about Karen, that's why I came over here. I hope you don't mind." Alma said she was glad to know he thought enough of Karen to watch out for her. They were caught only a few hours ago. They are down at the police station along with their folks now. Carl said, "I didn't know anything about what happened today. That R.G. told me everything. How the courthouse janitor got shot or hung himself." He was supposed to have stolen some tapes from the courthouse. What kind of tapes? I don't know. A couple of kids were going over to his house to get them. That's why they wanted me to lie about seeing them. Carl said he figured if he lied about seeing the two boys they would blackmail him into the club. Alma asked if they knew the two boys. Carl said he never heard who they were. He hung up the phone before the caller said the names. Alma told them both what the boys names were. She said they seemed like nice boys. They belong to the R.G.s. Their parents were all upset. The sixteen year old was Tory Cox, he was 2/3 Indian. The 15 year old was Phil Syzmansky. "Don't tell anyone about how you found out there names. They are minors and nobody is supposed to know." They told the police that because they belong to the R.G.s. That Judge Lipton would take care of them. That it was his tapes they were after. Carl said he knew the boys. He also knew that they belonged to the R.G.s club. He was surprised when he found out about them. He thought they both were good kids. Troy played first base on the Plantsville Cats softball team, and Phil was a couch on the little league team. It's hard for me to believe that they would do something like that.

Alma did some thinking,"... Who is the leader of this group? Are the two boys still involved? Are they receiving orders from Judge Lipton? Is Judge Lipton the president of the Club, or is Lipton going to deny everything and leave the kid's holding the bag." Alma looked at her watch; it was past midnight. She would look into this more in the morning. She was tired and wanted to go to bed. Carl said he had to get home before his mother called the police out looking for him. She would call the Chief in the morning and see what he had to say. Alma and Karen went right to bed; they both were tired and upset about this evening. The next day's paper had a small item about the hanging on the fourth page. Nothing was said about the break-in. Maybe it was because it was late in the evening. Alma called the Chief; they talked for about twenty minutes. He said he was home sleeping when all of this happened and hadn't had time to read the report through that was on his desk. He said he would call her back and hung up. Three days went by and not a thing in the paper about the boys breaking in to the Janitors house. The Chief never called back and nothing was said in the courthouse. She received a note, all that was on the paper was today 102630. She got home early and Karen was already home. They sat down and had a cup of tea. Alma had been doing a lot of thinking, should she tell Karen about Judge Hawter or not. Tonight she made up her mind; she was going to tell her. She figured Karen was old enough to keep things to herself. This also would let her know that her mother trusts her with very important stuff. She explained everything to Karen, how she trusts Judge Hawter, and because Judge Webster Said he was ok; that they had a code that whenever they wanted to meet, they would put the place and time and day on a piece of paper. She showed Karen the note she got from Judge Hawter today. Karen said that it didn't make sense. "What is all the numbers for, can't you just come right out and say meet me at so and so's place?" Alma told her that Judge Lipton had cameras all over the courthouse. "He will do anything to get something on a person. He then will use it to his advantage. That is why we have to meet away from the courthouse and the town. We are trying to get things on Lipton to get him out of town. This R.G. Club is one thing. In addition, he lies and is no good with the workers at the courthouse. They are all worried about there job's. He has called me into his office several times. That is the reason the boys were at the janitor's house, trying to find some tapes the janitor took to give to the two detectives. So please don't say a word to anyone, not even to Carl. Do I have your word on it?" Karen looked at her mother and said, "Mother you have my word I will never tell anyone, and that code is pretty cool." Alma took Karen's hand and gave it a squeeze. She told Karen how proud she was that she was her daughter. She looked at her watch and said, "My gosh, I have to go I'm late already, good by love."

That night Alma drove up to Miranda's; she got there just at six-thirty. Clarence was parked over on the side of the building. Alma pulled up in front, but a little to the left. She went in and got a booth near the back. Clarence came in a few minutes later. There were only a few booths empty. It was suppertime and people were eating out more often. They gave there order and started talking. The Judge told her how Lipton called the paper and told them not to put anything in about the boys. There was an internal investigation going on and it would ruin everything if people knew. He also sent a note to all the Judge's that these boys would be brought before his courtroom. He would handle this himself.

Alma told Judge Hawter about the two boys breaking into the janitor's house. They said, "They were looking for tapes that the janitor took from the courthouse." She said how she had called Chief Rose three day's ago. He was going to read the report and get back to me. As of yet he hasn't called. "Maybe the Judge is putting pressure on him also," she said half to herself. I wonder if they or anyone has found the tapes yet. What do you think of the idea of me having a talk with the younger boy? Maybe put a little scare into him. Explain the new club we are starting, and ask if he would want to join. Promise him nothing but a lot of fun. We need someone to help with the younger kid's, playing games and all. Judge Hawter thought that would be a good idea. Maybe talk with his parents first, and get there permission. Don't forget he is a minor. The waitress brought the food and drinks and left. While they were eating, they started talking about other things. Where were you born, what school did you go to, what friends, neighbors and some funny little stories. That got them laughing. Then they got to the serious side of things. "He was married for eight years. They struggled to make ends meet while he went to law school, they had two children. One day six years ago, he was nominated for Judgeship. To this day, I do not know who it was. I thank him every night in my prayers... we were celebrating my first year on the bench, my friends and associates gave us a big party. One of our female friends got sick and wanted to go home. My wife said she would be happy to take her and the kid's home. Our two children wanted to go with them, so they all piled in the car and drove out the driveway, that was the last time I saw them all alive. They got a few miles down the road; a truck with a load of hay came around the corner on the wrong side of the road and smashed into them. The hay cough fire and everyone was burnt beyond recognition. The three loves of my life were snuffed out in a matter of minutes. We held a service for all six of them. I put a stone with there names on it in the cemetery. The stone is there but no bodies. The lawyer friend who's wife and kid's it was, committed suicide a year later. I came close many time of doing the same thing. That is not what my wife would have wanted. We struggled to long and hard to get where we were, and to throw it away now would not be right. I have in the years past tried to be a good and fair Judge. Thinking my family would be proud of me." Looking around they saw that they were the only ones left. The waitress was cleaning up the place, getting ready for the morning rush. Clarence said," I'd like to hear your side, but let's make it the next time. It's late and I have a heavy load tomorrow." They split the bill and left. When she got home Karen was still up. She wanted to know how it went. Alma gave her the highlights but not all. It was late and they were both tired so off to bed they went.

Alma had a hard time getting to sleep. She kept thinking of the crash she was in years ago. Then she started seeing in her mind, what must have happened when the hay truck hit that car. It was just getting daylight when she got to sleep. The alarm went of, and it scared the daylights out of her. She got up and took a shower, got dressed, went down and had breakfast and went to work. All day she was thinking about what she was going to say to the fifteen year old. Should she talk to him alone or with his parents there? The more she thought about it the more she wanted the parents with him. This way they would know everything that was going on. As it got near quitting time, Alma looked in the phone book for there phone number. She called and Mrs. Szymansky answered. Alma told her who she was and why she was calling, and why she wanted to talk with her son. At first Mrs. Szymansky didn't want anything to do with her. Reporters were calling all the time, people she didn't know were calling and she was getting tired of it. The Judge Lipton who she doesn't care too much for, told her not to speak with anyone. He was the one that started all of this... him and that crazy club. He told Phil's parents that the tapes were of court cases and that he couldn't talk about them to anyone. That's why he called the paper and the Police Chief. He didn't want the word of the tapes being missing to get out. Alma said, "She would respect the privates of there conversation." Mrs. Szymansky said, "She would talk it over with her husband and call her back one way or the other." Alma said, "That would be fine and gave her the house phone number and hung up"... Just before seven o'clock the phone rang, Alma jumped to answer it. The call was for Karen. The Ballard's wanted her for Saturday night. They were going to a party and would be home late. She would have to sleep over if that was all right with her. They would bring her home around ten the next morning. She checked with her mother, and said that it would be ok. She just hung up the phone when it rang again, this time it was Mrs. Szymansky, Alma took the call, that would be fine, yes Saturday around seven or seven thirty would be ok. Would you care to come to my house? That's fine I'll see you then, and hung up the phone. Friday night Alma called Judge Webster. They talked for a long time. The Judge told her how the two men had gotten in touch with him and asked if they could stay and check this hanging out. Something didn't seam right, the report on those two needle marks hadn't come back yet. They believe they were made with a large needle that contained insulin. But they were still working on it. They also said something about some tapes that were stolen from the courthouse. The Judge told them to stay as long as it takes to clean this mess up. That was about all for now. Alma said "give my love to all, and tell Bessie I'd love to have her come out here and see my ranch." She said she would call him back next Friday night, unless something important comes up. Both agreed and hung up. Saturday afternoon Carl called, "And asked if she wanted to go to the basketball game that night?" Karen said, "She would like to go but she was working, taking care of the Ballard children." He said, "Some other time ok." and hung up. She though that was pretty brief, then her thoughts went to the TV. She hadn't seen HBO movies in a month. She could hardly wait. Mr. Ballard came and picked her up at seven thirty. This way the kid's could play a little, get tired and go to bed and go to sleep fast. Mr. and Mrs. Ballard looked real sharp; she had a low cut strapless dress that made her look ten years younger. Mr. Ballard had a pair of white duck legged pants and a shirt that looked like a button down but was really a pull over, that too looked great. They said, "They would be late so don't wait up for them." They left about eight o'clock. The children had taken their baths and were ready for bed. Karen gave them a bit to eat, and then sent them up stairs to bed. She cleaned the dishes and was about to go up when she heard a car pull up in the driveway. Looking out the window, she saw two men coming toward the front door. They didn't look to friendly. They rang the doorbell, she wasn't sure she should answer it or not. The kids started hollering, so Karen went to the door and said, "I'll be right back, she went up stairs and used the phone up in the master bedroom, and called the police." She told the children to be quite, and went back down stairs. She went to the door and asked what they wanted. They said, "They wanted to talk with her. She asked why. They said, "It was about the tapes that were missing from the courthouse." She said, "She didn't know anything about tapes, and if they didn't leave right now she would call the police." One of them said, "He was the police and showed her a badge through the window in the door. Karen was still not sure what to do. She said, "Wait a minute the kids are fighting, I'll be right back." When she came back downstairs they were just getting into there car. She took the marker number down and the color of the car. In about five minutes the police car came. She explained what happened. She gave them the marker number and the color of the car. One officer went to the car and radioed it into headquarters. They were told to get all the information they could and six it to headquarters. Karen was worried now, what would they want with her. She went over and called her mother, no answer. She did say she was going out, then it dawned on her, she was going to see that boy's parents. She asked one of the officers if he would go up to her house and look around just to make sure everything was ok. No problem, said one officer and he got in the car and drove off. When he came back, he said, "The house was locked and everything was ok." He looked all around and left. Just then the radio came in, car twenty call jimmy ASAP. The officer asked if he could use the phone, sure she said and showed him the way in. He made the call, gave his name and badge number. He listened for a few minutes then said, "... yes sir... yes sir...very well sir. We will do that right away sir," and hung up. The officer said, "That the car belonged to a police officer that was released from duty about three years ago. He started a private detective agency. He never did turn his badge in. They have been after him for a long time but he still has it. It was his car that was here. Any communication with HOT must be made by phone. He has a police scanner and can hear everything that's going on. He knew we were looking for his car, so he parked it out in front of his office". Back at HOT, one of the detectives happen to over hear the conversation. He went in and asked the officer in charge what was going on. The officer said, "He wasn't sure his self. Judge Lipton has been calling every half hour looking for the tapes." The detective wanted to know what tapes? The charge officer said, "It was a long story," the detective said, " He had a few minutes; he was just on his way home. The officer told him how the janitor hung himself, or they think some one hung him. The Judge thinks he took the tapes from the courthouse. Nobody can find the tapes. Judge Lipton is driving us nuts with phone calls. Who is working on the case? The detective was very interested. The officer told him, "Sunny Cloud was working the case." The detective asked, "If he thought he could be assigned to that case? The charge officer said, "To check with the Chief in the morning."

The detective checked with Sunny Cloud and went in to see Chief Rose. They both thought that detective Henry would be good for the investigation .They called him in and told him he was... now working on the case of the missing tapes. He was briefed on what has happened and was told nothing was to be said about this case outside of the people that are working on it. There are two FBI. Men who also are working on there own. We will help them all we can. Two days went by nothing new was found. Sunday was paper day, all the information that was collected during the week was filled away. Monday morning when they came in, they took one look at Clouds desk and said, "What the hell went on over the weekend." They sat down and started going through all the paper work. Judge Lipton called twice more Sunday. They were still tracing fingerprints that the FBI. Boys had given them. There was only about four that they could not find. Last week they searched the house, garage, the car, the trash, and everything, but couldn't find a thing. They though that maybe he might have mailed them to someone. No one has come up with them as of yet. Maybe today things will be different.

Alma was doing a little investigating herself. She wanted to fine out who the leader was. She also wanted to know what Judge Lipton played in the RG's club. Another thing she wanted to know was the janitor killed before or after he was hung. If he was killed before he was hung, maybe he hid the tapes back at the courthouse before they got to him. No one has looked in the courthouse, they have been spending there time at the house and garage. Alma called the Chief; he would not talk with her. He had gotten a note from the Judge saying, not to talk with anyone about the tapes, the more she thought about the tapes, the more she wanted to look around the courthouse. The first place to look would be in the janitor's room, then the boy's room, then the girl's room. No one would think of looking in the girl's room. Then look in all the trash barrels and under the plastic trash bags. She wanted to find out if anyone had checked the courthouse. She called the Police department again, this time she asked for Detective Cloud. The operator wanted to know who was calling. Alma wouldn't give her right name; she just said she had some information on the hanging, that's all. He said wait a minute, and put her on hold. A voice came on the phone, she asked, "Who is this?" The voice said he was Detective Cloud. She asked what his badge number was; he stalled and gave her a number. She said this is not Detective Cloud, now you either get Detective Cloud right now or I will hang up. The phone went on hold for a few minutes, then a voice came on and said Detective Cloud here. This time she knew it was him. She told him who she was and what her thoughts were. He told her, he never had given that a thought. He may have left them at the courthouse somewhere. She told him how she knows someone that goes to that school and is finding out things for her. If you want to know what I'm finding out take my calls, don't put someone else on the phone. If you are not there I'll leave you my home phone number and you can reach me there. I expect to have more information soon. She hung up. She met with Phil and his parents Saturday night at there house. Phil would not talk at first; he said, 'The Judge said, that if he says anything to anyone he would not help him out. Alma told him about the Club she is starting up; it's going to be a fun club. Not something like what you're in now. We are calling it the Plantsville Guardians and we are going to have a contest and prizes for the best logo. How does that sound? We will not stand for any stuff like what you have now. We want to help kids, not get them in trouble. We know a few things about Judge Lipton, they are not the best things a Judge should do. However he thinks he's god and can do anything he's a-mind to. Someone has to stand up to him. The more Alma talked about the Club, the more the boy and his parents got interested. Phil started asking questions, where do they meet, what games are they going to play, are there an age limit? Alma told them that they were looking for a place now. They would like to get a place big enough for basketball, plus other indoor sports. As the young kids get older, they can become Guardians and mates for the younger kids. That way, there will never be an age limit. As they get bigger they move up to playing baseball, soccer, hockey, basketball and so on. They will make crafts and sell things, that way the money they make would go to buying uniforms and equipment. Girls will also be able to join. We will be trying for all the parents to come and help out. Maybe the fathers could make a dollhouse big enough for the girls to go inside, the mothers could help, showing them how to bake cookies that we could sell. There are so many things that can be done to help the children stay off the streets and yet have fun. All they need is a little guidance, and the fathers and mothers can have a lot of fun also. Can't you just see on the forth of July parade, the hole town watching the Plantsville Guardians marching down the street from the little ones to the ball teams. They would all be in the same kind and color outfits. There would be large banners flying with the Plantsville Guardians logo on it. May be we could get enough for a band, there's no limit as to that we can do, if we all stick together. Phil wanted to know how much trouble he was in now, and can Judge Lipton help him? Alma said she couldn't guarantee anything, but would try to get them off with just paying for the things they had broken. She talked for a few more minutes then left to go home. They said they would get back to her. She did a lot of thinking on the way home.

The next morning she called Andy, the FBI Agent at the motel. He wasn't there but Jack answered the phone. She told him the same thing. He said, "They had planed on going over to the courthouse that night." She said, "She would like to meet with them sometime soon. He said, "Hold on a minute, when he came back to the phone, he said, "How about tomorrow night?" She asked, "If it would be all right if she brought Judge Hawter along. She said he's ok. He's on our side." He said, "He would talk it over with Andy and get back to her." He got her phone number and what time she got out of work. Then they hung up. She felt pretty proud of herself. Maybe she should have been a detective.

Andy was over talking with the ex-policeman. Wanting to know who told him to go see Karen, and what did he know about the hanging? The private eye told Andy to go to hell; he didn't have to tell him nothing. Andy went around behind the desk, grabbed the smart-ass private eye, and held him with one arm while he picked up the phone and was ready to call the police department when the door opened and there was Detective Cloud. Andy was happy to see him; he told Cloud how this asshole used his badge to scare a little girl out of her wits last night. He and another man came up to the house she was babying sitting and wanted to come in. He then flashed his badge; lucky for her she didn't answer the door. What I want to know is how you knew she was baby-sitting at that house. Who told you? The private eye said, "Go to hell, he's not saying anything." Andy let him go and came around to the front of the desk. Detective Cloud knew Andy was with the FBI Investigating Judge Lipton, so there wasn't much he could do or say. The ex policeman (Sam) didn't know that this big guy was a cop. He thought he was a friend of Alma's. Detective Cloud said, "He would take over from here. He also said he wanted to see him outside, now." They both walked out, Andy had his head down. When they got outside Cloud said, "What am I suppose to do," I guess I'll just say you're a friend of Alma's." Andy didn't say anything for a while; he was doing some thinking as to how to hand this. Andy said, "He thought it best if he kept in the background for a while. People maybe starting to put two and two together and if that's so Judge Lipton may figure things out also." Detective Cloud went back in; Andy went back to the motel. Detective Cloud said, "He was sorry about what just happened. But he did come over to ask a few questions, "One of them was How did you know the girl was going to baby-sit and at what house?" The second question, "Who was the man with you? Does he work for you or is he just a friend? And the third and last thing is...I have to pick up your old police badge, NOW. If you want a private eye badge, come down to the station, fill out the papers, and as long as you have no police record then there shouldn't be any trouble, especially since you being an ex- cop. Oh, by the way... Do you carry a gun? I didn't see any permits that you signed for one. Now let's start with the first question... who told you the girl was going to baby sit last night, and at what house? Remember if I don't get the right answers, I'll have to take you down to headquarters. That wouldn't look to good on your report for a private eye badge." Cloud walked over to the door and asked a uniformed officer to please come step inside." The officer was about six feet tall and weighed about two hundred and fifty pounds... all muscle... Sam the private eye said, "Look you know I can't tell you who I work for, That's employer-employee confidential stuff. Sorry I can't help you on that one. Now let's see, the second question... What was that? Oh yeah... I know who was with the person who went to that house. I don't know, I wasn't there, but I'll ask around for you and maybe I can find out.

Now the third question... The badge, "I don't have the badge, I lost that a long time ago. I went to give it back and couldn't find it, boy was I pissed. Someone must be flashing it around. Detective Cloud said, "I guess I'll have to take you down to headquarters; I thought we could handle this easy like, but I guess not. I'll also have to put this on record too. That means on your record. Cloud told the officer, "To put the cuffs on him". Sam is saying, "You can't do this to me I didn't do anything Why are you taking me down to headquarters for." Detective Cloud told the officer, "I want front and two side pictures, make sure they come out good, finger print him. You know the works, I'll be down later. I have a few stops to make first, if he causes any trouble put it on your report. I'll write it all up later. If he gets to excited put him in a nice quite cell and lock the door." Sam is hollering, "You can't do this to me, I didn't do anything. I know my rights." Just then Cloud said "Add this to that private eye permit list. He may never get his private eye permit. Now wouldn't that be sad.

While Detective Cloud was taking care of Sam the private eye, Andy went back to the motel. Jack was getting worried; he thought he should have been back long ago. He told Andy, "How Alma had called and they are to meet tomorrow night, she also is bringing Judge Hawter. She said, "He's on our side." Judge Webster told us before that Hawter could be trusted if we ever needed him. Andy started doing some checking. This private eye (Sam) got bounced off the police force three years ago. George Hewitt got put in jail three years ago. He was to serve ten years for rape. Now he's out after serving only three years. Do Hewitt and Sam have anything in common? Is there any connection between Hewitt, and Sam the private eye? Could Lipton be giving orders to Hewitt to be passed on to Sam.? If so...how would Lipton know that Karen was baby-sitting, only if the phone lines were taped. When the Ballard's called Karen and the phone was taped, Lipton could have picked it up right away. Called Hewitt and had Hewitt call Sam. The only other thing would be to check the Ballard's out. See if they have any connection with Hewitt, Sam, or Lipton. They seem to be going to a lot of all night parties. Maybe we should follow them some night and see what goes on Jack said, "maybe Lipton wants to put Sam back on the force so he can keep an eye on what's going on in the police dept. It was only three in the afternoon, which meant they still had a few hours to go. Jack got on the phone and called the Police headquarters. He asked to speak with the chief. The officer said one minute please. . . Jack waited for about five minutes, the officer came back and said he was sorry but the chief was in a conference, could he help him. Jack told him to tell the chief that Jack wants to talk with him now! The chief got on the phone and said, "He was sorry he didn't know it was him. What can I do for you Jack? He said, "Chief about three years age a police officer was discharged from the force. Could you tell us why he was let go?" The Chief though for a minute, that was a strange case. "It seems that Sam was caught sleeping in a patrol car one night. An alarm went in on a burglary and

Sam didn't hear the call, a backup officer was shot and wounded. He was all alone; Sam was supposed to have been there to help him. Sam said that his radio wasn't working. But we checked it out and went all over town and it worked well. He finely said how he dozed off. The board of police commissioners wanted him off the force. I said maybe a leave without pay for a few months. He was a good cop, the only thing was . . . he was trying to get his detective business off the ground and was working long hours. They wouldn't hear of it. They wanted him out. They felt they couldn't trust him on patrol anymore." Jack hung up the phone and told Andy what the Chief had to say. I wonder if that's the true story. Andy said he would ask the Judge tonight. , With Judge Hawter on our side, we should be able to find out a lot of things. Andy got on the phone and talked for a few minutes then hung up. About ten minutes later the phone rang, Andy said, "You have to be kidding is that the truth, brothers-in-law? Holy cow. Now all we need is the in person at the Capital. When we find that out our job will be finished. He said, thanks for the info and hung up. Andy sat back in his chair, clasped his hands and said... listen to this Sam is Hewitt's, ex-wife's first husband. That makes Hewitt, Sam the private eye and Lipton brother-in-laws. Can you beat that? What a small world. Now all we have to find out is what kind of connection and with whom, at the Capital."

Things were not going so good on the home front. They couldn't find out how Sam knew that Karen was baby-sitting, and at what house. The only ones that knew were Alma, Karen, and the Ballard's. There were no connections there. Could Alma's telephone be tapped? That's something I'll have to check right away. She called the telephone company and asked if there was a way that a tape could be installed on a phone without anyone knowing about it? The operator said please hold and I'll check. She came back a few minutes later, first she wanted to know what her name was, then the telephone number. Does she have a single phone line or more then one line? If more then one line how many more? How many phones does she have in the house? Alma said, "Please I do not want a phone tap, I just want to know if a person could tell if there phone was tapped." The operator said, "She was sorry but she though she wanted her line taped." The operator said, yes it could be done, however it would be against the law. Alma said, "Thank you and hung up."

She left a note under Judge Hawter's door. 102630. Before she left for home, she called the motel and left a message for room 172, "Will pick you up at 6:00." No name. The manager sent the boy up and had him slide it under the door. Andy saw it come, so he went over and picked it up, looked at it and told Jack it's 6:00. Alma got home from the courthouse early. Karen was working at Bill's Restaurant. She opened the door; there on the floor was a note. All it said was "I'm Sorry." This had her confused, maybe the note was for Karen. She called Bill's restaurant, Ruth answered, and Alma talked with her for a few minutes, and then asked for Karen. Karen came to the phone and said "Hi mom." Alma asked if she had gotten into a fight with anyone. She said "no, why"? Alma told her about the note she found under the front door. Karen knew nothing about it. Maybe someone put it under the wrong door or house. They talked for a few minutes; Alma told her she was going out for a while tonight. She told her she would tell her all about it when she gets home. She had to go now, clean up and change and said see you later. Love you and hung up. At 6:00 she picked up the two men and got to Miranda's a little before 6:30. On the way up Alma told them how she found the note under her front door. She said how she called Karen at Bill's rest and she knew nothing about it either. Jack said don't touch it anymore. We'll pick it up when we get home. Maybe we can lift a fingerprint or something. Detective Cloud hadn't gotten any further with the hanging. Detective Cloud was going to let the private eye do some thinking. Maybe that would make him talk. Right at 6:30 Judge Hawter pulled in. He got out of the car and went inside. A few minutes later the three of them got out and went in. Judge Hawter had gotten the same booth as they had before. Alma introduced the Judge to the two men. She said there names were Andy and Jack. The Judge nodded his head. They looked over the menu, saw what they wanted. When the waitress came they gave her the order. The music was country song's that kind of covered there voices, Judge Hawter seemed uneasy tonight. Alma noticed also. She asked if every thing was all right. He said he just had a bad day. Judge Lipton was on his case all day. He felt a lot better when he got Alma's note. As they talked waiting for there food, Jack asked how often do you come here? Alma said that this was the second time. Jack suggested a few other places. A little farther out of town. Don't go to the same restaurant every time. We know that Judge Lipton comes out this way and they shouldn't be seen together. The two men asked a lot of questions. Judge Hawter gave them the best answer's he could. Because everyone was so closed mouthed at the courthouse not to much talking got around anymore. There are a few girls that don't care if they do get fired. They would call the paper; tell them what they know about Lipton. Maybe Lipton knows that and is going easy with them. He's probably trying to get something on them. Maybe he's checking there personal file, he would do anything as along as it benefited him. He would check to see if any of them ever got caught playing around. If they owe anyone money. He could take over the payments and increase the interest. Who knows what else he would do. They saved the best for last. Jack said" Do you know that Hewitt, Sam the private eye, and Judge Lipton were brothers-in-law? Judge Hawter looked at all of them. Didn't say a word for a few minutes. He then said, "Are you sure about this?" Both Jack and Andy shook their heads yes. We just found out this afternoon. Sam is Hewitt's ex-wife's first husband. Hewitt's and Lipton's wives were sisters. How about that? For the first time today, Judge Hawter had a big smile on his face. What a small world he said, "Now we are getting some place. If we only knew how much power he has at the

Capital. We could pull the plug on him tomorrow. This is only the beginning; we will keep this quite till we know more." Alma couldn't wait to tell Judge Webster. First she has to make sure her phone is not taped. She did some thinking. Tonight I'll call Judge Webster from Bill's Restaurant, that way, if the phone is tapped, he wouldn't hear a thing. It was getting late and the crowd was just about gone. They got the check, split it four ways and left, when they got outside, Alma happened to look to her right. There was Judge Lipton's car. How did he know we would be here tonight? They didn't see him seated in there, Andy said lets stay and watch. Maybe we can learn something. They talked about the janitor. Did Judge Lipton have anything to do with his hanging? Maybe he called Sam, who called George Hewitt, who may have found a friend in prison that could handle this job. Andy said, "He would check and see who else the Judge let out, at or near the same time as Hewitt's." George may have promised the guy a lot, just for doing some odd jobs for them. They waited for thirty-six minutes. Out came Judge Lipton and a woman. Alma recognized the woman, My God Alma said, "That's Carl's mother." What would she be doing out with Lipton? What information could she give him that he could use on anyone? Jack wanted to know were she worked? Alma said she didn't know she was out at the house a few weeks back. It seemed that word was spread around that Karen begged Hewitt for sex. She was only eleven at the time, but stories went around the school. Her son Carl and Karen were good friends. Not boyfriend-girl friend just good friends. She didn't want Carl going out with Karen because Karen had a bad reputation, so somebody said and spread the word around the school. I invited her over one night and explained everything to her. I thought we were pretty good friends. Now I'm not so sure. What shall I do? Andy cut in and said, the way it looks, and he never saw us. He hasn't looked around for our cars. They may have come in later and didn't see us. Four people going out, he may not have noticed. Besides it was fairly dark in there. Judge Hawter said he would drive his car home, Alma could follow Lipton. After they drove out, Alma watched to see what direction they went in. She asked, shall we follow them. Andy looked at Jack, if we do keep quite a ways back. When you come to a crossroad turn your signal light on. That way it looks like your going to turn. Turn into the street and turn around and come out. Turn right and follow them at a safe distance. They went in the direction of town. He turned onto the street that goes to his house, not hers, she went down two blocks and came back and parked on the opposite side of the street. His car was out in front of his house. She said, "He probably had other things on his mind." I don't think we have to worry. She drove back to her house, went in, and picked up the note by using a spring-loaded clothespin. She brought it out to the car and let Andy hold it. She took them back to the motel. They told her not to forget, make sure you find two or three places farther out of town to meet. Use the same code you're using now, only in a week or so, change numbers for the restaurants. That way he would never know which one you were going to. They said good night, got out of the car, and went inside. As she was driving out of the driveway she looked in her rear view mirror. She jammed on the brakes. The room was engulfed in flames. A figure was running from the room. She parked the car and went after the figure that was running. The figure got into a car and took off. She was able to see and get the marker number. She ran back to the room, Jack and Andy was standing outside. They were badly burned, their clothes were still smoking. The fire truck and police cars were coming. Andy told Alma to get out of there fast. They would be all right, she got in her car and left. Days later she went to the hospital to see them; they were doing pretty good considering what they went through. She asked them what she should do with the marker number. Jack said to give it to him, he would have it traced. Their hands face and hair were burnt. The Doctor said he didn't think there would be any scarring, and that they should be out in a few days to a week. The paper said that a robbery was in progress when the two men came in and surprised them, the thief ran away. No clues as to what was missing or who the crook was. It was still under investigation. That's all, for the next four days nothing was printed. Detective Cloud had been in to see them a few times. Jack gave Cloud the marker number and the note, he asked if he would check the marker and to see if there were any prints on the note. They still were not able to find out who the four prints belonged to. No film has been found, Judge Lipton was worried. They had looked all over for the film. Nothing.... Andy got out of the hospital first. His face and hands were mostly soot and some burns. He had to watch out for the next few days so that they don't get infected. Jack got it the worst. He was farther back in the room when they turned the light switch on. They only got a glimpse of the figure. They were lucky to get out of there alive. Now comes the question... Was the place being robbed or were they planting a bomb? Are they known as FBI or what? The Fire Marshall came over to see them. Hoping to get some information from them. While the fire Marshall was there Chief Rose came in, then the Fire Chief. The room was getting crowed. Andy said maybe he could answer the questions because Jack was all bandaged and didn't see anything. The Fire Marshall asked if he saw anyone leave the room. He said, "Yes he did, however not too clear. He looked like a white male, dressed in black. The Fire Chief wanted to know what they were doing in town. They told him and the rest that they both were told to come here and check a complaint on Judge Lipton, and that's what they were doing. They were getting ready to leave town and write there report, when they heard the janitor of the courthouse was hung. They thought they would hang around for a few more days and see if they could help. The Fire Chief asked if they found anything out about the Judge. Andy said, "Only that he wasn't very friendly, and was all business. He took his cases very seriously and it appears he was a hard working man. If you have something to add to that, we would like to hear it. You can talk now or we'll stay and you can talk with us later.

Judge Lipton doesn't seem to be very popular in town. The former Judge Webster was a well liked Judge. So far we haven't heard too many good things about this Judge. I would like to say this, "Anything that is said in this room, must stay in this room. Is that understood? If not you can all leave now, and nothing more will be said. You never know when some idiot may try and do you harm. Understood, good. Close the door and let's talk, This was not a robbery, we have nothing in our room that contains fuel of any kind and there are no gas pipes, so who ever was there was looking for something in particular. If they couldn't find it, and they though that it was hidden in there they wanted to make sure no one else found it. He looked at the fire chief and said, did you find out what caused the fire, and where did it start. The Chief said they think it was a bottle filled with gasoline and a rag stuck in the neck. You could smell gasoline all over in the room. Andy said my theory was right then. I'll bet they were looking for the tapes. They didn't have time to search good when we came back so they lit the fuse and ran. Have you found anything else out?" Both the Fire Warden and the Fire Chief said, "They were still working on it." Andy said, "To please let him know if they find anything else out. He said I know you men have a lot to do so you can go back to work. And thank you both."

Andy asked if they had gotten any reports back on the marker plate or prints from the note. The Chief said "the marker plate and car belong to a Mrs. Shirley Gates" and the fingerprints were smudged but what they could get from them, it looked like one of the prints we couldn't identity. This Gates woman is the mother of Carl Gates. Carl is the boy that hangs around with Karen. Everybody seamed to think he's a pretty nice lad. Why would he be mixed up in something like this... unless he's a member of the RG's? Why would this Gates boy want to blow up the motel where these two men were staying?Unless somebody told him to. Somebody that had a lot of pressure on the kid. Maybe like we'll harm your girl friend if you don't do what we say. Or we would do something to your mother. Andy thought for a minute, on the way home we followed Judge Lipton's car all the way to his house. Alma said, "She knew the women that got into the car at the Restaurant, she even said her name, Shirley Gates.I'll bet anything that's what happened; they put so much pressure on the kid he had to do it. We have to talk with Alma and Karen before we talk with the Gates woman.

They left the hospital and went over to Alma's house. They rang the doorbell. Alma had just dialed the number for Judge Webster; she hung up the phone and went to the door. The Chief and Andy were outside. She told them to come in. What can I do for you gentlemen? Andy said he needed some information. "What do you know about Carl?" She looked surprised, why do you ask? Andy told her, "The marker number she gave to him was from Mrs. Gates' car." Alma couldn't say anything for a few minutes. "Carl" what would Carl went from these two men. She started thinking. Carl called and wanted to talk to Karen, he wanted to take her to a basketball game. Karen told him she had to work, baby-sitting at the Ballard house. Carl was not too happy and hung the phone up. That would mean Carl was the only other person that knew Karen would be at the Ballard house. What we need now are fingerprints from Carl there's a possibility that he may have left that note. The next question is why? Why would he want to hurt Karen? Is he under Lipton's finger too, or is he the leader? He must be hanging around our house trying to find out things. He then would report back to Judge Lipton. Lipton would call Hewitt and Hewitt would call Sam or vice-versa. They would get one of there people to do the dirty work. If he gets caught, he would go before Judge Lipton, and Lipton would get him off easy. That sounds reasonable; now what kind of power does he have at the Capital? This is the big question. We still haven't been able to figure that one out. Andy asked Alma, have you called Judge Webster yet? I remember you saying you were going to call him. She said "no" she hadn't. Things have been happening too fast around here. She said she just hasn't had time to figure everything out. As a matter of fact, I had just dialed the number when you rang. I hung up before it had a chance to ring. Now I'm pretty sure my phone is not tapped. Carl was the one that said Karen was over at the Ballard home. He must be the one that told Judge Lipton. Why would he leave a note under our door? Maybe he thought Karen would be home before me. Let's have a talk with Carl maybe he's home now. How do we get to his house? I would like a full set of fingerprints also. Maybe, before we talk with Carl we should talk with Judge Webster. Andy asked Alma if she would ring that number again. She said no problem, she picked up the phone and pushed redial. The phone rang a few times, and then Bessie answered. Alma was so happy, Bessie how are you all? This is Alma. I've missed you all so much. They talked for a few minutes, and then Alma asked to speak with the Judge. Bessie said hold on a minute, I'll have to go out and get him, and he's working in the garden. Alma looked at her watch; gosh she said I forgot there is a time difference out there. She looked at both of them and said, "He's out in the garden working." She's gone after him. That was Bessie, the owner of the Ranch. She's almost 100 years old. What a lady and she still has young ideas too. While she was waiting, she told them a little about the Ranch. How she makes everyone that lives there work. They pay her about $10.00 a week, that's for lights, heat; water an a few miscellaneous things. They have to work for their keep. If there's any money left over, like when I was there, they would have a big outdoor cookout. What a time that is, she started to tell them about it when Judge Webster got on the phone. He was happy to hear from her. He had a lot to tell her; he started by saying he found out what hold Lipton has at the capitol. Lipton's former wife is married to the Chief Justice and guess what? She hasn't gotten a divorce from Lipton. The Chief Justice will do what ever she wants him to do. He doesn't want it gotten out about his wife. Plus the fact that she's a lesbian. How does that sound? We are checking now to see if the governor is involved. What a mess this will be

if he is. Half of the Capital building will be guilty of
something. First they would check all the Lawyers,
then all the contractors, all the elected people. Did
anyone get paid off for getting certain jobs, receive
gifts or money. Did they have work done around their
homes, or property no charge? This could take weeks
or even months, maybe even years. What a time, this
could even go right down to Washington with the
senators and state representatives. I hate to think of
what could happen, all because a Judge thought he
was God. This will have to be kept quiet for a while;
I have a lot of checking to do before this gets out.
Now he said, "What do you have to say?" She told
him Chief Rose and the F.B.I. Man Andy was with
her. He wanted to know what happened to Jack. Alma
started telling him all about the problems back here.
How the janitor was found hanging in the garage at
his house. How they are checking the needle marks
out and trying to find what they are from. The big
news is this, Hewitt, my ex -husband, the one you
sent to prison, Well, we found out his first wife and
Sam the ex -policeman's ex- wife were the same. We
also found out that Judge Lipton's wife and Hewitt's
wife were sisters. That makes Hewitt and Sam plus
Judge Lipton are all Brother-in-Laws. NOW you tell
us that Lipton's former wife, who is not divorced from
Lipton, is married to the Chief Justice, what a story.
Judge Webster cut in and said, I will want all the
facts you can get for me? In the mean time, we will
be working on what's going on back at the Capital.
Who's involved in what, with whom? Don't forget,
don't let this out yet.

Alma left a note for Judge Hawter. It read 101600.
She wanted to tell Judge Hawter all about what Judge
Webster had said. This was a complicated mess, and
there was a lot more that has to be looked into. What
about Carl and his mother. What about the janitor
and the missing tapes he's looking for, what do these
tapes hold? Will they hold incriminating, so-called
facts on all the people at the courthouse, including
me? If that's the case, then he's really in hot water. He
may figure that he has everyone in the courthouse
under his thumb. What about Sam the ex-police
man, what kind of a hold does he have over him? His
wife is divorced from him so what has he got left, or
does Sam have something on Lipton. Maybe about
his wife breaking the law by not getting a divorce and
marrying the Chief Justice. That would make Lipton
look bad. These are just a few things that she will
talk over with Judge Hawter. At 6:00 sharp he pulled
into the rear parking lot. Walked down between the
cars and the lake. She said she would like to go some
place different. He thought that was a good idea.
This time they picked a restaurant about eight miles
out at the south end of town. That would be number
three. They would look for another place some other
time. He suggested Sunday afternoon. She would
have to check with Karen first, she may be working
at Bill's, if so Sunday would be fine. They stopped at
number three and had supper and talked. She told
him everything that happened. He had heard about
the fire and two men getting burnt. He said he didn't
realize that it was Andy and Jack.

Alma told him what Judge Webster had told them. Then she added what Andy and Jack had found out, to that. Now she started asking questions. Should she go to see Mrs. Gates and find out what was going on? What does Lipton have on her or her son? Does she know anything about the tapes? Judge Hawter smiled and said, "You should have been a lawyer." They both laughed. Judge Hawter said, "As long as you know Mrs. Gates, why not give it a try, she may be looking for someone to talk to. What have you got to lose? She also wanted him to write down everything that he could see wrong with Judge Lipton. This is one case we have to make sure is right. We have to have enough on him so that he can't squeeze out, by telling a bunch of lies.

Friday night Alma called Mrs. Gates, she asked her if she wasn't doing anything Saturday, she was going to have a cook out. Just a few friends from the courthouse, NO JUDGES. Also a few neighbors. At first she said, "She didn't think she could make it." With a little begging and persuasions, she said, "She would come." How about three in the afternoon? I'll make some steaks, salads, and some cool drinks. Bring Carl to if he wants to come. Karen should be home here also. Alma sent a note around to all the help in the Court House, inviting them to a cook out including Mrs. Gates. Alma made sure Shirley Gates got introduced to all the people. The weather was great, there must have been about eight or nine people there. Carl came later in the afternoon. Karen worked at Bill's till three thirty, by the time she changed and all it was close to four when she got home. She had just gotten in the yard when Carl came driving in. Karen was cold toward Carl, she hardly spoke to him. He was trying to break the ice. Finally he said, "We need to talk. Can I see you later tonight?" Karen said, "Yes, but I think we should have our mothers present. I am not in a very good mood today." The cookout went great; the party broke up around ten that night. The office girls really enjoyed them selves. This is like old times, one girl said, Remember how we use to have parties. It seems like every weekend something was going on. Now nobody wants to talk with anyone. I think this get together today is the best thing that could happen. Because of that conversation, people started talking. They had a few drinks in them and they started talking about Judge Lipton, and how he treated everyone differently. He tried; to blackmail everyone in the Court House. Those cameras he has all over, I'd like to rip them out of the walls. Some of the girls got together, let's block off the cameras so he can't see or hear what's going on. One of the girls said lets buy playboy and put a bare-ass babe in front of each camera. He's always trying to make time by blackmailing us girls; we'll give him something to look at. We will have to stick together and not let him know who did it. They all agreed, the next day he leaves early we will paste bare-ass babes over each camera. One of the girls said ...make sure you wear rubber gloves, knowing him, he'll send the pictures out, and have them fingerprinted. One girl was going to buy playboy, another was getting some rubber gloves, and another was getting some masking tape.

One girl said maybe we should use condoms, they all laughed. Another said... don't stand in front of the camera they may be still running, he then would know who did it. Jane said let's make sure that there's none in the ladies room. Maybe we should put a stiff you know what in that one if there is one. Again they all laughed. I don't trust him. When Shirley Gates heard what was going on, she started doing some talking to. But she mostly listened. It seemed like everyone there had something to say about him, and none of it was good. They decided to have a get together again next weekend. Two of the girls couldn't make it on Saturday, so they made it for Friday night. They all held hands and agreed one for all, and all for one. If he fires one, we'll all walk out regardless of what they were doing. We are many, he is one. I don't think he would like to see this in the newspaper. If he thinks he has anything on us. We will not heed to his wishes. He would not dare buck us. The hour was late when the party broke up. Everyone said" see you all next Friday night. Someone said, where shall we meet'? The women" Pearl" that works for Lipton said "how about my house at 7:00, we'll have tea. That's a good idea; we'll call our selves "The Tea Club."

They all laughed, and though that was a great name. Alma talked with Mrs. Gates for a few minutes. Karen said Carl wanted to talk with her. She wanted both of us there. How about tomorrow afternoon around 5. Mrs. Gates thought that would be ok. She said" how about at my house" Alma said fine. She called Judge Hawter and told him she would have to be back by five. And she told him why. He said. "It stays light late now, how about Monday when we get finished working. We can go for a ride and when we find a place that looks good we can go in and try there food. Alma thought that was a great idea.

At 5:00 Sunday, both Alma and Karen arrived at Shirley Gates, house. Mrs. Gates came out to meet them. My, what a lovely place you have here. Mrs. Gates said thank you, let's go around to the back. I have a surprise to show you, as they rounded the comer, she had a picture perfect view of the setting sun. They sat down, she asked them both, what would you like to drink? Alma and Karen both said Ice Tea would be fine. Alma was trying to figure out what the surprise was. Mrs. Gates came out with a pitcher of tea. Right behind, Carl came out with something in his arms. He went over to Karen and said, "Karen I'm truly sorry about the other night. I would like to make it up to you. He handed Karen a cute little dog. As he did, he said again, "I'm sorry, please take this as a peace offering." You can pick a name for him, he is house trained and very lovable, and she held him in her arms and started kissing him. He's adorable. She looked at her mother and asked, "Mom can I have him? I'll take good care of him. I promise." Alma looked at her and said, "If you promise to take good care of him, I'll let you have him but... if you don't take good care of him, I will return him to Carl, how's that. They all laughed. They sat down and started talking. This man gave Carl two tickets to the basket ball game last Saturday night. He said to take a friend. Carl thought that was great, so I called Karen. When she said she had to baby-sit, I was disappointed and hung up. The man was still there when I called. He asked me where she was setting. I told him tonight at the Ballard's. He said that was too bad. Maybe I should try someone else. I called this friend of mine and he said he'd like to go. So we went. The next day I heard what happened. It was my entire fault. That's when I came over to see you but no one was home, so I left the note under the front door. Alma asked if he knew the man that gave him the tickets. I said, "Not really, he had seen him around a few times." He didn't know his name, but maybe somebody would know. He said he would ask around. Alma again asked if he was a member of the R.G's. he waited a minute before answering. Finely he said he was. He got into a fight at school. Someone called the police and they took only me. The other kid that started it was a member of the R.G.'s. So he wasn't arrested. Judge Lipton said that if I cooperated with him, I would get off easy. That was about two weeks ago. By being arrested, he made me join the R.G.'s. I told him I didn't want to join. I didn't believe in it. He told me too bad... but I still have to join. He said if I didn't he would take my mother's drivers license away and mine also. I told him I'd see our lawyer, he said I would be sorry. The next day he called my mother, and very nicely asked my mother to go out with him. He said he had something very important to talk to her about. He picked her up at the house. They went to a Restaurant and had supper. What he wanted to talk about wasn't that important. He then brought her to his place. He tried to Rape her.

He said if she didn't cooperate, he would make sure I would be in real trouble. Very calmly she told him this is not the right time. He let her go. He said he would see her another time. They got in the car and he drove her home. She told me what happened; I was ready to kill him. He told me he would have me put in jail if I told anyone. What kind of Judge is he? Alma told them how these two men are looking into things they have heard about him. They are working on the hanging of the janitor also. Only that is on the Q.T. so please don't say anything about it. All this will be in the report that will be filled against him. It would be good if you could write all of this down just the way you told me. The date and time and the place you went too, everything including him trying to rape you. What he said about putting Carl in jail if you said anything. Carl looked at Karen and said I truly am sorry if I had known, I never would have told him about you. Please believe me... Karen got off her chair and went over and gave Carl a big kiss on the cheek. Both Alma and Mrs. Gates felt a lot better. Alma said if Lipton calls again, stall about the time, tell him you will have to call him back if it's ok with him, be nice. Then give me a call, I'll see that you are followed all evening.

Nothing was said at the Court House about any meets, at least as far as Alma could see or hear. Everyone acted the same as before, no one talking with anyone. But they couldn't wait till Judge Lipton left early so they could cover the cameras. Just for spite, he worked late every night. She started wondering if maybe someone may have told him what we were going to do. She thought for a while, who should she watch. Who would be the ass-kisser? Would he have enough on someone to threaten them maybe! She started thinking the only outsiders that were at the house was Shirley Gates and Carl and Karen. Alma was almost positive that it wasn't any of them. Carl wouldn't tell anyone... I don't think he would, but he belongs to the R.G.'s. Now... Maybe, just maybe. She started going down the list... first was Pearl she's the secretary in Judge Lipton's chamber. Then Ruby, she was Judge Hawter's secretary. Then Jane, she was new; she had only been there about six months (possible)... Marge was Judge Silverman's secretary. Neither one like Lipton. Alma started thinking, Jane... she was a floater, she covered for all the secretary's when they were out, or over loaded with work. All the rest had been there for a long time, at least for four years if not longer. She kept thinking of Jane... WHY. ? She was pretty, had a good figure, great personality, and always had a smile. She was the life of the party. What did she do before she came here? Alma thought she would get to know her better. For that matter, maybe she could have Jack or Andy check her out. What was her last name? Friday before she left the Court House she went into the personal office. Alice and Alma started talking. Alma asked Alice if she wanted to join our Tea Club. She explained everything to her. Alice got all excited; she said she would love to join. Anything for a little excitement, this place is like a morgue since Lipton got here. As Alma was about to leave, she got to the door, turned around and asked... Alice, what's Jane's last name? Alice thought for a minute. Hardwick. Jane Hardwick. Thanks said Alma and left. When she got home she called the motel.

Andy was going over the Police report on the Janitor's hanging, and the car. That's funny he thought, fresh tar on the tires. Where had they tarred the roads? He'll have to check that out, and drew a line under tar, and started to read on. That fingerprint showed up a few more times, on the door handle, back of the mirror, and glove compartment door. In the ashtray was a key, they thought it was his locker key at the courthouse; he drew a line under key. They went to try the key in his locker, but the locker was open so they didn't bother. They just put it back in the ashtray. He wanted that key. The needle marks were made from a size twenty-one gauge needle and they found traces of a heavy dose of insulin in his system. He is not diabetic and never used insulin. That's what they figure killed him, an over dose. The rest of the report was pretty much routine. He was very interested in the tar, and the key. He called the Chief and asked if he could find out where the most resent roads were tarred, also what was at the end of each road. The Chief said he would try and get back to him. Andy went out and bought a map of the town, the only problem was, it didn't say what was on each street, or at the ends. Right now he was more interested in the tar. He had just put the report down when the phone rang. It was Alma, first she wanted to know how Jack was. He told her, he thought he would be coming back in a day or so. She was happy to hear that. Then she asked if he could do her a favor on the Q.T. He said he would try. "What do you need?" She told him about this new girl at the Court House named Jane Hardwick, she would like all the info that she could get, and also on Shirley Gates.

That night all the girls met at Pearl's house. Alma started by telling the new girls that the talk at this meeting was going to be about Judge Lipton, and if they didn't want anything to do with the conversations, they could leave now. They stayed; Alma introduced them to every one. Alice was down in personal, and Nancy was secretary to Judge Bill James. They talked about how Lipton had cameras all over and that they were going to cover them up. She also said if Judge Lipton had any personal vendettas against anyone, this is the club to be long too. We will stick together, regardless. Nancy was a blonde about 5' 10" and built like a brick... very pleasant and easy to talk with. Alice was 5' 2" and had reddish brown hair. She, like Nancy was a divorcee. Both of these girls would be a catch for Lipton. Make sure that you don't get caught in his web. They were both extremely good-looking girls. And very friendly. I'm sure Judge Lipton must have tried to make a pass at you both some time or another. "That's ok if he has, just be careful." That goes for the rest of us to. He will use anything he gets his hands on, so keep one arm over your chest and the other down below. They all laughed. I've been through it, so I'm talking from experience. Pearl brought out the tea and cake she made, and also some sugar free cookies. They all let their hair down, they were talking about everything, problems with there ex-husbands, boyfriends, neighbors. You name it, the subject was brought up. They all had a great time. The girls that worked with Judge Webster were talking how they use to meet once or twice a month and have a ball.

Like this meeting, only we didn't talk about the Judges. They were all great. We had Christmas parties, Birthday parties, showers, you name it, and we had a lot of fun. Then this jerk came along. Everything changed, we don't even smile anymore. He would hold that against us. Please, don't say anything about these meetings at the courthouse. If you went to talk, send a note, but make sure that it is sealed. Isn't this disgusting, that's probably why he wants those tapes. He said they were personal cases, and didn't want anyone looking at them. "Bullshit, if I get my hands on these tapes, I'll stay up all night looking at them. We'll show them at our next meeting. But we'll have to find them first." It was getting late and some wanted to go home. They all joined hands and swore, no outside talk about these meetings and planned for the next meeting to be in about two weeks unless something important comes up.

Monday Andy and Jack got a message from Headquarters, they have checked out the two women. Jane Hardwick, Age 38, was born in Ohio. Went to High Boardman College in Boardman Penn. Graduated in Business. She worked her way up to manager of field sales. She was in charge of all the sales people for the medical supply division of the company. She worked there for 18 years. She got married when she was 24, to one of the top salesmen of the company. Everyone thought, that was the marriage of the year and it would last forever. They got a divorce after 10 years. He was an alcoholic, and he played around. His sales went down to practically nothing so the company dismissed him. She worked there for about eight years more, but the company started going down hill because of foreign products coming in at a lower price. They are now in chapter II. She took a few years off, did a few odd jobs, and then got the one she has now. She came with very good references.

Shirley Gates, age thirty-nine, was born in Utah, went to Yale in New Haven, Connecticut. She didn't graduate. She was very sick for about three years. She missed one year of graduating. She married Howie Gates. They were married for eleven years. Six years age he died in a plane crash. She received a nice piece of change from the insurance company. She was a stay-at-home mom, till he got killed. She went to work as a sales manager in a ladies dress store. She worked there for two years. This job was closer to home so she left that one and took his one. She works for an insurance co. her base pay is $59.000.00 per year plus expenses. She has some traveling to do...but not to often.

Jack came back to work Monday. He still has bandages over some of the burn areas. He wanted to get out of the hospital; it was driving him crazy doing nothing. Andy made sure that he didn't do any manual work.

He could answer the phone and write out reports for Andy that's all. He called the police station and asked for Detective Cloud. The operator said he was not in at the present time. He asked, if she would have him call when he gets in. She said, "One minute please. He waited a few minutes and Cloud came on the phone." He asked if there were any bus stations between here and downtown. He also wanted the key that was in the ashtray of the car. Cloud said he never saw a key in the cars ashtray. What kind was It.? Jack looked at Andy. He doesn't know anything about a key. Detective Cloud said, "There must be a mistake. He'll get right back to us, and hung up." Thirty minutes later, Chief Rose called, He said, "There was a bus station about three miles at the north end of town. The road had been tarred about a week before the janitor hung himself. As far as a train station, besides the one in town. The next was about 10 miles north, up in Forestville. The only trouble there was, no roads had been tarred near or around the area. Andy asked him if he had the key that was in the ashtray of the janitor's car." He said no, "He had not seen it but he would check with Detective Cloud and see what he has to say. He said he would call us back, and hung up." Andy and Jack looked at each other, what the hell do we have here a dishonest Police Department or a crooked cop? Andy said, "It says right here in the report that there was a key in the ashtray." Jack said, "He was going to call the police station and find out who wrote this report, and did the Chief or Detective Cloud read it before it was sent out. He also wanted to know the names of the officers that checked the car over. There names were not on the report, why?" Andy said "I think I'll take a ride over and take a look at the car myself." Jack wanted to go, but Andy wouldn't think of it. He was gone for over 3 hours. When he came back, he had a stack of notes that he had made, plus the notes that he found on the seat of the car. The ashtray was missing, he asked one of the inspectors what happened to it? He said, "He though they sent it out to have it checked for fingerprints. There seamed to have oil or something on it. They wanted the State Police to check it over. Where are the Lab men that went over the car?" Andy asked, "They only come when they are needed? The officer said. Andy wanted to know what they did in the mean time. The officer didn't know. The Chief or Detective Cloud could probably give you the answer. Andy left and went back to the motel. Detective Cloud hadn't been to the garage, so he must have talked with the Lab Men that checked the car. When Andy got back to the motel, Jack had some news. The Chief said, "He was on vacation and at a police Chiefs convention when all of this happened." Detective Cloud hadn't called in as yet so we don't know what's going on with him. Andy started reading some of the notes that were left on the seat. They had check marks that covered just about everything. The engine was gone through; the interior of the car had been vacuumed out. The inside had been gone over for fingerprints and blood. The trunk was vacuumed out and also checked for blood and any other things that they could find. Detective Cloud called back, he sounded irritable. He said he had glanced at the report, but was very busy because the Chief was on vacation and at a convention and he was in charge. He had them make some copies and send them out to you. He didn't remember reading about a key. He called the Lab boys that went through the car from bumper to bumper. They said the ashtray had something like an oily finish on it. They sent it to the State Police Lab. To have it checked out. The key must still be in it, he's checking it out now. Andy asked what the inspector's did when there's nothing to inspect. Detective Cloud said, "Right now they are going through the dust and dirt the vacuum cleaner picked up from the front of the car. That will take about a week, then the same with the back seat and floor. Then they have the trunk to go through. They hit the high spots first. They will be working on the tires later. Jack took the phone and asked what he thought of Judge Lipton? Cloud said he thought the guy was a little nuts, he isn't a well-liked man, that's for sure. Andy and Jack looked over all the notes and material that was left on the seat of the car. They could find nothing, except for the key. They were hoping Cloud would call and say "we found the key" but ...we'll have to wait and see.

Monday after work, Alma met Judge Hawter and they drove west out of town. They went for ten or twelve miles, they didn't find anything that looked decent. They decided to turn around at the next intersection, and maybe take another road home. They made a left turn at the light; there on the left was a restaurant that looked pretty good. There were a number of cars outside so they thought they would give it a try. This place was not a diner but a very nice restaurant. They were shone to a booth and given menus. Water was brought over and a very nice waitress asked if they were ready to order. They said "Yes and told her what they wanted". After she left, Alma started telling him about the TEA CUP CLUB. How all the girls at the Court House were going to stick together and not let Lipton boss them around. Judge Hawter (Clarence) said" don't get too smart, this man has a lot of power so be careful, it's better to get something on him, then to just talk." They talked for a long time. Clarence looked at his watch. My gosh, it's getting late. Karen will be wondering where you are. When they got to the car, he reached over and opened the door for her and helped her in. She didn't say anything but" THANK YOU." As they drove up the road, he looked at her and said "do you suppose we could go out on a date some time? I mean someplace where we don't have to talk shop all evening. She put her hand on his arm and said I'd like that.

Eight o'clock Tuesday morning, things began to happen. The phone rang in the motel. It was detective Cloud, they found the key. He said they are bringing it over to you now. Second the fingerprint that they couldn't identify belonged to the janitor's wife. Third the ashtray that had that oily stuff on it, well that. That oily stuff happened to be cosmetic preparation for the skin. It was wiped off, that's ware the oily look came from. They did however remove a fingerprint. It looks like a female, by the size of it. Either that or a small hand from a man or child, this is going to make it harder to find. Females don't have there finger prints taken that much unless they have broken the law. Could he have had a girl friend? Cloud said he had a meeting to go to but he would call back later. Just as Jack was hanging up the phone, there was a knock at the door. Andy went over and opened it. A plain clothed man handed a small package to him and left. Not a word was said... he opened the package and found the key. That's what he was waiting for. Andy told Jack he was going down to the train station, if he had no luck there he was going over to the bus station... he took the map with him. He figured he would go by the same route from the Court House that the janitor would take. He went to the train station first. There keys were different from what he had. He went out and got in his car and drove over to the bus station. He could see that the road had been oiled not to long ago. He pulled over on the side of the road, got out and checked the tires, there was still some tar stuck to the tires. It was a warm day so the tar was still a little soft. Andy pulled up in front of the bus station, got out of the car and went inside. He walked over to the lockers and checked the keys. The one he has matched some of the others. Now witch locker does this one fit. He started checking one by one. The manager came over and asked what the hell you think your doing. Andy told him he was trying to find the locker that this key fits. The manager said" give me the key and get the hell out." Andy reached in his pocket and showed the man his badge. The manager said he was sorry, he didn't know. Andy said" he was proud of the man because he was protecting people's property." The man asked for the key, looked at it, and said that locker is over here. He put the key in the lock and turned it, the door opened. Andy opened the door; there must have been a dozen tapes. Andy asked if he could us the phone. He called the police station and asked for Detective Cloud or Chief Rose. Cloud came to the phone, Andy explained where he was and wanted someone to check for fingerprints now and hung up. Detective Cloud and two other Detectives were there within ten minutes. There were 27 tapes, the two Detectives checked each one for fingerprints and numbered them. Now to check them out. We have to make sure these tapes belong to the Judge. Detective Cloud and the other two Detectives worked there for more then 2½ hours. Cloud asked Andy if he wanted to run them and make sure these were Judge Lipton's tapes. Andy looked at Cloud and said, "I think we auto, they could be tapes that belong to someone else, and maybe even they could belong to the janitor." The detectives boxed them up and taped them. The manager came over with some papers for Detective Cloud to sign. The detective said, "This could be evidence on a case we are working on." They took the box back to the police headquarters. Andy went back to the Motel and picked up Jack, he wanted him to see them also. Detective Cloud had the two Detectives, Andy and Jack along with himself sign a paper that what they are about to see, unless as evidence would not be told to anyone. They took the tapes at random and started showing them. This was going to be a long night. The first tape was showing Court Trials, they went halfway and stopped. Cloud said we could see the rest another time. Make sure you mark the tape as such. Andy didn't like that, there could be something at the end, Andy agreed and ran the hole tape, only now they played it at fast forward. They still could make things out... Tapes two thru eleven were all the same. Tape twelve showed Andy and Jack talking with the janitor. The sound was very clear and they could hear everything. They didn't play the complete tape, they would do that later. The next few tapes were ok; tape seventeen had the janitor talking with Judge Lipton. The janitor was yelling at Lipton, he wanted out. He didn't care what he had on him; Lipton told him he could have him put away for a long time. The janitor said he didn't care. If he went so would you {meaning the judge) the Judge was livid... He said he had too much power to even think about going. They were screaming at each other. They stopped the tape and put that one side with a note on it. The next four tapes showed what went on in other parts of the building. Lawyers talking with clients, secretary's talking with each other, and etc. The tape was put aside and marked also. Tape twenty-four showed Alma in the Judge's chambers, going through some files. She found one and read it. She had her back to the camera and replaced the file. Lipton thought she took the folder out of his office). the film showed she went out empty handed. He had a special mark put on that one. That last tape showed the janitor and one of the secretaries making out in one of the chambers. That tape was also put aside and marked. Eight tapes had things that didn't belong to the court... 19 were court related. This alone is enough to convict him and have him thrown off the bench. The next thing is... why or who hung the Janitor? They still think it was murder.

That night when they got back to the motel, Andy called Alma. He told her all the tapes were found, there is a lot of things on them that are not court related. Eight out of twenty seven were personal, things like watching what goes on in the hallways, listening to the different lawyers talking with their clients, and so on. He wanted to get all the evidence together and send it to Judge Webster. We will print out what we find on the tapes, plus what ever else we can get on him. Alma was so excited she could hardly sleep. Wait till she tells Judge Hawter. Andy said to keep it under wraps for a while. They want to spring it on him when Judge Webster say's it's ok to do so. He wants all the evidence he can get. They still have the hanging of the janitor. Once we get Judge Lipton. We should have the people that did the janitor in. If I'm right, when Lipton gets caught and can't get out. He's going to cry like a baby. He'll spill the beans as though what happened, and blame everybody else. I can just see him now hollering "I AM GOD; you can't do this to me." The next two days they went over the tapes with a fine-toothed comb. They made copies of the most important stuff and had it sent to Judge Webster. The judge went over all of it, plus all the paperwork on what he has done to all the help. Every woman that worked in the courthouse had something to write about Judge Lipton, the God. Even Mrs. Shirley Gates sent a letter, telling what he tried to do to her and her son. She told everything. Alma did the same. Karen wrote and told how the R.G.s that was run by Judge Lipton almost ruined her life, and the lives of a lot of other good kids. Judge Webster called Alma and told her he had some good news and some bad. First he was happy to think that at last we have enough on Judge Lipton. But after checking real deep into the workings of the state capitol, we find a lot of corruption at the same office building. We are still checking and it is getting deeper. A lot of big names come up. We haven't received anything bad so far on the governor. He looked pretty clean. If we can find nothing on him in the next couple of weeks I'm going to call him, and have him come down here. I think he would be happy to. He seems like a straight shooter. How are we going to get rid of Judge Lipton with all this hanging over our heads? He does have a lot of power at the Capitol. For now we will have to wait and see how the Governor makes out. If he's clean, I'll bring all this to his attention. This will be a big problem for him.

After Judge Webster hung up, Alma just stared out the window. What are we going to do with Judge Lipton? We have so much on him and can't use it. She looked at the time, ten o'clock. No wonder she felt tired. She went into the kitchen, heated up some milk and went up stairs, changed into her nightclothes. Drank the milk and went to bed. The next morning at the Court House, everything seemed different. It seems everyone was talking with each other. She went over to one of the girls and asked, what's going on? Pearl asked" didn't you hear? Alma said, "For heaven sakes, hear what? Sue Ann's husband killed the janitor. He caught them making out. They're both down at the police headquarters, that new detective found out what was going on. That's all we know now. I always' thought Sue Ann had the hots for Judge Butler, a couple of the girls said the same thing. Just then Judge Hawter came around the corner on his way to his chambers. He stopped, looked at all the women, they stopped talking when they saw him... He smiled said "good morning" and went on. A few girls said they would like to work in his chamber. Alma didn't say anything, she just listened. She never gave it a thought as how the females talked about the Judges till now. She happened to look up, there on the air duct was a picture, and it looked like a nude girl. She looked around and started to laugh. The rest hadn't noticed it before. When they looked up, they all started laughing. Alma waved her arms and motioned to be quiet. They all moved out and went there separate ways. At lunchtime they all went out into the parking lot to eat. The big news was Sue Ann and the nude pictures hanging over the air conditioner vents. They made out that they new nothing about the pictures. Just in case he was watching and was lip reading. All together they found six cameras and covered them all with the nude girl's pictures. They thought eating outside in the good weather, was fun.

It was a few day's later that everything came out in the paper. Sue Ann's husband was a diabetic, a very bad diabetic. She hadn't had any loving in a long time so the janitor had gotten a room in a motel out on route 41. They would meet once a week. Her husband followed her one afternoon and "bingo" there they were. He had a gun and barged into the room, held the Janitor against the wall. Took his insulin needle and gave him 2 big doses of insulin. Then he left, he never said a word. Got in his car and drove home. Sue Ann came home an hour later. She walked into the bedroom and started packing. Her husband came in, and wanted to know what she was doing. She hung her head and said in a low voice, "I'm sorry... I'm very sorry. I just needed some loving. You are a very good husband, but I needed more... You never hold me, or give me a hug once in awhile. You never put your hands on me. You never make love or even run your hands over my body. I needed some attention. I didn't mean to cheat on you, I just wanted some attention. I know you can't make love like we used to do; I would have been satisfied with just some heavy petting. I just wanted some attention. He hung his head and started crying, He said "what have I done? I have maimed him, I lost my head... At least I'm glad I didn't kill him. She looked at him and said he's in my car now... He passed out. He ran out to tell him he was sorry. When he got to the car, the janitor was slumped down in the seat. He opened the door, the janitor didn't look good, he tried to get a pulse, but he could feel none. He started to panic, he ran back into the house yelling for Sue Ann. He told her the janitor is dead. I killed the janitor, oh my god, what am I going to do. He thought for a few minutes. He then told Sue Ann what he had in mind. She never said a word. They drove back to the motel and got the janitors car. They then went to the janitor's house. They were going to leave him in the garage, and then he said "Let's make it look like he hung himself. That's what they did, and that's how they found him.

The newspaper had big headlines, for a few days. Sue Ann's husband was held under $500,000.00 bond and Sue Am] under $25,000.00. Alma called Judge Webster, he new Sue Am very good, she used to work in his Court Room. Judge Webster was sorry to hear about it. He liked the Janitor and Sue Ann and her husband. Now if only we could get Lipton out of the way, things would be back to normal. He said, "He would get back to her in a day or so." There was a few thinks he wanted to do first. He knew the Chief Justice very well. He worked in Judge Webster's Court Room when he was a lawyer, years ago. Years later he was appointed the Judge ship. About 7 or 8 years ago he was appointed Chief Justice. He had a lot of pull in the Capital even at that time.

Judge Webster made a person-to-person phone call to Chief Justice Frances Ramprest. The operator said" I'm sorry, but Chief Ramprest is busy at the present time, can you call back another time. Judge Webster was getting angry, he told the operator he wanted to talk with Judge Ramprest NOW, not later but NOW. She put him on hold, a few minutes later Judge Ramprest got on the phone. Hello Judge Webster... sorry for the mix up. We have a new girl on the switchboard. What can I do for you? I'm pretty busy, but let's see if

I can help you. Judge Webster asked him if he knew Judge Lipton. The Chief said... yes he had heard of him, what's the trouble? The Judge said you must know him; he took over my Court when I retired. The Chief said yes... He requested the position and it was open. Then you knew that I requested Judge Hawter for the job. The Chief said, yes... but it's too bad the request didn't come sooner. We had already given it to Judge Lipton. Judge Webster very quietly said, that's strange, the request I sent was three months before I retired. No one, even my staff didn't know I was retiring. Now you are telling me you didn't receive it. I have here in my hand a signature, signed by you, that you received my request. Now, let's not play around. Your wives husband is in hot water, and I can assure you, you will be swimming in the same mud pond that your wife... her husband... Her sister and her two husbands will be in. This Lipton thinks he's God. I have received a lot of complaints about him. I've sent 2 men over there to find out what's going on. I have a stack of papers plus tapes of your wives husband that will put you and him, plus your wife in jail for a very long time. If you don't think so, try me. I may not be setting on a bench anymore, but I am still a high Court Judge. Now let me ask you, how much time do you have now?" The chief said, "There must be some mistake; my wife had gotten an annulment from Judge Lipton shortly after her sister got hers." The Judge said, "That's strange; my people went through all the records and didn't find a single sheet of paper that said she got a divorce. I also understand your wife and her sister are lesbians. I also understand that your brother-in-law thinks he's God. This I know, as a fact. I have a big stack of papers here that were written by independent women. Women that don't know what the other one wrote. They all say the same thing. I would think that would mean Blackmail. Telling everyone, you have to do it my way because I am GOD, or I am Judge Lipton and if you don't do it my way you will be sorry. You and I know different don't we Judge. I want you out to salt Lake City tomorrow afternoon, be at the Court House no later then 5 PM our time. If you do not come, I will guarantee you, the headlines in Friday's paper; all over the country will have your picture on the front page. Judge Webster hung up. He was sweating when he got off the phone.

Chief Justice Ramprest called his secretary into his office. He said, "Cancel all my appointments for the rest of the week. I have some personal business in Salt Lake City; get me a plane ticket for either tonight or the first thing in the morning. He looked at her and said "DON'T JUST STAND THERE DO SOMETHING." He called George Hewitt. He was at work. He called there, the phone operator wanted to know who was calling, the Chief was getting pissed, I want to talk with George Hewitt NOW, and if you like your job, you'll get him NOW. Do you under stand? She said very sweetly, mister I don't know who you are and I don't give a damn; you can take this job and shove it. "I Quit" she got up from her desk, took off her earphones, through them on the table, and walked out. The Chief Justice was left holding a dead phone. He hung up, called Judge Lipton, the operator was very sweet, and asked may I help you? He said, this is Chief Justice Ramprest, and I want to speak with Judge Lipton at once. She said one mo-mite please, Judge Lipton got on the phone. "What the hell do you mean, calling me away from my bench? What the hell do you want?" The Chief told Lipton what happened, he then said," What kind of hell have you been raising? You thinking you're GOD... I have to meet Judge Webster at 5 o'clock in the Salt Lake City Court House tomorrow. He will not stand for any bullshit. I'm not sure how I'm going to handle this, but believe me; I will not go down alone. Lipton said, "He has nothing on any of us." The Chief said, "That's what you think. he knows about our wives, he knows about getting George out of jail, he knows about all of your freaking' cameras in the court house, he knows about all the females you've screwed and blackmailed in the court house and outside of the court house, and that's only the beginning, and your telling me, he has nothing on us. You had better straighten your act out, starting right now." Ramprest called his wife; "Did you get an annulment from Lipton before we got married?" She gave a little sigh, why do you have to bring that up now, I'm just going out to do some shopping, he said, "Screw the shopping, answer me yes or no? I think I forgot to. Why do you ask? He hung up the phone. He was really worried now; he could just see the headlines now CHIEF JUSTICE RAMPREST NOT MARRIED TO HIS LESBIAN WIFE......

He started pacing the floor back and forth, back and forth. How did I ever get myself into this mess? That fucking lesbian woman I married, everything was fine till then. Well, almost ok. I had Lipton on my ass all the time. Now I'm going to lose everything I've worked hard for, all because of that ass hole Lipton, and his family. Thinking he's God, I could see the devil, but not God... Now if Webster starts checking deep enough, he could probably bring the whole capitol and everyone in it down. I know that half are crocks, and the other half I wouldn't bet on. The only one I would trust would be the Governor. He is an honest man. He has a lot to learn. What am I going to do... it's getting hot in here; now the air conditioning has broken down. What next, as he loosened his tie and top button of his shirt He opened the bottom drawer of his desk and took out his bottle of VAT 69 Blended Scotch Whisky. A contractor would show his appreciation for his good deeds and send him a case of his favorite booze every few   months. After a few big slugs of VAT 69, he said to himself, I think I'll write down everyone's name and the graft they have been taking and for how many years. If I don't do it now, I would forget it later. Including the past Governor and right on down to the floor sweeper. If I go everybody goes. That includes JUDGE LIPTON, George Hewitt, Sam the private detective, plus the two Lesbian's and everybody else. He looked at his watch, it was getting late He checked with the secretary, how did you make out on the plane tickets? She said the best she could do was 12 noon our time. He started figuring 12 noon our time, that's 3 hours earlier there time which would be 9 o'clock our time. That would bring him into Salt Lake City round noon there time. He then would have a few hours to look around. He had never been that far west. He would need some time to think things over before he met with Webster. The plane was a little late coming and going, so he didn't get into Salt Lake till a little after 1 o'clock. By the time he got a cab and got down to the center of town it was around 2:30. He found a hotel and registered for one night and possible two. He went out and started looking for the Court House and the Police Headquarters as he was looking in a store window he had a feeling someone was following him. He went across the street and was looking in a men's store window, again he saw this man in the window. Now he was getting nervous. He made sure he stayed where there was a crowd of people. Why did he bring his brief case with him? All he had in it was the notes he made the day before in his office. He turned the comer and as he did, a bunch of kids were practicing for the shows that go on in the winter. For a few minutes he forgot about the man that was following him. He started to mingle with the crowd. As he was watching, people were pushing trying to see better. He felt someone push, there was a burning feeling, and he went down. A man beside him said" this man has pasted out, someone call an ambulance, hurry." A policeman came running over to the man that was lying on the sidewalk. The man that was standing next to him had disappeared in he crowd. A few minutes went by and the ambulance came and took him to a hospital. He was in critical condition.

As they were removing his shirt they found it was full of blood. They ripped off his shirt and undershirt. There was a bullet hole. They called x-ray and told them they were bringing a patient up with a bullet hole, clear the table. They didn't see where the bullet had come out. He had lost a lot of blood; one doctor asked if anyone knew him. They started checking his pockets, they found his wallet. He is a Lawyer from New York, then someone said" He's Chief Justice Ramprest from Albany. Did he have any luggage, an over night bag or anything? He had a briefcase when they brought him in. Someone check and see where it is. Is he married, how about a phone number? If not somebody call the Capitol in Albany. They should have a lot of information on him. We need his wife or someone to give us the ok to operate at once. They took him up to x-ray to find where the bullet is lodged. Hopefully by then, they would have his wife on the phone.

Judge Webster was walking by when a large crowd gathered around a man on the sidewalk. The ambulance arrived and took a man away. It looked a little like Ramprest, but he was to far away to be sure. He walked down the street, taking his time because he was plenty early. He still had the picture of that man in this mind. He hadn't seen Judge Ramprest in a number of years, thinking back it had to be ten years if not more, since he had seen Ramprest. He was only a Judge then. But when you know the right people, the sky's the limit. Judge Webster went down to the Court House to see some of his old pal's. He was greeted with open arms. He saw friends he hadn't seen in years. He was a Judge here years ago. When the job opened up in Plantsville his wife wanted to get into the country more, she never cared for the real cold like they have out here. They went into one of the Judges chambers. They wanted to know what he was doing; he told them the whole story. He glanced at his watch and said, 'He was going to meet Judge Ramprest here at five o'clock." He was just getting out of his chair when there was a knock at the door. One of the Judges went over and opened it. The man whispered something in the Judge's ear, the Judge said, "Are you sure?" The man shook his head; the Judge thanked him and closed the door. He came back to the table and sat down, taped his fingers a few times. Then looked at Judge Webster and said, "I have some bad news, I was just told that Judge Ramprest has been shot and is in critical condition at the hospital." Judge Webster looked at him in disbelief. What happened? The Judge said, "All he knows is someone shot him in the right side." They are operating on him now. Would you like to go down to the hospital? At first he said, "No! then the more he thought about it he said, "Yes he would go." They called one of the marshals and asked to have his car brought around. They got to the hospital in no time flat, went up to the desk and told the girl who they were and why they were there. The girl said let me check. She called someone, talked for a few minutes and hung up. She told them someone was coming down for them. They waited for about 10 minutes. A nurse came down and asked for them. She took them up to the third floor, surgery. They sat and waited till one of the doctors came out. He went over to them and explained what happened, at least what they knew. His condition is critical, but I think he will make it. The bullet missed a few vital spots that could have done him in. He lost a lot of blood; he'll be out of it for the next twenty- fore to thirty -hours. Judge Webster asked if he had any baggage with him. The Doctor said he would check. A detective was assigned to the case, and came right out. He was an old timer in the detective department and he knew what to do. Judge Webster saw him when he was a Judge in Salt Lake years ago. The Judge introduced himself and started giving orders. First he wanted to know where the briefcase was. The Judge also asked if they could keep it quite for a few days. Maybe say, a man had gotten shot, as of now he is unidentified. If anyone has any information in this shooting please call the police headquarters at once. Maybe this would give the person that shot him a little time to think; maybe I did shot the wrong man. Maybe in a few days say that the man is in critical condition but should make a full recovery. Then put a guard in his room twenty-fore hours a day. No one is to be allowed in that room with out an escort, Doctors, nurses or anyone, including the cleaning people. Is that understood? The detective said he would do his best to watch over him. He turned to the Judge and said" Sir... Do you mind if I ask you who this man is." The Judge said that it would be better if he didn't know who this man is. This way if anything leaked out you couldn't be blamed for it. I will tell you one thing: he is a very important man. Now if that hit man was from Salt Lake City and had only a picture to go by, he may be worried that he did get the wrong man, and who ever hired him would be pissed.

Judge asked again, make sure you find that briefcase. For some reason Judge Webster had a funny feeling about that briefcase. It may hold a lot of information. The detective called for an assistant. This was getting too big for one man to handle. The two detectives called the judge into a private waiting room and started asking him questions. First they wanted to know what he was doing in Salt Lake City. The Judge told them most everything. This is the reason he does not want this in the papers. We are doing a lot of undercover work, if this gets out, all our work would be in vain. The detective asked, "Who would know you were coming out here? Judge Webster said, "He had no idea. He was from Utah. He is carrying on this investigation thru the FBI... All questions and answers can be asked by them. He gave them Alma's phone number. She in turn will get in touch with the 2 men. The younger detective looked at Judge Webster and said, " Sir are you bull shitting us? I wouldn't like it if you are. But if you are telling me the truth, we will need some more help. How long are you going to be here in Salt Lake?" The Judge said, "He could stay for a few days. He would check into the hotel and come back to the Court House if he had time." Otherwise he will be at the hotel for at least the next twenty-fore hours. He wants to be around when this gentleman comes to. He will be doing a lot of work, he again asked the detective about the briefcase. The detective said, "He knew nothing about a briefcase." He went out and called the doctor. He wanted to know who the ambulance company was that brought the man that got shot into the hospital. The doctor said, "He would check in the emergency room and get right back to him." Ten minutes later the doctor came back and told the detective. They had left it with the patient in the ER. Some one down there must have it. He went down himself to the E.R. They remember seeing it but don't know where it is now. The Judge said keep looking, I need that briefcase. It contains some things we need. The Judge said he was going to the hotel and check in. I will be back at the Court House for a few hours and then back to the Hotel. I have a lot of work to do. I want to be at the hospital when this man wakes up.

He started walking down the street, as he was about to cross a car came speeding down the street. It missed him by a fraction of an inch. He was able to get a part of the marker number. He wrote it down on the palm of his hand before he forgot it. When he got back to the hotel, he asked if there were any messages, she gave him a few. He thanked her and got into the elevator, by mistake he pushed the wrong floor button. This one took him one floor above his. He didn't realize it when he got off. But the floor numbers weren't the same. He saw the exit stair sign and decided to walk down. It was only one flight and he could use the exercise. Just as he opened the stairway door, he saw a man come out of his room. Who would be coming out of my room, when I have the only key? He waited till the man left, and then with a handkerchief over the doorknob, he went inside. Every thing looked the same as before, but he had a funny feeling. He looked around the room, looking for a bug. Looking at the phone he picked it up and removed the mouthpiece, just as he thought. There was the bug. He removed it, called the police headquarters, and asked for the chief. The operator started to give him a hard time, he told her who he was and that got her going. A few minutes later the chief got on the line. Hello Judge Webster, long time no hear. How are you doing? The Judge said he would like to talk with him as soon as possible. Could you spare a few minutes right away. The Chief said, "For you sure, how would it be if I picked you up now? The Judge said, "That would be fine, and could you make it behind the hotel and Chief, could you have your fingerprint man go over the door knob and telephone in my room. He gave the room number. Will take care of it at once. The Chief said... "Stuff the latch so my men can get in. I'll be there in ten minutes." The Judge went out the back entrance which leads to the back alley. He looked all around, no one was there. A few minutes later a car pulled up and the Chief said, "Hop in Judge, it's a nice day what do you say we take a ride throw the park. Maybe stop and get an ice cream cone." The Judge thought that was a good idea. After getting the ice cream, the Judge told him everything how Judge Ramprest was as crooked as they come, and someone tried to kill him. Now some one is trying to do the same to me. They tried to hit me with there car, I have the marker number here. And someone bugged my phone. I was careful to use a handkerchief so I wouldn't destroy the prints. The Chief took the marker number, drove to a pay phone, and called headquarters. Gave the desk Sergeant the numbers and said he would wait for the answer. The sergeant Came back and told him, as far as he could tell it was an out of state car, and it was stolen from. We don't know what state as yet. The Chief said to put a watch out for the car and he would call back later and hung up. He went back to the car and told the Judge what he found out. He told him that they have a watch out for the car, this way if they can find the car and keep an eye on it they may try and use it again. Then we can nab whoever is in the car. They rode around for over an hour. The Chief pulled over at a phone booth and called headquarters again. The desk officer said they haven't been able to locate that car as yet, and they haven't found what State it came from. Would the Judge have any idea what kind of car or what color it could be? The Chief said, "Hold on and I'll ask him." He went back to the car and asked the Judge. He thought the color was either a dark green or dark blue, and it looked like a late model car. That's all he can tell them. They went back to the motel and the Chief let him out at the back entrance.

The Judge checked his watch, it was close, but he still had a little more time. He went up to his room, checked it all over, and found nothing. He called the hospital to see if there had been any changes. The doctor said there had not; they will probably let him sleep till tomorrow. He happened to remember the messages that he picked up. Looking at them, he had gotten three messages from Bessie; he called her, she was happy to hear his voice. They talked for a few minutes. Then she told him that she had received three calls, two from Alma and one from Andy and Jack. He thanked her and called Alma. She was happy to hear his voice. She told him how Jack and Andy had been trying to get in touch with him. He was wondering how Jack had gotten his phone number at Bessie's place. She said how they had called so many times that it would be better that they call Bessie. She told him everything that went on in Plantsville. The hanging of the janitor and a few other things. He told Alma how Judge Ramprest had been shot, but no names had been put in the papers as yet. He didn't go into any details. She did tell him how the FBI Headquarters had called Jack and Andy saying that a secretary that works in Albany had called and wanted to talk with an agent. They new Jack and Andy were working on this case, so they contacted them. They in turn wanted to talk with the Judge first, to see what he had to say. He gave Alma his Phone number at the Hotel, and told her he would be there for the next few days. She gave him Jack's phone number at the Motel. This way he could talk with them. He happened to think of the time difference, let's see there's three hours different between here and there, that makes it six o'clock there time. He rang the motel, and Andy picks up the phone. He was happy to hear the Judge's voice. He told the Judge what they had found out and what Headquarters had to say. This secretary called and wanted to talk with an agent, there was a lot of things going on that was not legal. She wouldn't give her name or where she was calling from. She would call back later, she had to hang up. The Judge said that if she should call again have her give me the call, or get a phone number and I will call her anytime. (The Judge was really getting into it now.)

The next day at noontime the phone rang, it was the Chief; the hospital called and said the Judge was coming out of this long sleep... He would have his car pick him up at the rear of the Hotel. The Judge hung up, put his jacket on, and went down stairs. He looked around, and went out the back door. Within a matter of minutes a car pulled up, and Judge Webster got in. They went straight to the hospital. They went up to the third floor. The Doctor told them to wait a few more minutes longer. In the waiting room sat a man the Chief knew. He spoke to the Chief; the Chief asked what he was doing there. He said that he was following up on the story about the man that got shot a while back. The Chief looked at the Judge, the Judge nodded his head. The Chief said he knew the man, as a matter of fact, that's why we are here now. The reporter asked if maybe he could get a story out of it. The Judge said" let me explain. I came into Salt Lake On business, I know the Chief so I stopped over to see him. He told me how Chief Justice Ramprest had been shot, and was in the hospital. To myself I asked, why would anyone want to shot the Chief Justice, there must be some mistake. His secretary said he went on vacation and was going to see some old friends in Reno. From what I can make of it. Someone mistook him for someone else. The Doctor came out and said the" Judge was doing very well and should be out in a week or so." He asked if we wanted to see him, but he said only two at a time and that was only for a few minutes. They said they would like to see him and went in. When they came out the reporter was gone. Ramprest said," He never saw the man that shot him, but there was a man following him." He tried to lose him in the crowd. Judge Webster asked, " Who in his office knew he was going to Reno, Ramprest thought for a minute, my secretary for one, she got me the ticket. My chauffeur, he took me to the airport, and my wife. That's all that I can think of. Both my secretary and chauffeur have been with me for the past seven years. I would trust them with my life." The Judge looked at the Chief and said that leaves only one. Did she know how crooked he was? Was she trying to blackmail him? Did she call someone out here and tell them he was coming." Who would she know that lives out here? How about insurance? Did he have a large insurance policy on himself and was she the beneficiary? Did she want him out of the way so she could collect the insurance money? Judge Webster was writing all this down in his little black book. He said, "Let's start from the top. Does your wife know how crooked you are? The Judge said, "She did not." ok... Was she trying to Blackmail you? No she was not... OK. Did she know anyone out here that she could call and tell you were coming? He thought for a long while it's a possibility. She would go on trips with her lesbian girl friends. I never knew where they went. She never told me and I never asked. I was happy to be rid of her. Where you and your secretary lovers? He looked at both of them and said quietly" yes."

The next day on the front page of the paper CHIEF JUSTICE RAMPREST OF NEW YORK SHOT BY MISTAKE. Police are still investigating. Chief Justice out here for a rest and to see some old friends, Judge Webster a retired Judge who served in Plantsville N.Y. was one of them. He is expected to be released from the hospital in a week or so. That was about all that was printed. The room now was placed under guard twenty-four hours a day and the guard was inside the room. The Doctors and nurses had a password to get in. Three days went by, nothing happened. On the forth night, late... The door opened very slowly, the officer inside was watching, he got up and went behind the door. As the door opened a little more, the officer grabbed the doorknob and gave it a good yank. A figure came flying into the room. The officer had his gun in his hand and pointing at the figure on the floor. Hot coffee and donuts went flying. When the officer saw who it was he gave a shy of relief. It was one of his buddy's and was bringing him coffee and some donuts. The one on the floor looked under the bed and there was the coffee with the lid off and spilled all over the floor. The donuts were ok, the guard started to laugh, he felt bad but he was still laughing. The coffee man said he should have known better and knocked first. But he said at least you were on the ball. They talked for about 1/2 hour then he went home. It was getting time for his relief to come anyway. The officer wrote in his log just what happened. He thought they would get a kick out of it. When the next shift came on everything was back to normal. The Judge was getting out on Sunday. He had been in the hospital for just over two weeks. The first thing he asked for when he came too was his briefcase. They still hadn't found it. The judge was very upset. In it were all the notes he had written the night before he came out west. Some of it was in his scribbling; only he could read. But there were a lot that was done in long hand. Judge Webster walked down to the hospital witch was only four blocks from the hotel. He also had a funny feeling that some one was following him. He would look in a store window to see if some one was there, but he could see no one. He just had that feeling when he got up to Judge Ramprest's room; he first checked the telephone to see if it was bugged. He looked around and checked everything out. The officer was still there. He watched the Judge go through his usual routine. Every time the Judge came in, he would do the same thing. He called the Chief, they put him right through. He told the Chief he had this feeling that someone was following him and was being watched. The Chief said, "Don't worry about it; it's one of my people". He also told the Judge," That the fingerprints on the doorknob and the telephone in his room were not clear enough to make a comparison match, he also said they had not seen the car and were afraid that by now they have changed the marker plates. The Judge said" thanks" and hung up. The day after Judge Ramprest got out of the hospital, Judge Webster made arrangements for one of the Salt Lake City Judges and a secretary to listen to what Judge Ramprest had to say. It was also to be taped. They met at the Hotel in a private room. This way neither the two judges had to leave the building. They met at 3 in the after noon, at five they ordered supper and called it a day at II:00 that night. All four of them were tired by this time. Judge Ramprest came clean on everything that was going on at the capital. Because the Governor had just gotten into office, he was clean. At 4:30 the following morning Judge Webster got a phone call from a secretary in Albany. First she apologized for calling at this hour in the morning. She felt that this was the safest time to call. She would like to meet someone and tell her story. He asked for her phone number, and told her he would call her right back. He didn't want his phone number on her records. She gave it to him and they hung up. He called her right back she answered the phone on the first ring. He wanted to know where and when would be a good time to meet. She said she was going on vacation, and was planning on going to Las Vegas. Is there any chance they could meet out there? He asked her if Reno would be any inconvenience to her. She said "No they hadn't made any reservations as yet." He said for her to make arrangements to come to Reno and give him the name of the hotel. He asked for her name and they would meet there. He also asked if she was traveling alone. She said she was coming with another secretary. The judge said that would be fine. She gave him her name which is Gina Parker and her friends name is Deborah Franco. They would call back when everything was set three days later he got a call at four o'clock in the morning. Only this time it was Debbie calling. The Hotel is called the Dove Palace and the room number is 6110. We should be there around 4:00-4:30 Monday afternoon. The phone number is 1-775-755-6110. The judge said that would be fine, and my name is Sam Webster. He called the Dove Palace and got a room next to 6110. He then called Miss Bessie at the ranch. He explained to her why he hadn't been back and why he was going to Reno. He started thinking ...now... let's see what's going to happen. He called an old friend. He wanted information on a Gina Parker and Deborah Franco. Both live in or around Albany New York. He gave his phone number. Later that day, his friend called back. Gina Parker work's in the District Attorney's office in the Capital building. Deborah Franco work's in the Governor's Distribution Department, also in the Capital building. Gina has worked there for 3 years, and "Debbie" as she is known by, has worked there for 9 years. Her boss has been there for 4 1/2 years. Neither women have ever been in any trouble, they are well liked and hard workers, they both are from New York State and attended New York colleges. They are trustworthy and honest. Not even a parking ticket between them. Right now neither has a steady boyfriend. There jobs seem to come first.

The Judge was doing a lot of thinking. It had to be the Judge's wife that wanted to get rid of him. She had to have called someone out here, and tell them that the Judge was coming, and she didn't want him to come back home alive. It seemed funny that the man never grabbed the briefcase when he shot the Judge.

He must not have known what was inside it. He got on the phone again to his friend. He asked if he would check the phone bill of Judge Ramprest home phone and see if any calls were made out this way. If there has ... Try and find out who the party is, and where they live. I'll wait for your call and hung up. The next thing is where is the briefcase now? It was brought in with the Judge, so it must be someplace in the Hospital. But who took it? The Judge answered every question. He knew he was, or is in deep trouble, so he might as well cooperate. Maybe things will go a little easier. Now... what about the two secretaries? What kind of story are they going to tell? Will it match the Judge's? At 3:30 he got a call from his men. There was a call made, From the Judge's house to a party in Modesto California area code 209-333-0111. The number goes to a private home. I tried to call that number but it has been disconnected, I'll need a few days to trace this one down. The Judge said" I need it" and hung up.

Monday at 4:05PM two girls walked into the Dove Palace lugging two large suite cases. They went up to the desk clerk and gave there names and waited while the clerk got the papers and keys. He also gave them a note that was left for them. He rang a bell and a buss boy came over, took there luggage and put it on a rake and lead them to the sixth floor. When they got off the elevator they turned left and went down five doors on the right. The buss boy who was really in his mid thirties, opened the door, and went in, looked around and waited for his tip. Debbie gave him two dollars. He looked at the two one-dollar bills then at Debbie and walked out. Debbie said to Gina, "What does he think we are, made of money." Gina opened up the note; all it read was 61130, that's all just 61130, what does that mean. Debbie said, "I think it's a room number, ours is 6110. I think he just added a zero." They got talking about the slot machines and everything else about the hotel, when there was a knock at the door. Debbie opened it, there stood an elderly gentleman. He asked, "If this was Debbie and Gina's room.? She said, "Yes, he asked if he could come in for a minute. At first she was going to say no. Then she thought he must be Sam Webster and stepped aside so he could come in. Once he got inside and closed the door, he told them his name was Sam Webster." Gina came over and introduced her self and Debbie did the same. The two girls looked at one another and smiled, Sam said, I hope you weren't expecting a handsome young man. They looked at each other again and Gina said, "We will take you any day." He never told them that he was a Judge, so it was Gina, Debbie, and Sam. He told them, "That he was in room 6113 one door down. I put the zero at the end in case someone found it. When you get settled, I'd like to have a talk with you two, if it's all right with you. They said, "They would like to unpack and maybe have something to eat first." Sam said that would be O.K. with him. When you feel up to it come to my room, it's the next one down, same side. He opened the door and left. They looked at each other again, could he really be an FBI. Man? He must have makeup on to make him look older."

They put everything away. Then went down to the second floor and had some lunch. They took the elevator down to the first floor and started looking for the nickel machines. All they could find was the quarter and half dollar machines .they played those for a while. Gina felt rich ...when she got back to there room she started counting she had won two dollars and twenty-five cents Debbie had lost two dollars. They were both tired from the flight, and getting up early and all. They wanted to rest for a while, but they also wanted to talk with Sam. They liked Sam, he was like a father to talk with, and at least that's what Gina thought. They decided to go and have a talk with Sam now. They were about to leave the room when the phone rang. They didn't know anyone here and no one new them, so let it ring. They went down to the next door and knocked. They heard noises but no one answered the door. They tried to open it but the door was locked. They went back to there room and called the desk for help. The assistant manager came up with the master key and opened the door. Sam was lying on the floor holding his chest, the manager got on the phone and called for help. The EMT people came and determined that he had swallowed something and it got lodged in his throat, and could hardly breathe. They gave him a slap on the back and something came flying out of this mouth. The color started to come back and he was able to set up. He said, "He tried to call next door but got no answer." Gina felt real bad for not answering the phone. They got him some water and helped him to his feet. He felt much better and thanked them all. He told the manager he and the EMT'S people could go now. He was fine, they wanted to stay a little longer, but he said they didn't need to. So they left. The judge felt much better. They sat down and the Judge started asking questions. First of all, one of you had called before; you said you wanted to talk with an FBI agent. Your next call was transferred to me. What can we do for you? Gina said, "She and Debbie are worried about what may become of them if they tell everything they know." The Judge told them that if what they say is true, did they have proof. Every one of them will end up in jail. The Judge also said that they have been looking into things in Albany themselves and also Washington. We will take care of both of you that I can assure you, Gina why don't you start..."The District Attorney where I work is money hungry. Everything goes through channels. That way his name is never mentioned. If he should get caught, there's nothing they can pin on him. But he gets about two-thirds of everything that comes into the Court House. All the projects that Debbie handles are mostly bought. The extra money comes through channels, and goes into private accounts with a fictitious name. When the account gets to large, stocks and bonds are bought with a phony name on the top and his name on the bottom. Then he sells them and gets the money and puts it into his account. If he hears of some good stock from inside traders, he will transfer some of his stock over to the high paying dividend stock and have it come to the office each month. Debbie let's me know when a large contract is coming up for bid. My boss wants to know everything, so I have to send him a note on plain paper. This way if anyone finds it, he says he's checking them out. He wants to see how honest they are and don't want anyone to know what he's doing." Sam asked, "What kind of proof do you have on what you are telling me? Have you ever deposited any checks for him from these contractors? Have you ever seen any payoffs? Do you know what the account numbers are on his personal accounts? This way we may be able to check the incoming deposits and see where they are coming from. We also would like the fictitious names that he's using, on all of his stocks and bonds. We would also like the names of the stockbrokers he does business with. They get a commission on what they sell; does he get a piece of that commission also? From what we have checked the Governor knows nothing about what's going on. Could that be right, it's going on right under his nose?" Debbie said, "She didn't think he would stand for anything dishonest, he seems like a straight and honest man." She did say, "How a couple of lawyers had taken her and Gina out and tried to get us drunk, they wanted us to go to bed with them and tell them who the contractors on the new bridge was going to be. They figured if we went to bed with them, they would have us on there side and let them know everything that goes on. But it never happened, we didn't get drunk and we didn't go to bed with them. They got mad and we never heard from them again." The Judge asked, "How many people are involved in this scheme." This has to be a large-scale operation. If everyone is involved, and getting a little something from the action, this has to be a large payoff. With the D.A. Getting the lions share, that leaves only a third for the rest. Somebody is getting screwed. Gina said, "The D.A. Thinks he has enough on everyone so that they wouldn't talk, he would make it hard for them to get another job. I guess they are happy with what they are getting." The Judge asked, "If they ever heard of Judge Lipton.? Gina said, "She has, he has sent some big time gamblers up to Judge Ramprest, he in turn for a small fee would lower the sentence and the bond, and most of the time they would walk out free. The money collected would go to the D.A. With a kickback to the Chief Justice. What a deal they have going on here. Now all we need is proof. Something that will stand up in court." Gina wanted to know how she could get in touch with him if she had to. He gave her Alma's phone number, and told her any time you need me, give Alma a call. "She keeps tabs on me most of the time. I would prefer calling around ten pm your time. That is if it's all right with you? Unless I'm out and she can't get me. I should call you that night. If it is an emergency, tell her and she will get someone to you at once. But please both of you, be careful. If you need help, we will try and get you some help. If you are going to write anything down, do it in such a way only you can understand it." Sam asked, "How long are you planning to stay here?" Debbie said, "About a week or until the money runs out. Sam laughed;" he said, "make sure the plane fare home and the hotel room are paid." Also save enough for a phone call back home. They hadn't thought of that, but that's what they are going to do tonight. Figure out how much everything is going to cost, and put that money aside. Now they know how much they can spend ...gambling, food, souvenirs, etc. Sam also told them to hide there money someplace, in case some one breaks in to your room. They would not find it. Maybe in your shoe or in your underwear. Sam told them he was staying till the following day. If there were any questions or they need help with anything to come and see him. This may be the last time we will meet, but not the last time we will talk. That I can be sure of." They got up and started toward the door. Gina turned and asked him, "If he was going to be all right?" He said, "He felt fine, and not to worry." She said, "If you need anything knock on the wall or give us a call... Please"... Sam smiled and said, "He would now you two go on downstairs and have some fun. And win! I have a lot of work to do. I will talk with you tomorrow."

Judge Webster stayed up late, writing everything down that would help the girls get evidence. What to look for, the time it happened and where it happened. Names of all his friends, addresses, and phone numbers, if you can. Have you seen any weapons, are any of the guards involved, if so who? Any local police, lawyers, anyone that you think may be involved in doing something wrong. Make a note of it as soon as you can so that you don't forget. Check the plate numbers on there cars, try and get the make and color of the car. Most of all don't go looking for trouble. Be yourselves. If they receive phone calls that you answer, make a note of the time and who is calling. After you have read this over a dozen times each please destroy by tearing it up in small pieces and flush down the toilet. Good luck Sam

Three weeks went by; nothing was heard from the girls. Alma was getting worried, she was wondering, should I call them or go see them. She was ready to call, when the phone rang. It was Gina, she was all excited. Judge Lipton wants to come out and see Judge Ramprest. He thought he would take a few days off. He had planned on Oct. 5th thru the 8th. That would be Columbus Day weekend. Judge Ramprest was mad; he wanted to go fishing that weekend. Now this jerk wants to come out. Judge Ramprest was telling Debbie all about it. He was trying to find a way out. Judge Ramprest was only working part time, but his two buddies only had this weekend off. He started thinking I'll tell him I have to go back into the hospital for tests that weekend. How about that? Debbie thought that was a good idea. The judge left, but...listen to this. They found the Judge's briefcase. An orderly picked it up and put in a locker. He went on vacation and forgot about it. There was no name on it so he didn't know who it belonged to. One day he read a note on the bulletin board about the briefcase, he called the Doctor whose name was on the card. It was taken up to the Doctors office, he in turn call the Chief of police. The Chief himself came down and picked it up. The Chief called Alma, she was happy that it was found. She told him not to say anything for the time being. Some one will get back to you shortly. They made some small talk for a few minutes and hung up. That night at eight-thirty Alma called

Judge Webster. She told him what Gina had said. The Judge said he would call the chief and take care of it. The girls were doing a great job of keeping their eyes and ears open. If only they could get something solid. In the mean time everything was going like before. A few more weeks went by before Alma heard from the girls. This time it was only a few days before the holiday. Judge Lipton had decided to come out and see the Judge anyway. Judge Ramprest was all upset, what should he do? Debbie told the Judge to leave a day early. If Lipton says anything, Debbie would tell him the hospital canceled the tests at the last minute, so you went someplace and we didn't know were. Judge Ramprest thought that was a great idea and left Friday morning. Gina and Debbie got together that night for supper and a little talk. Things should start to fire up now. When Lipton comes out here and Ramprest is not here. We will have to keep our ears and eye's open now.

Judge Lipton went first to Judge Ramprest's house. He went up to the front door and rang the bell. He waited a few minutes, the door opened and there stood his ex-wife, only she is not his "ex" as yet. He pushed his way into the house, looked around trying to see the Judge. She told him the Judge had left with a few men and would not be back for a few days. Judge Lipton started yelling, "He knew I was coming, why didn't he wait?" I have something to tell him. Where did he go? His wife said she didn't know. He pushed her out of the way and went up stairs. Looking in all the rooms. He came to the master bedroom, opened the door. And there on the bed were two girls making love. He stopped and watched them for a few minutes. They never stopped doing what they were doing. He started to get excited; he ran into the bedroom and started to undress. The two girls let out a scream. They didn't want anything to do with him. His wife came to the door and wanted to know what he thought he was doing. She left and went into another bedroom, opened a drawer and took out a pistol, walked back into the bedroom, pointed the gun at Lipton and pulled the trigger.

Judge Lipton took his dive on the bed. She told the girls, he was hitting on them for sex. They wanted no part of him. He started fighting with them. They screamed, his wife came up and shot him. She turned around and picked up the phone. She asked the operator for the police department. The desk officer answered. She told him everything. He told her his men were on the way, and so was an ambulance. He kept her on the phone till he could hear the officer's voices. They got on there two-way radio and called for detectives. Nobody move or touch anything. The detectives came and she had to go through everything, and so did the two girls. Now they had put on there bathrobes. Because this was Judge Ramprest's house and nothing was said for a while. The ambulance and the EMTs came in and checked Lipton out. One bullet in the chest. Mrs. Ramprest gave the detective the gun. She admitted she shot him in self-defense. She didn't know were her husband had gone, he said he was going fishing, but he didn't say where. They put out an all points bulletin for him. It was two day's later that he came home and found a mess. He was relieved in a way that Lipton had been shot. He never trusted that man, he was always for himself. He would hurt anyone that didn't do what he wanted them to do. The Chief of Police called Plantsville Police Chief Rose and told him what happened. He thanked the Chief for calling. Chief Rose called Alma, told her what he knew. She in turn called Judge Clarence Hawter, he felt happy and sad. Now maybe it was his turn to be the top dog in court.

Judge Lipton went to the hospital in critical condition. They didn't think he would make it. They operated and removed the bullet. It came within a fraction of his heart; His condition was not made public for almost a week. Judge Ramprest was worried; all that had to happen was for some reporter to start digging into the past of Lipton. It was placed in the paper that Lipton was shot by accident. Very little was said in the papers about the mishap. If they started to dig and found out about Ramprest wife, and how Lipton is involved, you can just see the headlines now: Extra... read all about it... Ramprest's wife not really his wife she is Judge Lipton's wife. How can the Chief Justice do something like that? Was there blackmail in there someplace? Was that why Lipton was at the Chief Justice's house? Was he messing around with his wife...that couldn't be, she is a lesbian? That's right folks Chief Justice's wife is a lesbian. What were the two young girls doing at his house?" Is she keeping a house of lesbians? The Judge started to wonder if he would be able to sit back on the bench, then he thought, instead of setting on the bench in a courthouse he'll be setting on a bench in a jail cell. With his luck, he would have Lipton in the cell next to him. On the other side will be the whole bunch from the Capital, plus all the contractors and lawyers. Except the Governor, Alma, Judge Webster, Judge Hawter... and all the other ones that were taking the abuse from Judge Lipton felt relieved. The Righteous Guardians will be disbanding, and the Plantsville Guardians will take over. Bill's Restaurant will be one of many, Alma and Clarence Hawter got married, and Harvey Binder is back part time as boss at the courthouse. Everyone in Plantsville is talking with everyone again. What goes around comes around. Chrissie is engaged. And Chris is a grade one detective. Sitting in Bill's Restaurant here in Plantsville, looking out the clean window, and thinking where the time goes. Seventeen years have gone by; things have been pretty good these last years. Now let's see, today is Oct. 21, 1989. Bill's Restaurant has grown to twelve; he really worked hard with the lobsters and shrimp. Ben and Karen were a big help in placing the Restaurants all down Route 95 from Maine to the New York border. Connecticut seemed to be the best spot. They built the buildings all the same, after the one in Maine... simple, clean and friendly. Not to bright and not to dim. The prices are within reason. Ben and Karen are still running the friendly restaurant in Maine. Bill and Bee are managing the restaurant in Plantsville and Alma and Karen and Carl are in charge of the rest of them. Let's see now. I didn't tell you about Karen and

Alma yet have I? Karen and Carl got married, which was no surprise to anyone. They have two children, a boy six, and a girl three. Both are spoiled rotten, but good kids. Carl went on to college and is now the assistant city planner. On the QT he helps Karen with the bookwork. Karen went to business college; Alma is in charge of all the ordering. She has four people that do the hard stuff. She just makes sure that it's done right. She left the courthouse about ten years ago. Once a month they have a meeting, they all get together and talk. It's more of a family get together then anything else, which is nice. On the 4th of July they all close and have a family picnic for all the help. What a time... about three hundred people show up. Most have been with them from the day they opened. They are treated very well so no one wants to leave. They rent a Motel in Old Saybrook for the weekend, and go boating, swimming and getting a suntan (or bum). Awards are given out to the oldest employee, and the one that's been there the longest, at each Restaurant. Everyone gets a bonus. They have a waiting list a mile long for people that want to come to work for them.

Judge Webster and Miss Bessie came out about fifteen years ago. Judge Webster couldn't get over how the little town had changed, they stayed with Alma for three days, and Miss Bessie wanted to get back home. She thought the place would burn down if she wasn't there. Judge Webster was welcomed with open arms. They had a parade for him; there was a little tear in his eye. Miss Bessie at that time was 102 and still going strong, and Judge Webster was in his late 70's. She died when she was 106. Up till the time she died she ran the Ranch. They found her at the kitchen table paying bills. Judge Webster took over the Ranch, that's what was in the will. When it got too much for him, he turned it over to the town. They had to use it as a children's retreat. Anyone of the old help could live there the rest of there lives no charge. The children could help keep the place up. The Judge died five years after Miss Bessie. Sheriff Roper has taken over the Ranch; it's still used for disturbed children, both boys and girls from all over. Miss Bessie had saved enough in the bank so that the interest would cover the taxes and a lot of the expenses.

The Righteous Guardians lasted about 2 months. Nobody wanted to run it. The Plantsville guardians took over. The membership now is about 200. They run in age from 2 thru 65 years old. I think Harvey Binder is the oldest member. He's still going strong. He rides his electric scooter all over town. He still goes to the Court House every day, unless it snows or rains. The mayor of Plantsville gave Alma a citation award for fighting the crocked Judge that started Righteous Guardians. She has it hanging on the living room wall. Ruth, Bill and Bee's daughter went out west and opened her own Fish and Chips Restaurant. She calls it "Karen's Own Fish and Chips". She got married and divorced in the same year. She has a new boyfriend, she say's she's not in any hurry to get married now. She has hopes of opening a few more Restaurants. Ruth would like her mother and father to come out and help. The weather would do them both good. It's time they retired and slowed down.

Charlie and Clare, the past owners of Alma's house, passed away about 10 years ago. They were a fine couple. Alma got a letter from there lawyer one day. It said how Clare had pneumonia in a nursing home and pasted away, and a few weeks later Charlie pasted away. They were very devoted to each other because they had no family; they left everything to Alma and to Karen. They both went down to Florida for a week and took care of everything. For the time being they will keep the condo. They figured there were enough folks that could use it. The money they had left paid off the mortgage and Alma sent some out to the Ranch.

The Ballard's have stopped partying, like they were before. The Kids are still in School. Jamie is going to be a doctor, and Joanie is also going to college. She wants to be a teacher. This will be her last year. She's going to take a special Ed course next year. She wants to teach handicapped children.

Chief Evan Rose is retired. He got injured in a car accident. He was going on a robbery call when a drunk went through a red light and hit the chief's car broadside on the driver's side. The Chief was unconscious for weeks. He finely came to, but was never in any condition to go back to work. The driver of the other car got a cut on his forehead. They closed it up with a band-aid. Detective Sergeant Sunny

Cloud was voted into the Chiefs job. He has changed a few things but all in all, he's doing a pretty good job of running the department. He has made a few promotions and the men are happy about that, plus he has added more men to the police force. Ex-officer Sam moved out of town, he screwed up so bad that he couldn't get his private eye badge in Plantsville. Tory Cox and Phil Syzrnansky along with the other kids that were in the Righteous Guardians where all let go. Tory Cox is a paid EMT and Phil works the 911 hot line for the city. Tory has a girl friend, Phil say's he doesn't have time for girls.

Jim Bob, the prosecutor in Alabama, was replaced. He did wrong and admitted it. He should have checked everything out better. It was time for him to retire anyway. He spends most of his time fishing. He loves catching Bass. He say's he has a few ribbons. (I never saw any.) Attorney Steven Ryan is still going strong. We saw him and his wife at Miranda's Restaurant. They think their food is the best, next to Bill's of courseThe two FBI men Andy and Jack are still doing there job checking on crooked judges and cops. They stop in once in a while, when they are in the area. They often talk about the time they spent in Plantsville. Chris and Chrissie well, Chris got promoted to the Detective Division, he cracked a big case. Him and his partner that is. He got promoted to Detective First Class. He has been engaged to his partner for almost ten years. He doesn't want to rush things. They bought a house together, one of these days they may get married. Chrissie got married to her high school boy friend. (I think Chris is watching to see how Chrissie makes out, before he tries it.) Her husband has a good dental business. She is expecting twins the last week in March. They have all come up for a few days in the summer. We will go down there for some of the holidays. They are just like family.

Jay Johnson installed new windows at Shirley Gates' house, she thought he did such a fine job she invited him for supper one night, guess what... she wanted a new front door. He took her up to Alma's house and showed her the kind he put in for her. That's the kind I had in mind, she told him. I want one just like it, he ordered one and installed it. That called for another supper. The next meal was on him. Jay and Shirley got married about five years ago.

NEWS FLASH: With an election coming up, a reporter starting to do some digging on some senators and state representatives. He found that a senator and his wife were getting things for nothing; siding for there home, a vacation in France, Hawaii, and a lot of other things. After further digging he found that Judge Ramprest was the go between with all the contractors. For small favors the Judge could get friends anything from the contractor. If they wanted the jobs, they had to pay the price. There were two secretaries (who's names were never given) that let the reporter in on a few deals. Judge Ramprest may go to jail for a long time. The case is coming up in a few days.

Who am I... the one that's telling you all about Plantsville? I'm Alma's husband.

Senior Judge Clarence Hawter. Yup... Alma and I got married, July 4th, 1979. Karen was our little flower girl. Only kidding... she did stand up with us though. It's the best thing I have ever done. Alma is the most b-u-t-full person in the world. If she can be of any help to anyone, she'll be there. It seems good to think that everyone is talking to everybody again.

ABOUT THE AUTHOR

This is my first book and it was started quite by chance. While visiting my wife in a rehabilitation hospital; I met a lovely ninety-two year young lady. We started talking and I told her how living alone was a very lonely and boring life. She suggested I write a book. I had never thought of writing a book, or for that matter even how I would start one. She told me all I needed was a first line and a last line, then fill in the rest. So, I started the first line and the rest began to fall into place.

A lot of things have happened since I started the book. I've made many friends that I won't soon forget. These friends have given me the courage to carry on when I was ready to call it quits...I thank them. The woman at the nursing home passed away about a month after I started the book...I will never forget her. The strange thing is; I never got her real name. An author herself, she always used a pen name. I hope everyone enjoys the book, and keeps their eyes open for the next one...yes I'm hooked.